The Pe

Janet Tanner is the well-loved author of multi-
generational sagas and historical Gothic novels. Drawing
on her own background, Janet's Hillsbridge Sagas are set
in a small, working-class mining community in Somerset.
Always a prolific writer, Janet had hundreds of short
stories and serials published in various magazines world-
wide before writing her first novel. She has been trans-
lated into many languages, including Russian, Hungarian,
Polish, Romanian and Hebrew. Janet also writes as Amelia
Carr and Jennie Felton.

Janet TANNER

The Penrose Treasure

CANELO

First published in Great Britain in 2005 by Severn House Publishers Ltd

This edition published in the United Kingdom in 2022 by

Canelo
Unit 9, 5th Floor
Cargo Works, 1-2 Hatfields
London, SE1 9PG
United Kingdom

A CIP catalogue record for this book is available from the British Library.

Print ISBN 978 1 80032 822 8
Ebook ISBN 978 1 78863 629 2

Look for more great books at www.canelo.co

Printed and bound in Great Britain by Clays Ltd, Elcograf S.p.A.

As the bedchamber door closed after his visitor, the old man's eyes misted and for a moment he stared unseeingly into the gathering gloom whilst fragments of the past flickered like moths in lamplight. Then he heaved a sigh, scarcely audible above the painful rasp of his laboured breath, and, with an effort, summoned what remained of his failing strength.

He had done what he could to protect the inheritance; he prayed it was enough. He could think of no safer hands into which to entrust the secret of the Treasure, no one else in whom he could place his trust. Now there remained one last thing to be done, and it required all his fading concentration.

With enormous difficulty he inched his fluid-heavy legs towards the edge of the great four-poster bed in which he lay, then, taking the weight of his swollen body upon his once powerful arms, he shifted his bulk into line with them. The effort exhausted him; it was a few minutes before he recovered sufficiently to take up the quill and paper which lay on the table beside the bed and pull the well of ink to within his reach. Then he began to write in spidery, sloping script.

> My son. I pray to God that one day you will return
> safe to these shores. When you do, I fear you will
> find me gone to meet my maker and unable to tell
> you face to face where to find the Treasure that

has been handed down through our family from generation to generation. You will know without me describing it what it is of which I speak. My greatest fear is that the Treasure will fall into the wrong hands and will be disposed of for its monetary value rather than preserved for its much greater intrinsic worth. Men have died to possess it; men have died to safeguard it. My life is almost over, by the will of God, and yet I still fear that in my weakness I may fall prey to those who would stop at nothing to gain possession of it and use it for their own ends, though it pains me greatly to admit this.

The Treasure is concealed in a place of safety where it has been hidden these many years and which is known only to me. Now, in my hour of trial, I have entrusted the secret of its hiding place to one who loves me. I have asked them, when the time is right, to seek you out and reveal all that you need to know. I have every confidence that you will act with the wisdom I believe is yours — though God alone knows, there have been times when I have despaired of your worthiness to carry the burden which history has laid upon our family. You have not always behaved, my son, as I might have wished. Some of the family traits which showed themselves in you are not the ones I could have hoped you would inherit. But youth is rash and foolish. I can only trust that the years, and your experiences since last we met, will have mellowed you and brought forth the fruits of wisdom and honour that I would see in you. The wisdom and honour that are so necessary if you are to become the guardian of the Treasure.

My time is now short; yours, by the grace of God, will be long enough to do what has to be done. Do not fail me. Do not fail the inheritance.

God be with you.

Your ever-loving father,

Ralph Penrose

The final stroke of his signature formed, the old man waited whilst the ink dried on the page, folded it, and secured it with a blob of sealing wax melted in the flame of the candle beside his bed. Then he reached for the bell pull and tugged upon it.

The servant who entered the bedchamber was almost as old as he, and had been in the service of the Penrose family since he was a boy, and his own father still squire. But though her once trim figure was now stout and her chins wobbled ponderously over the neck of her calico gown, her silver hair was still shot through with black, her legs still did her bidding, if a little more slowly than of old, and her hands were as steady as they had ever been. Trudy Billing was as strong as a moorland pony, he thought ruefully. Would that he had been blessed with her rude health!

'Oh sir!' she admonished him now, hands on ample hips. 'What in all the world have you been up to! You look terrible, and that's not to be wondered at! First visitors, and then letter-writing! You know what Dr Warburton said. You need to rest.'

'Some things are more important than rest, Trudy,' he managed between rasping breaths. 'This letter is for Adam.'

Trudy fixed him with a beady stare.

'We don't know where Mr Adam is to send him any letter, sir. We don't even know if he's alive or dead. And America is a big country, so they say.'

'Give it to him when he comes home,' the old man managed.

3

'If he comes home!' She crossed herself. 'This terrible war…'

'Keep it safe, Trudy. Deliver it into his hands, and no one else's.'

'Oh, whatever you say.' She took it from him, tucking it into the pocket of her apron.

'Promise me, Trudy. To no one but Adam. Promise me now!'

'Oh very well – I promise. If you promise to get some rest…'

The door closed after her. Ralph Penrose sank back against his pillows, drained by the efforts of the last hour. It was out of his hands now. He had done all that he could. Now it was up to others, and the will of God.

He closed his eyes and drifted into exhausted sleep.

One

As the coach jolted and swayed down the steep hill, I sat forward in my seat, pulling aside the dusty brown velvet curtain so as to catch my first glimpse of Truro. The impatience to be home that had simmered in me, not just for the duration of the journey, but for the last two weeks since news of Mammy's illness had reached me, grew ever more insistent, so that it seemed to me the horses' measured pace was impossibly slow. It was all I could do to keep from throwing open the door and leaping out to run before them down the rutted road, petticoats flying, bonnet hanging by its ribbon round my neck, as I had not run since I was a child.

But of course I could do no such thing. I was twenty years old, and young women of twenty years old did not run like scruffy urchins, even if such a thing would not be foolish in the extreme. Some of the snow which had delayed my journey home still lay in stubborn patches where the sun had not reached it; the treacherous surface most likely accounted for the care with which the coachman was descending the hill. Why, on Bodmin Moor the drifts had looked still deep enough to swallow a man whole, and if I gave in to my rash impulse I would doubtless be flat on my back before I had gone more than a dozen yards. But I wriggled in my seat all the same, so that the clerical man beside me, who had had his nose in a book for most of the duration of the journey, huffed reprovingly and moved a little further away from me, and the rosy-cheeked woman who sat opposite, a baby on her knee, smiled at me knowingly.

'You from round these parts, dearie?'

'Mallen.' But I could scarcely tear my eyes away from the window to look at her.

'And you're in service somewhere, I'll be bound. And coming home to visit.'

I frowned. Was it so obvious?

'Launceston,' I said. 'I'm in service in Launceston.'

She pursed her lips, satisfied.

'I knew it! You're eager to see your family again. There's nothing like distance to make you want for your own.'

She was right, of course. When I had first obtained my position in Launceston it had seemed as if I had gone to the other side of the world. Many had been the night I had cried myself to sleep, so homesick for the little cottage in Mallen where I had shared a bed with Ellie and Ruth, my sisters, and the warmth of Mammy's kitchen where we all clustered together in the evenings, and the salty smell of the wind when it blew in from the sea, that I simply could not stop the tears. The first time I had come home to visit I had been almost as impatient as I was today to see the smiling faces waiting for me and the familiar sights of home. I had wondered how I would ever tear myself away again, and each passing hour had been a little death, taking me relentlessly towards the moment when I must wave them all goodbye again and put those cruel miles between us. But gradually, of course, I had grown used to it. I could not be homesick for ever. My life had resolved itself, and never again had I felt such sharp sadness at leaving, nor such eager longing to be in Mallen.

Until now.

The letter from my sister Ruth telling me of Mammy's illness had reawakened all the old sense of isolation, and far as I was from home, I had instantly feared the worst. Ruth was no letter writer, she had never taken to books and learning as I had. Papa had insisted we all learn to read and write, but whilst I had been an eager pupil, she had grumbled at being torn away from her play to sit around the table in the flickering light of the reed lamp whilst Papa patiently taught us our letters. None of the other children in our little hamlet were put upon so, she complained. Why should she be different?

Papa was, in truth, the only man in the hamlet who could read and write, and though he toiled as a miner at Wheal Henry for his living, he was regarded as something of a scholar for it. In the end he had his way. Ruth had learned as we all did, though it came harder to her than to the rest of us. I could well imagine how she had laboured over this letter to me.

The spelling and the sentence construction would no doubt have had Papa turning in his grave if he had seen it, but Ruth's meaning was clear enough.

Mammy had caught a chill early in the winter and could not shake it off. Rather than improving, she had grown worse. The thick sea fogs of November had sent the infection to her chest, she coughed day and night, sometimes bringing up thick phlegm, sometimes wracked by the pain of not being able to move it at all. Her breathing was terrible; at times, it seemed to Ruth, who lived in the little cottage next door with Jed, her husband, and her two children, that Mammy would choke. And she had lost weight – my Mammy, who had seemed to me never to have been any bigger than a sparrow – had lost weight. Dear God, I thought, there could be nothing left of her!

Anxiety had risen in me in a great wave, making the breath catch in my lungs as if, like Mammy, I was choking. I reread Ruth's letter, and my fear grew. Mammy was no longer a young woman. The years had taken their toll of her, and that was hardly to be wondered at, even if age alone was not itself a cruel master. I was just seven years old when Papa died of the illness that took the lives of so many copper and tin miners. Mammy had been left to raise us alone, we three girls and the two boys, John and Luke. Times had been hard; Mammy, a seamstress by trade, had sewed long into the night to make enough money to put food on our table. When Ellie was old enough, she took employment at Wheal Henry, much to the distress of Mammy, who had hoped for better for us. But, as a girl, Ellie's earnings were even more meagre than if she had been a boy, and the constant strain of stitching by lamplight was doing untold damage to Mammy's sight. She found it harder and harder to complete her commissions. Yet still she worked on.

It was not only hardship and endless toil that had taken its toll of Mammy's strength. She had endured more than her fair share of grief, first the loss of Papa, then both her sons. First little Luke, who died of a fever when he was just three years old, then John, who was thirteen when he was killed in a terrible accident.

Why he should have been at the old mineworkings at Wheal Martin, known locally as Old Trevarrah, we never knew; he had been warned often enough to stay away from them. But boys, I suppose, will be boys, and he must have been out for mischief and adventure. The rotten rungs of the ladder into the shaft gave way beneath him, and poor John plunged to his death in the filthy water far below.

His death almost destroyed Mammy; though she dearly loved all her children, there could be no doubt John had a special place in her heart. Not only was he her favourite, he was also her hope for the future. Yet Mammy was strong, so strong. Somehow she rallied and carried on.

It was how I had always seen her, a brave warrior who took everything that life threw at her and remained the one constant in our lives. But as I read Ruth's letter and grasped the seriousness of the situation that had brought her to write it, my heart trembled with the sudden real- ization that Mammy could not always emerge victorious from her battles with fate. She was only flesh and blood; one day she would fail. She would not always be there at home in Mallen waiting for me.

I was wracked then by urgency. I must ask leave to go home and see Mammy whilst there was still time. If she should succumb and I not there... If I should never see her again, never hear her voice or feel her arms embrace me... Far away as I was, busy with my own life, I had not stopped before to think of it. I had taken it for granted that whilst I was in Launceston, life as I had always known it in Mallen had not changed at all, but remained in some kind of timewarp. Suddenly I was all too aware how precious my family was to me.

When I took my predicament to them, my employers were understanding and generous, as I had known they would be.

Mr Ronald Melhuish was a banker who had overseen the rise of the family enterprise so that it was now the principal financial institution in the town, and his wife, Dorothea, had come to treat me more as a companion than as a lady's maid.

'I shall miss you dreadfully, Tamsin,' she said. 'But, of course, without question, you must go and visit your poor mother. I would never forgive myself if I deprived the dear soul of sight of her daughter. You must go at once!'

But I could not go at once. Winter had set in, as hard a winter as I could ever remember. Snow had come, falling for the best part of a whole day and night, falling so thickly that a man could scarcely see his hand in front of his face if he tried to walk in it, and when at last it stopped, the whole landscape had been transformed into a white wilderness. Hard frosts followed, so there was no chance for the first falls to melt away before more followed. The road south across Bodmin Moor was deep with drifts, they said, and impassable for the coach. There was no way I could get home to Mallen, and I could do nothing but wait, fretting and worrying, until it cleared somewhat.

That wait was torture for me, cut off from my home and my family, cut off even from any word of how they fared. Mammy could be dead and buried and I would not know it. Day by day I watched the sky for a break in the weather which so cruelly thwarted me, and questioned anyone who could tell me as to the state of the roads, though all the while I knew I was wasting my breath and their time. It seemed to me the snow would last for ever, and I began to despair that the moors would ever be green again, or even muddy brown.

The thaw, when it came, was slow, which I suppose was a mercy, for if it had melted all at once the ground could not have absorbed it and the roads would have been submerged before the water ran away to the sea. At last –

at last! – just when I had thought I could not stand another day of waiting, word came that the road was passable.

All my feverish anxiety came to a head then, bubbling up like the stew in a pot when the heat beneath it is too high and the lid left on.

'Tamsin, my dear...' Mrs Melhuish's soft, puffy little face was drawn with anxiety for me. 'I do not wish to be a Job's comforter, but I do wonder if you should prepare yourself for the worst.'

Hearing my own fears spoken aloud made my stomach clench, but I managed to return her gaze evenly.

'I have already done that, madam.'

I saw the compassion and concern in her grey eyes as she looked at me silently for a long moment.

'Yes,' she said at last. 'Yes, Tamsin, I am sure you have. And for your sake I hope very much that things will turn out not to be so bad. I realize, my dear, how you have missed your family these last years. My gain has been their loss – and yours.'

'No,' I said, anxious to show my gratitude for the kindness she had always afforded me. 'I am very happy with my position here. No girl could wish for a better.'

Her lips twitched suddenly. 'Except one where there might be a young man to take your fancy, perhaps.'

'Oh, I am not interested in young men!' I replied with a hint of my usual asperity.

'That's because you have not yet met the right one, Tamsin.' She folded her hands in the warm wool of her skirts, regarding me shrewdly.

That, I had to agree, was true enough. There had been those who had shown an interest in me, in particular a young blacksmith who looked after Mr Melhuish's horses, and I had walked out with him a few times on my afternoons off. But my heart had never lifted to see him in the way that I had hoped it might, and in fact, after he had tried to steal a kiss, and I felt only panic and revulsion, I had begun to dread seeing him at all. I had ended the association with some difficulty, for he had proved very persistent, and, ever since, I had been careful to avoid entangling myself so.

Sometimes I wondered if it was unnatural for me to feel such reluctance when other girls simpered and flirted and batted their eyelashes whenever a presentable young man put in an appearance, but there it was. The only man who had ever made my heart beat faster was the handsome son of Sir Edgar Trevoy, a friend of Mr Melhuish, and an investor with the bank. But our relationship had never gone beyond a few exchanged glances, his admiring, mine shy, and I knew it never would. Not only was Garth Trevoy engaged to be married to Miss Elizabeth Dalgleish, he was also out of my class. It was unheard of for a gentleman to have a decent, licit association with a hired servant, though dalliances were not uncommon. I had no intention of being drawn into such a shameful arrangement, which would, as like as not, end in nothing but disgrace for me. I ensured I was never alone with Garth Trevoy, so that I could not be tempted by the flattery of his attentions or the treacherous pull of attraction I could not help feeling when he brushed my hand with his or held my gaze a moment too long, inviting me with his dark, narrowed eyes to forget myself.

One day, perhaps, I would meet a man who could rouse those same feelings in me, who was not either spoken for or out of my class or both. I hoped it might be so. But until then I was satisfied enough with my situation. Certainly,

I was not prepared to settle for anything less than a true meeting of hearts and minds and bodies, just for the sake of it.

'Perhaps,' Mrs Melhuish said now, 'there is some young man in Mallen?'

'Madam, I have been with you since I was fifteen years old,' I said frankly. 'Any young men I knew in Mallen will have long since wed, and no doubt will have a family of little ones to provide for.'

'Well perhaps.' She smiled briefly. 'I should be most grieved if you decided not to return to us. But you have your life to live, Tamsin. You are young and beautiful. I would not wish to see you grow old and sour – if the Good Lord grant that I shall live that long.'

I hid a smile at her words. I would scarcely have described myself as beautiful. The face that looked back at me each morning from my dressing mirror did not entirely displease me, but my mouth was too large and my curious grey-green eyes too slanted to be credited with such a description. Elizabeth Dalgleish was beautiful, with her big brown eyes and hair the colour of corn on a summer's morning when the sun lights it. My hair was reddish brown and unruly; it was all I could do to keep it neat under my cap. No, I was not beautiful, though I hoped by the same token never to grow pinched and ugly with age. Mammy was not ugly, for all the cruel blows fate had dealt her. She was still a handsome woman – or had been when last I had seen her, her hair greyed but still luxuriant, the lines merely adding character to her even-featured face. I hoped that I might be served as kindly by the years.

The thought reminded me all too sharply of my concern for her, the frivolous thoughts of the last moments forgotten.

'I am not going home to Mallen to find a husband,' I said. 'I am going to see my mother.'

And: 'Of course, my dear. Forgive me,' Mrs Melhuish said, her expression of concern returning. 'Now, I wish to send some small token with you that may help to make life a little more pleasurable for you and bring some comfort to a woman who has been sick. I thought perhaps some preserves, and a jar of honey.'

'Oh no, there's no need, really!' I protested, embarrassed as I so often was by her kindness – and by the implication that my family was lacking in the provision of material comforts. How often as a child had we had nothing on the table but dry bread and a bowl of vegetable broth, supplemented perhaps by some of the poorer quality catch which had come in on the fishing boats and was not fit for the tables of folk who could afford to be choosy with their diet, or a pheasant or a hare, which sometimes appeared miraculously upon our doorstep. Mammy always frowned when she opened the door and found some such offering lying there. She knew it was illicit game, poached from one of the big estates and left there by someone who took pity on poverty, and she did not like it on either score. She was a proud woman as well as an honest one. But she could not afford to look a gift horse in the mouth. To keep her children from going hungry, she overcame both her scruples and her pride.

Sometimes, when she did sewing for Alicia Penrose at Trevarrah House, she would come home with leftover food from their kitchens, pressed on her by Trudy Billing, the housekeeper there, and though she liked that little better, seeing it as just another manifestation of charity rather than as part payment for her hard work, we children always fell upon the packages eagerly.

How those Penroses ate — especially when they had been entertaining guests! French cheeses, slices of cold ham and capon, rich fruit cake, tiny, melt-in-the-mouth sweetmeats. How the Penroses and their guests could bear to leave them uneaten on the table was a source of amazement to us children, but I suppose where there is no shortage there is less appreciation, and the dishes presented in all their glory doubtless never tasted as sweet to those spoiled rich folk as they did to us, for whom they were a rare treat.

Now, I accepted Mrs Melhuish's kind gifts with as good a grace as I could muster, knowing that they would doubtless bring as much pleasure to Mammy and Ruth and Jed as those titbits had brought to us children all those years ago. The preserves and honey were packed in my bag along with the clothes I thought I would need for my visit, my hairbrush and items of toiletry. Then, with the impatience to be home once more bubbling in my veins and the knot of anxiety as to what I would find when I got there growing and tightening in my stomach, I took my leave of the Melhuish household and boarded the coach bound for Truro.

I had sent word ahead of me on the faster mail coach that I would be arriving, but I had no way of knowing whether my letter had reached Mallen in time for Jed to come over and meet me, and as we reached the bottom of the hill and turned into St Austell Street I peered eagerly through the windows of the coach again, anxious to catch a glimpse of my sister's husband, though common sense told me that if he had indeed come to Truro, he would be waiting outside the Red Lion Inn, on the other side of the river, where the coach had its stopping place.

The street was deserted but for a few scruffy urchins who raced behind the coach, shouting, and a bent old man picking his way carefully over the still-treacherous cobbles. The snow here had mostly turned to slush, but it was still slippery enough to make for hazardous walking, and most sensible folk had chosen to stay indoors. The coach took the narrow bridge over the river, creaking loudly, and at last turned into a street of close-knit little houses with lace curtains covering their bow windows, as a girl's long hair may cover her face when she takes it from its pins and shakes it loose. The moment the coach came to a stop outside the Red Lion Inn, I was on my feet, shaking out the folds of my skirt, which clung to my legs after the long ride, and setting my bonnet straight. Then, aware of my unseemly haste, I sat down again to let the rosy-cheeked woman and her child leave the coach first.

She smiled at me.

'Go on, dearie. Your haste is greater than mine.'

I flushed, but indeed my anxiety was turning my limbs to worms, crawling over my skin, itching in my veins.

'Thank you,' I said.

The post boy handed me down and I stood for a moment, looking around me at the familiar street, searching for a face I knew. At first I thought I was to be disappointed, and I was just thinking I would have to arrange to make my own way to Mallen, when a voice I knew called to me, and I spun round to see Jed picking his way across the cobbles through the ankle-deep slush.

'Jed!' I took a step towards him, slipped and almost fell.

He put out a hand to save me, a big, countryman's hand, roughened from hard work and engrained with the dirt from the mines, which no amount of scrubbing could wash away entirely.

'Steady on now, Tamsin! You'll do yourself an injury!'

'Oh, Jed!' I leaned upon him for a moment, grateful for his calm strength. Suddenly, for all my anxiety to hear the latest news of Mammy, I wanted to postpone the moment. I was so afraid what that news might be; until I heard it from Jed's own lips, everything was as it had been.

But I could not delay the moment for long. I levered myself away from him, my eyes searching his weather-beaten face.

'Mammy... How is Mammy, Jed?'

It seemed a lifetime passed as I waited for his answer. Then a slow smile lit his eyes, and he nodded.

'Praise the Lord, and we think she's turned the corner, Tamsin. This cold snap has done her chest the world of good. 'Twas the damned fog she couldn't stand, I reckon. She's picked up since the snow came, day on day. We needn't have fetched you home, I reckon.'

'Oh Jed! Oh, that's wonderful news!' Relief was making my knees go weak and my heart felt lighter than it had for more than two weeks. 'I was so afraid that... Oh well, let's not think about that now. As for fetching me home, well, I'm just glad to be here! I miss you all so much. When Ruth's letter came, it made me realize just how much I miss you – how much I wanted to see Mammy.'

'That's all right then.' Jed was a man of few words. 'We'd best get you home.'

'You rode over?' I asked, envisioning that I would have to ride back to Mallen up behind on some horse he had borrowed, somehow juggling my bag.

17

'I done better'n that!' A slow grin split his face. 'I prevailed upon old Ross Parry for the loan of his trap.'

'Oh, what luxury!' My relief was making me gay; I laughed in delight. 'Oh, I am spoiled, Jed, and no mistake!'

'And not just you neither,' Jed returned. 'Ruth took the chance to come into Truro with me, and young Charlie too. They'm off picking up the provisions now; they'll be here any minute. We left little Billy with your ma.'

Billy, their youngest, was just six months old. If he had been left in the care of Mammy, she must indeed be much recovered! Again I felt a surge of joy, both for Mammy's returning health and the fact that I would see my sister and nephew sooner than I had expected.

Ross Parry's pony and trap were drawn up on the Red Lion courtyard; Jed took my bag and stowed it, and I watched the corner of the street eagerly, looking for Ruth's return. The slush had already soaked through my boots, made for town wear and much thinner than the stout ones worn by country folk, but I scarcely noticed. The sun was out, bathing the old stone with sharp, pale light, the sky a clear blue. The sharp air had the unmistakeable tang of home. Everything, I thought, was right with the world.

When Ruth at last rounded the corner, my first thought was how much weight she had gained since last I saw her. As children, we had all been skinny, and I, too, had filled out somewhat since then. But I was still lithe enough, whilst childbearing and a better diet had made Ruth unashamedly plump. But the face above the grey woollen cape was unmistakeably my sister's, and wreathed now in smiles as she hurried towards us as fast as the slush underfoot would allow, thrust her purchases at Jed and threw her arms around me.

'Oh Tamsin, it's so good to see you!'

'And you!' We hugged, and I looked down at little Charlie, who was hiding shyly in his mother's skirts. 'My, Charlie, how you've grown! Why, you're quite the little man!'

'He's three years old now,' Ruth reminded me. 'Come, Charlie, give your Aunt Tamsin a kiss!'

Charlie hung back even further, burying his face in Ruth's skirts, and I laughed.

'Never mind, Charlie, there'll be plenty of time for that later, when you know me better.'

'We'd best be heading for home then,' Jed said. 'There's places where the snow still lies, and we want to get back before the light starts to go.' He glanced at the sky. ''Twouldn't surprise me if we have another frost when the sun goes, neither.'

'And Billy will be ready for a feed too,' Ruth added. 'He's a hungry one and no mistake. And after all the trouble I had getting this one to take the breast, too.'

Already, though it was so long since I had seen my family, we were falling back into our old, comfortable ease in one another's company.

We climbed into the trap and set off, Charlie squashed in between me and Ruth, but still hiding his face in his mother's ample bosom.

'I cannot tell you how relieved I am to hear that dear Mammy is so much better,' I said as the trap jolted over the cobbles. 'I was so worried, Ruth, when I received your letter.'

'Oh, we were all worried,' Ruth replied. 'I'd never have written you otherwise. I couldn't see a good outcome, and that's a fact. But you know Mammy. Her spirit is that strong, she don't know how to give in.'

'It wasn't her spirit I doubted,' I said.

'No, they're all getting older,' Ruth agreed. 'Tessie Paynter died round about the time Mammy was taken bad – now there was a shock. And Ralph Penrose is in his grave too. He had the dropsy, so they say, but I reckon he died of a broken heart.'

I looked at her sharply. 'Why a broken heart?'

'Word had it that Mr Adam had been killed in the fighting in America. He's a captain in the army, you know, and his regiment was sent over there to help defend the colony against the rising. Mr Ralph still had Mr Nicholas, of course, and him now wed to Miss Isobel...'

'Nicholas and Isobel are wed?' I interrupted. 'But I always thought that she and *Adam*...'

As a child I had known the Penroses well – Adam, the elder by less than a year, Nicholas his younger brother, and Isobel Fletcher, Ralph's ward. She and I were of an age; when Mammy had been working at Trevarrah House, stitching new drapes and bed coverings, or fitting gowns for Alicia, she had used to take me with her, and Isobel and I had played together through long summer days, and become great friends. But I had always thought that it was Adam she would wed if ever she wed either of them. Certainly the last time I had seen them together, shortly before I left for Launceston, they had had eyes only for each other.

'Like I told you, word was Adam had met his end in America,' Ruth said, a little impatiently. 'I suppose Isobel thought to make the best of it and settle for Nicholas instead. If she wanted to go on living in luxury on Penrose money, she had little choice.'

'Oh Ruth, Isobel isn't like that!' I protested. 'Such a thing would never enter her head, I'm sure!'

Ruth pulled a face. 'If you say so. I never cared for her myself, but you know her better than I. Whatever, she's wed to Nicholas now, and if she still carries a candle for Adam, she'd do well to hide it.'

'He came home safe and well after all then?' I asked.

Ruth cast me a knowing glance. 'What's it to you?'

'I wouldn't like to think of Adam dead before his time in some far-off land,' I said.

'Well, you need not worry on that score,' Ruth assured me. 'He did come home, though he walks with a limp, and he bears a scar to mar his good looks. But he wasn't in time to see his father. Ralph died last May Day, and 'twas well into autumn when Adam came home. Like I say, I reckon 'twas a broken heart finished Ralph off. Adam was always his favourite, for all that he caused him endless trouble, if talk is anything to go by.'

'I'm very sorry to hear that he's dead,' I said.

'Oh – and Trudy Billing. There's another one. You remember old Trudy? Fell down the stairs and broke her leg and Isobel had her shipped off to her sister in Penzance rather than look after her at Trevarrah. But she's gone too now, I hear.'

I shivered suddenly.

Mammy might be better, and that was a wonderful relief. But death and decay were all around. Suddenly, inexplicably, I felt a weight of depression deep inside me, and it frightened me.

Sometimes, without warning, these feelings overcame me. They had begun when I was just a child, a sense of foreboding that made me cold and heavy with fear, and which seemed to come from nowhere. But almost without exception they were the harbinger of something bad. For a time, fantasizing, I had imagined that perhaps I had been cursed with 'the sight'. After all, had I not been told that I had been born in a thunderstorm, when the skies had darkened so suddenly that the lamps had to be lit so the midwife could see to deliver me, though it was the middle of the day?

I had soon come to realize, though, that to credit myself with 'the sight' was an exaggeration. I did not see the future any more than anyone else. But I did seem to know instinctively when something terrible was about to happen. I would, perhaps, fall asleep at night perfectly happy and content and wake in the morning filled with dread, or suddenly, as now, feel my mood change so markedly and for no apparent reason that there was no denying it. And I had learned to trust those feelings and fear them, no matter how I tried to reason myself out of it.

Now I gave myself a little shake and tried to tell myself the mood was nothing but an echo of the past weeks of anxiety, reawakened by the news of the three deaths. Mammy was recovering, Ruth and Jed would never otherwise have left her alone, and certainly not with little Billy in her charge. And the deaths of Tessie Paynter and Ralph Penrose and Trudy Billing had nothing whatever to do with me.

By the time we reached Mallen the sun was low and pink in the pale sky and I knew Jed had been right to make haste. Already there was a sharper nip in the air, and, with dark, the frost would come quickly, hardening the ground where the snow had melted.

As the row of cottages, straggled at right angles to the track, came into sight, my anxiety to be home quickened once more.

The cottage in which I had been born and raised was the very last in the row; the one which Ruth and Jed occupied was next door to it. When we were young it had been the home of old Mother Tripp and her two sons, simple-minded Frank and Joshua, who was something of a villain. Many was the moonlit night we had seen Joshua creep out of the house with a bag in his hand and a gun under his arm, and we suspected that the poached game that appeared on our doorstep might have met its end in the sights of Joshua's gun or in one of his traps. In the end, of course, he had been caught and brought before the magistrates.

Ralph Penrose had been the chairman of the bench – and it was his land Joshua had been poaching on. On the first occasion, Ralph treated him with surprising leniency, sending him to jail for just a short sentence. But when he was free and resumed his old ways, Ralph lost patience with him. When his case came up at quarter sessions he was sent for deportation to Australia.

Old Mother Tripp had never recovered from the shock of it, and she had died soon afterwards. Poor simple Frank was sent to the asylum, where he too died. The cottage had lain empty then for some long time, and was in such a bad state of repair Mammy was afraid the rot would spread to our own. But when Jed had come courting Ruth he had seen the possibilities it offered. He had persuaded Ralph Penrose to rent it to him and had worked hard to make it habitable in time for the wedding. Now it was a cosy, watertight home for them and their growing family, and I knew it pleased Mammy that Ruth was so close by. With me in Launceston and Ellie married to a Redruth man and moved away, it was a great comfort to her.

We rattled along the track that snaked back and forth above the fold in the hill that sheltered our houses. Since, apart from the bends that lessened the incline, it ran more or less parallel with them, I glanced down eagerly, straining my eyes towards my old home. Then I started suddenly.

'It looks as if Mammy is expecting us! She has the door open ready.'

'Oh surely not!' Ruth followed my line of vision and frowned. 'You're right! The door *is* open! Whatever is she thinking of? It'll let all the cold in, and if Billy takes a chill…'

'Lord bless us, we'd better make haste!'

Jed urged the pony on so that the trap swayed danger-ously around the last sweeping bend and rattled along the track so violently I felt sure it would fall to splinters.

As we came to a halt outside Mammy's cottage we could hear the unmistakeable lusty wail of a baby. Ruth was up and out of the trap in an instant, leaving little Charlie pouting on the seat beside me.

'Mama!' he wailed indignantly as she disappeared into the house.

'It's all right, Charlie,' I pacified him. 'I'll lift you down, never fear.'

But I was almost as anxious as Ruth. I might not have her maternal instinct to alarm me, but the feeling of foreboding was back, constricting my throat.

The door was open to the bitter cold, the baby crying… Something was wrong. I knew it in my bones. I lifted little Charlie down, but for some reason held on to his hand to keep him from running after his mother into the house. And as he struggled to free his hand from mine, I heard Ruth scream.

Jed moved fast then, dropping the reins and leaping down from the trap. And in the same moment, Ruth appeared in the doorway. Her face was ashen; baby Billy was wailing loudly in her arms, but she paid no heed to him.

'Mammy!' she gasped. 'Mammy…'

Jed strode forward. 'A turn for the worse?' he asked grimly.

'No – no!' Ruth grabbed at his coat, holding on to it for dear life as if her legs were giving way beneath her. 'No – somebody's done for her, Jed! Some varmint's murdered my mother!'

Two

All the blood seemed to leave my body in a rush; I felt my own legs go weak.

It couldn't be true! Who would murder an old woman in her own home in broad daylight?

Jed was standing as if turned to stone by her words; little Charlie, frightened by his mother's screams, began to cry loudly. Ruth grabbed him, clutching him to her so that she was all but hidden by the two wailing children.

Jed moved then with such a burst of speed as I had never before seen in a man of his size, running towards the cottage, and I followed close on his heels, my thin boots skidding on the already hardening ground.

The front door of the cottage opened directly into the living room, with the small scullery beyond and the stairs leading to the two small rooms upstairs rising from the corner.

It was dim inside the cottage even when the sun shone brightly in the noon of the day; now, with the light failing, it was a moment before I could see anything but the dark shapes of the wooden settle and rush chair and the fire burning low in the hearth. Then Jed let out an exclamation, and, hurrying to his side, I saw her, a huddled form at the foot of the stairs. 'Mammy!'

For a moment every nerve in my body froze, then I pushed past Jed and fell to my knees beside her. She lay

26

crumpled backwards, one foot on the second step up, the other bent beneath her, her head, face upwards, lying on the rough floor. Her snow-white hair was clotted darkly at the temple, more dark stains lay in thick rivulets down the side of her face and pooled beneath her on the floor. I stretched out my fingers to touch, and they came away sticky and dark as the wound.

Blood.

At first, still scarcely able to comprehend that someone should have done this to her, I thought she must have lost her footing and fallen, knocking her head on the edge of the stair or the floor as she fell. But in almost the same instant I realized it could not be so. If she had fallen down the stairs, she would be lying, not on her back, but on her face. Rather, it was as if she had been trying to escape her attacker, and failed.

'Oh Mammy!'

I bent over her motionless body, bemused, horrified, stricken by grief. And as I did so, caught the faintest whisper of rasping breath.

'Jed!' I bent closer, putting my ear to her face. A lock of my hair escaped its pins and brushed over her eyes; I pushed it impatiently aside and bent my head again. 'Jed – I believe she's still alive!'

'Good Christ!' Jed fell to his knees beside me. 'Tamsin, I believe you're right!'

His fingers went to her neck, feeling for a pulse. 'She is alive – just!'

As gently as he could, he lifted her in his arms, freeing her trapped leg, and as he did so she moaned softly.

'Fetch a blanket, Tamsin!'

I needed no second bidding. My feet flew me up the stairs, where I pulled the blanket from Mammy's bed and grabbed up her good feather pillow.

As I emerged once more down the stairs, I saw that Jed had lain Mammy on the rag rug before the fire; saw, too, Ruth standing in the doorway, afraid to come in again, especially with little Charlie, yet anxious to know what was going on.

'She's alive, Ruth,' I said.

Jed, still kneeling beside Mammy, looked up.

'Take the children home, Ruth. This is no place for them.'

'But...'

'Do as I say now! Tamsin's here. We'll do whatever is necessary. And you might call Ross Parry or young Jim Weaver to ride for the doctor. Go on now, woman, stir yer stumps! She's in a bad way.'

For a moment longer Ruth stood there as if mesmerized, then she was gone. The sound of her shrill, panicky cries for assistance floated back into the cottage along with the cries of the two children.

Jed placed the pillow beneath Mammy's poor head and I bent over her again, anxious to see if I could discern any other injuries before covering her with the blanket. Her ankle, where she had fallen on it, was twisted at an odd angle and swollen to almost twice its normal size, otherwise I could see no obvious signs of harm. But Jed, arranging Mammy's head upon the pillow, let out a low exclamation.

'She has a wound on the back of her head, Tamsin.'

I slid my fingers beneath Mammy's disarrayed hair and felt them sticky with blood. It was not just her temple that was injured, then. Cautiously I explored the wound.

An indentation, as if she had been struck sharply with something heavy and blunt.

'Oh Mammy, what have they done to you?' I whispered, distressed.

'Best wait for the doctor,' Jed said. 'He'll know what's to be done.'

I bit my lip, looking down at the still form and listening to those faint, tortured whispers of breath rattling in her throat.

Dr Warburton was much respected in the district; he attended gentry and humble folk alike, even though he had to wait for his payment from them more often than not, and sometimes never received it at all. But I wondered, with a sick heart, whether there was anything that he would be able to do, clever physician though he was. Mammy had been severely injured, one did not need medical training to know that, and she had only just begun to make a recovery from a life-threatening illness. Even a young person, with all their health and strength, would be in mortal danger from such injuries; Mammy was nearly fifty years old and worn out by a hard life and a serious bout of sickness.

But Jed was right on one score. I had no idea what to do for the best except for keeping Mammy warm and making her as comfortable as was possible. We could only wait for the arrival of Dr Warburton and pray that he would be able to work some miracle.

Between us, Jed and I spread the blanket and laid it over Mammy's still form, tucking it around her. Then I lit the rush lamp and some candles, for it was growing rapidly dark.

It was as I carried a candle to the table that I noticed something lying on the floor, catching the flickering light of the candle and glinting softly. I set down the candle and bent to pick it up, holding it in the palm of my hand.

'A silver button!' I murmured, puzzled, and then, more loudly, to Jed: 'There's a silver button here, rolled into a corner!'

Jed pulled himself to his feet and came over to join me, first peering at the button in my hand, then taking it from me and examining it more loosely.

'Well, it's a button all right,' he said, scratching his head. 'But silver? Surely not! Your mammy doesn't have such luxuries as silver buttons.'

'I know that,' I said impatiently. 'But suppose it belongs to whoever attacked her? Suppose there was a straggle of some kind and she pulled it from his clothing?'

'Could be, I suppose.' Jed scratched his head again. 'But *silver*? The sort o' varmint who did this wouldn't be likely to have silver buttons neither.'

'Unless it's his practice to rob wherever he can,' I said. 'Oh, what does it matter anyway? I'll put it away for safe keeping in case it may help to identify her attacker, but I can't be bothered thinking about it now. Mammy is my only concern. Is there nothing we can do whilst we wait for Dr Warburton?'

'We could try a drop o' brandy, I suppose,' Jed suggested doubtfully.

'You have brandy?' I exclaimed.

'I came by some cheap last summer,' Jed admitted, a little sheepishly, and I guessed the rest. Contraband. Sometimes the smugglers who ran the gauntlet from the hidden coves along the coast to France let some of their booty go cheaply to locals, though most of it went up the line inland to more profitable markets. Someone had owed Jed a favour, perhaps, and repaid him with a jar of good brandy.

'Well, why didn't you say so?' I dropped the button into a cup on the top shelf of the dresser and hastened to the door. 'Will Ruth know where it is?'

'I reckon so,' he replied wryly. 'She's not averse to a drop herself when the children are in bed and asleep.'

I hurried out of Mammy's cottage and into Ruth and Jed's. Charlie, exhausted no doubt by his trip to Truro and his fright on returning, was curled on the settle, fast asleep, whilst Ruth sat in the wicker rocking chair, baby Billy at her breast. She glanced up anxiously as I came in, the shadows cast by the rush light accentuating the deep lines of worry in her plump face.

'Tamsin… is she…?'

'She's still alive,' I hastened to reassure her. 'But she's still senseless, too. She's taken two bad blows to her skull, Ruth – one at the back as well as her forehead. You've sent for the doctor?'

She nodded, wincing as Billy sucked hard and the two little teeth that were breaking through fastened painfully on her nipple.

'Young Jim Weaver's set off post-haste riding his father's pony. She's a fleet little horse. He'll be at the doctor's in no time. Just as long as the doctor isn't out attending a patient in some far-flung part. Mrs Thorne, the actuary's wife, is close to her time, I know for a fact, and a lady of her standing is sure to want the doctor in attendance for her confinement, not just the midwife.'

'In that case we must pray she's not chosen today to go into labour then,' I said shortly. 'Jed says you've some brandy in the house.'

Ruth's lips pursed. 'He shouldn't be drinking brandy at a time like this. He needs all his wits about him, not befuddled by blessed brandy!'

'It's not for Jed,' I said impatiently. 'It's for Mammy. You never know, it might help to revive her.'

'It might, I suppose.' Ruth jerked her head in the direction of the dresser. 'It's in there, on the bottom shelf...'

I crossed to the dresser and took out the jar I found there. One sniff told me it was good cognac, not the rough brew that sometimes passed for brandy amongst the poor. A whole keg of this would be worth a pretty penny, if I was not much mistaken.

'Oh Tamsin, who could have done such a terrible thing?' Ruth was saying. 'Why would anyone attack poor Mammy? She's nothing worth stealing, God knows. And why did no one hear the rumpus and come to her aid? Mammy's not one to give in without a fight. But Jim Weaver says they heard nothing and saw no one.'

'I suppose the weather is keeping the women in beside their fires,' I said, 'and the menfolk would still have been at the mine, or out in the fields, taking feed to the cattle. But never mind that now. We'll think about it later. For the moment I can only concern myself with Mammy.'

I started for the door, the jar of brandy in my hand.

'Oh, I could do with a drop o' that before you take it,' Ruth said urgently. 'I'm that shook up...!'

I fixed her with a hard stare.

'And risk getting little Billy drunk as well as yourself? I don't think so, Ruth. The time for brandy is not whilst you still have a child at your breast.'

Her eyes, a little ashamed, dropped from mine, and I took pity on her. The Good Lord alone knew I could use a little sustenance myself, and I was not a drinking woman.

Ruth, in being the one to find Mammy, had had an even worse shock than I.

'Oh, I suppose a little nip wouldn't do you any harm, so long as you take some water with it.'

I found a cup, poured a small measure into it, and topped it up from the ewer on the dresser. Ruth took it from me gratefully, juggling Billy on one arm as she sipped, and instantly I saw a bit of rosy colour come back into her pale cheeks.

'I must go, Ruth. I'll let you know at once if there is any change.'

I hurried back to Mammy's cottage. Jed was still kneeling beside Mammy, rubbing her cold little hands between his own to try and chafe some warmth into them.

'You found the brandy?' he asked.

'Yes.' I did not tell him I had administered a medicinal dose to his wife. He would not approve, I thought.

I fetched the smallest glass I could find, one that Mammy had used as an eye bath when we were children and got a fly or a speck of dust in our eyes, and poured a drop of brandy into it. Then Jed raised her head as gently as he could and I put the glass to her lips.

But Mammy still lay totally inert and the brandy merely trickled in a thin stream down her chin.

I dipped my finger into the glass and moistened her lips with it. Still no response. I did it again, managing this time to get a few drops on to her tongue, and this time her mouth moved a little, smacking her dry lips together feebly.

I dipped my finger in the liquid again and scooped some on to Mammy's tongue.

'Not too much now,' Jed said warningly. 'It's strong stuff, and we don't want…'

'I'll try some water.' I fetched Mammy's pitcher and repeated the exercise, then poured a little into the tiny glass and put that to her lips. Most of it, however, merely trickled down her chin.

'Oh Jed, if only she could rally a little!' I groaned.

'If anyone can rally, it's your mammy,' Jed said. 'But she's in a bad way, and no mistake.'

'Hush!' I said fiercely. 'Don't let her hear you say such things!'

'She ain't able to hear...'

'You don't know that!' I said fiercely, bending over my mother and smoothing the hair away from her ashen, clammy face, and the angry wound on her temple.

'Mammy,' I said softly. 'Don't be afraid. You're safe now, and the doctor is on his way. You are going to get through this, I know. And you know who I am, don't you? It's Tamsin, come all the way from Launceston, just to see you. So just you open your eyes and look at me! Can you do that?'

Mammy's eyelids did not so much as flicker.

'For me, Mammy,' I urged. 'For Tamsin!'

'It's no good.' Jed's tone was low and despairing.

'Don't say that!' I admonished him, but I did not try to get Mammy to wake again. Perhaps I was wrong to do so, perhaps this unnatural slumber was nature's way of helping her to recover from whatever terrible ordeal she had endured. I did not know. I really did not know what to do for the best.

'Everything is going to be all right, Mammy,' I said softly.

I sat beside her, my legs curled up beneath my travel-dusty, crumpled skirts, and took her hand in mine.

There was nothing now to be done beyond waiting for Dr Warburton's arrival.

And even after that, perhaps, still nothing to be done but wait.

–

Darkness had fallen before we heard the clip-clop of hooves on the track outside, and there was still no change in Mammy's condition.

The moment we heard the horse approaching, Jed leapt up and went to open the door, and then the portly figure of Dr Warburton appeared in the doorway.

His wig was a little awry, his face even more flushed than the usual high colour which a liking for too much port had daubed in his cheeks. He had ridden hard, not a doubt of it, and I felt grateful to him. It was not as if we could afford to recompense him generously for his trouble. He came into the living room, taking off his hat and depositing it, together with his medical bag, on the table.

'Well, what's to do? There's good reason for young Jimmy Weaver to have dragged me away from my fireside on a night such as this, I hope.'

'Indeed, Doctor, I wish there was not!' I said sharply. 'We came home and found Mammy half dead upon the floor.'

He peered at me closely, straightening his wig.

'It's Tamsin, isn't it?'

'Yes, sir.'

'Thought you were away in service.'

'I am, but I'm home now.' I moved impatiently. 'Please, Doctor, won't you take a look at Mammy? She's still breathing and I think her lips moved when I tried to give her a mouthful of water. But she doesn't move nor speak, and her head is hurt very bad.'

'Hmm.' For the first time he seemed to acknowledge Mammy, lying there on the rug in front of the fire. 'Let's see now.'

With some huffing and puffing he managed to get to his knees beside her, then grunted incomprehensibly as he made an initial examination.

'A blow to both the front of the head and the back, too,' he said at last, straightening and stretching out a hand for a cloth to wipe his hands. 'How did this happen?'

'We think she was hit from behind by an attacker,' I said. 'Perhaps she hit her forehead when she fell, but we really don't know. She was alone in the house at the time.'

'An attacker!' Dr Warburton looked startled. 'Well, they've made a pretty mess of her and no mistake.'

He bent to examine the wound once more whilst I held a candle close to enable him to see the better.

'The bleeding seems to have stopped of its own accord,' he said. 'I'll cleanse the wound if you'll bring me a bowl of hot water, and then perhaps we'll know more. The danger is that it may still be bleeding inside her skull, where it can't be seen. Maybe if I were to apply the leeches it would help. Draw some of that excess blood off. Otherwise... well, much as it pains me to admit it, there's little I can do. Your mother will either regain consciousness or she won't. That's all there is to it.'

'Have you seen patients recover from such a condition?' I asked.

'I most certainly have! Owen Trewith, but for one, took a bad fall from his horse and hit his head on a stone. He lay knowing no one for the best part of a week. Now

36

he rides with the hunt again, regular. But I've seen them fade away, too. It all depends. You must prepare yourself for the worst, Miss Hardy. And pray for the best. I can't say more.'

It was less than I had hoped for, but no more than I feared.

'Let's have a good look at her then.' He pulled the blanket aside, running his hands over Mammy's inert body in a way that would have horrified her had she been aware of it. 'Hmm... that ankle looks bad, but a cold compress should see it right. No bones broken that I can see. Has she a nightgown? Best get her into it, then I'll give you a hand to get her into her bed. Then all you can do is try to get her to take some water and hope for the best.'

Whilst I ran upstairs to prepare Mammy's bed and fetch her nightgown, Dr Warburton applied the cold compress to her ankle and cleaned her wounds as best he could. Then Jed carried her up the narrow stairs in his arms as one would carry a child and laid her down. Between us we got her out of her rough woollen gown, and I was about to lift the nightdress over her head when I noticed a patch of dark bruising around her midriff.

'Doctor – what's this?'

He moved from the window where he had been staring out into the darkness.

'Another flurry of snow... I mustn't delay my return home too long... What's that? What did you say?'

'Here!' I indicated the bruised area, then noticed more dark marks on her arms, just above the elbows. 'And here! Look!'

'Hmm.' He touched the bruised area of her ribs, probing gently, then examined her arms. 'If she were a young ruffian, I'd say she'd been in a fight. It looks to me like she's been punched – or kicked. Could be a rib or two cracked there. We'd best get a tight binder on her. And these…' He pointed to the smaller bruises on her thin arms. 'These, damn me if they don't look like finger marks! Someone has held your mother by her arms and shaken her, if you want my opinion. A bad business, Miss Hardy. A very bad business.' He turned accusingly to Jed. 'Are you sure you know nothing of this, Carrow?'

Jed bristled. 'What are you saying, Doctor? That I'd do something like this to my own mother-in-law?'

'It's not unknown,' the doctor returned, unabashed. 'The old can be enough to try the patience of a saint and make him snap with rage. Especially when they ain't your own flesh and blood.'

'Jed had nothing to do with this,' I said quickly. 'He and Ruth were in Truro meeting me when the attack took place, and in any case, my mother was not of the temperament you describe. I cannot think of anyone in the world who would wish her harm.'

'Someone did, Miss Hardy. That much is not in doubt.'

He returned to the window, looking out for a moment.

'This snow is coming thicker. I must be on my way, or I'll not make it home tonight. Can you attend to binding your mother's ribs? I'll leave a potion too – administer a few drops if you can get her to take it. Beyond that there's nothing to be done but let her rest.'

'Will you come again, Doctor?' I asked.

'Weather permitting. Though I don't know what good it will do.' That was, I knew, a hard admission for any doctor to make. 'When she comes round – if she comes round – keep her quiet and send for me. Otherwise, it's the parson you'll be needing.'

I showed him downstairs and watched him mount his horse and ride off into the falling snow. Then I went back into the house and upstairs. Jed, good soul that he was, had waited with Mammy until my return so that she would not be left alone.

'You must go to Ruth,' I said. 'She needs you, and you heard what Dr Warburton said. There's no more you can do here.'

'He said to bind your mother's ribs,' Jed reminded me. 'I could help you with that.'

'I don't think we should disturb her,' I said. 'It's not as if she's moving about. If she should come round, then perhaps I'll do it. But just for now she's taken enough manhandling for one day.'

'Should I ride over to Truro, do you think, and alert the law that there's a dangerous man on the loose?' Jed asked.

'Not tonight,' I said. 'It's snowing hard, and what good will it do? The constable won't be too bothered with the likes of us. If it were one of the gentry harmed so, it might be different, but as it is…'

'You'm right there,' Jed agreed bitterly.

'In any case, whoever did this is long gone,' I continued. 'I doubt we'll ever know who it was, for there's no rhyme nor reason behind it. 'Twas a wandering madman, no doubt.'

But even as I said it, I was thinking of the silver button. It might well provide a clue as to the identity of my mother's attacker. Certainly, if a man was apprehended and found to be missing such a button, the proof of his guilt was downstairs, in a jug we used for keeping oddments, on the top shelf of the dresser.

But with no suspect and no motive for the crime, a single button would be little use to the constable or anyone else. Better to keep it safe until we had had the chance to talk to our neighbours or anyone who might have seen a stranger in these parts this afternoon. For my mother had not been attacked by anyone from our hamlet, of that much I was certain.

'Go to Ruth, Jed,' I urged. 'She's in no fit state to have sole care of the two little ones. It's what Mammy would bid you do if she were able.'

Jed lumbered to the door. 'Maybe you'm right, Tamsin. It's a good thing you're here, is all I can say. But, Judas God, what a homecoming for you!'

I had never before heard Jed curse so; he was a quiet, God-fearing man who never blasphemed, though he never went to services on a Sunday either. But just now I could not find it in my heart to blame him for it. What had occurred here today was enough to make the most pious soul irreverent.

'It wasn't the homecoming I hoped for,' I agreed. 'Nor the one I feared either. I was so afraid the Good Lord might have taken Mammy – but in her own bed, of natural causes. I never for one moment dreamed...' I broke off, tears springing to my eyes as I looked down at her, so tiny and frail beneath the bed covers, and so frighteningly still. 'But yes, thank God I am here. At least I can do my best to care for her.' I touched her hand, and added for her benefit, just in case she could hear me: 'And nurse her back to health, for that is what I intend to do. She'll be fine in next to no time, Jed, just see if she's not!'

Jed made no reply. At the door he looked back.

'You know where we are if you need us, Tamsin.'

I forced a smile. 'Thank you, Jed.'

Then he was gone, and I was alone with Mammy. I pulled a chair up beside her bed and sat down, taking her hand in mine. For all my brave words, Mammy's recovery from this was something I did not dare hope for.

Why? Why? Who had done this terrible thing? And *why*!

A sprightly little breeze blew a flurry of snow against the window, and still I sat. I had had nothing to eat all day but a wedge of bread and cheese when the coach had stopped at an inn to change horses, and that had been hours ago. There was food in the scullery, I knew – Mama would have had something ready for my supper – but I had no appetite at all and could not imagine I ever would again.

All that mattered was pulling Mammy through this. For the moment I could think of nothing else, not even discovering who had done this terrible thing.

The anger and the desire for retribution would come later, I knew. Then, if I could learn the identity of Mammy's attacker, I would pursue him to the ends of the earth to gain justice for her. Why, I would see him hanged for it, me, who hated violence of any kind, and I would feel no shred of pity. I would do it myself, given the opportunity!

But for now I could think of nothing but the threads of breath that were the only sound in the quiet room, and my prayers to a god whom I was not even sure I wanted to pray to, given that he could allow something like this to happen to a dear, loving woman who had lived her life thinking only of the good of others.

'Oh Mammy,' I whispered. 'Oh, Mammy, please come back to me!'

It was going to be a long night.

Three

There was no change in Mammy's condition. I stayed all night at her bedside, making myself as comfortable as I could in the wicker rocker, which I dragged up from the living room and equipped with pillows and a blanket.

When the first grey light of dawn came creeping in I threw back the shutters and blew out the guttering candle which I had left burning and which was now reduced to a small stump.

The snow had come to nothing this time. It must have petered out under cover of darkness and something of a thaw set in, for the moorland on the other side of the valley had a grey and sodden appearance, more depressing somehow than the crisp white I had expected, though of course a great deal less inconvenient.

I went downstairs, lit the fire and set the water to boil to make myself a dish of tea, then poured some water from the pitcher into the small glass and took it upstairs to try to give Mammy a drink of sorts. This I managed more successfully than before, though perhaps that was simply because I was becoming more practised at dripping it into her mouth, and not, as I desperately hoped, that she was a little more responsive. Whichever, I managed to get at least half of it into her.

I had just finished and was wiping her chin and doing my best to tidy her hair when I heard Ruth's voice calling from below and her footsteps on the stairs. Then her anxious face appeared in the doorway.

'Tamsin…?'

'There's no change,' I said wearily.

'Oh, I've barely slept for worrying! And baby Billy woke three times during the night, and Charlie too. He knows something is very wrong.' She glanced at the rocker. 'It doesn't look as though you had much sleep either, Tamsin.'

'Oh, I'm all right,' I said impatiently, though in truth I was very stiff and there was a horrid taste in my mouth. 'Don't concern yourself with me, Ruth. You do what needs to be done to look after your own family. There's no point two of us just sitting here worrying.'

Somewhat reluctantly Ruth left to go back to her own house and make breakfast for Jed and Charlie and feed little Billy, and I was left alone once more.

I was not to be alone for long, however. Soon, a procession of neighbours began knocking at the door, first the men, before leaving for their day's work on the land or at the mine, then the womenfolk. All were concerned to know how Mammy fared, and shocked by what had occurred. The news had spread like wildfire from house to house as such news always spreads. But none could shed any light on the events of the previous day.

The men, as I had thought, had all been at their work, the women busy in their sculleries at the rear of the houses. No one had seen a stranger, nor any visitor to Mammy's cottage. Alice Weaver, Jim's mother, thought she had heard a horse some time in the early afternoon, but she had paid no attention.

'I thought 'twas Jed and Ruth back with Ross Parry's horse and trap,' she said. 'Though now I come to think of it, 'twas too soon after they left. Oh, if only I'd come out to have a look-see! Maybe I'd have frightened the varmint off, whoever he were.'

'And maybe you'd have a broken head too,' I returned. 'It's no sense blaming yourself, Alice. And we don't even know if the attacker came on horseback. He might have come across the moors on foot. Mammy's would be the first cottage he came to if he did.'

'I still can't make out how we heard nothing,' Alice argued. 'I know I'd have kicked up one hell of a row if I'd found a strange man in *my* house, and your ma would have done the same. She wouldn't be one to give in quiet-like.'

'From the injuries she received, it's clear she did not,' I said grimly. 'She had been beaten or kicked as well as hit over the head.'

''Twas fair bad luck he came when Jed and Ruth were over to Truro.' Alice shook her head, then drew her breath in sharply as another thought occurred to her. 'P'raps, though, that's a blessing in disguise. If Ruth had come running and those little ones with her… Oh, 'tis terrible enough that your poor ma took the brunt of it, but if anything had happened to those babies…'

'Baby Billy was here,' I told her. 'Ruth left him with Mammy rather than drag him to Truro in the cold. He must have been in his basket all through the attack. He was crying pitifully when we got home and found him.'

'Sakes alive!' Alice's hand went to her breast. 'It's a wonder he wasn't done away with too! If he'd woke and started that crying… oh Lord, it don't bear thinking about!'

'Well, he wasn't harmed, thank God,' I said. But a chill ran through my veins all the same. If Billy had drawn attention to himself, then it was all too possible the attacker would have silenced him. A baby's cry at the best of times can drive the most placid of souls to distraction and raise a violent response that must be kept under control. What would it have done to a man deranged or dangerous enough to have attacked my poor defenceless mammy in such brutal fashion? Especially if he had feared the baby's cries would alert someone to his presence here, where he had no business.

It seemed inconceivable that Billy could have slept through such a commotion as there must have been, yet miraculously he was unharmed.

'All I can say,' Alice went on, 'is that if ever we get wind of who done this to your ma, there's no way he'll ever get to be brought up before the magistrate. The men'll get together and see he's treated to their brand of justice. By the time he's hanging on the end of a rope, he'll be glad for death to put an end to his misery, and that's a fact. And my Jake and Jim will be amongst the first to give him his just desserts. They'm both in a terrible way about it all.'

I nodded. 'Thank you, Alice. I'm sure they are. And thank your Jim, too, for going for the doctor as he did. You're good neighbours, and always have been.'

'Yes, well, we've gotta stick together, ain't we, and stand up for one another. Lord knows, there's nobody else to do it for us. Not since Mr Ralph Penrose took bad and died. He were a good squire in his way. He treated us fair enough, and did look after his tenants. But this one... I'm not so sure about he. We haven't seen hide nor hair of him since his father died.'

'Mr Adam, you mean?' I asked.

'No, Mr Nicholas. Oh, the squire should have been Mr Adam, I grant you, him being the elder of the two by a year. But he was off in Americky, fighting for his country

45

when his father pegged it. Word was that he'd been killed in action. By the time he got home – and wounded, too, I might add, Mr Nicholas had set himself up as squire. And married to Miss Isobel too, who was always, as we thought, Mr Adam's sweetheart. Now whether Mr Ralph, thinking as how Mr Adam was dead, made the estate over to Mr Nicholas legal-like, or whether he just took it upon himself, that we don't know. But whichever, 'tis Mr Nicholas living at Trevarrah House, and Mr Adam in the keeper's cottage.'

'And Isobel the mistress of the house, I suppose,' I said. 'Well, unconventional it might be, but I suppose it makes sense. It was always her home, too, after all. Even though she was not his flesh and blood, Mr Ralph always treated her like a daughter.'

'He did that. But his boys never treated her like a sister – or not as a sister *should* be treated in a decent world. A sight too fond of her for that. And Mr Adam always the wild one, too, causing all kinds of bother for his poor father, and him a magistrate. Though these days, 'tis rumoured Mr Nicholas is near as bad if not worse. He gambles a great deal more than he can afford, it's said, and could be running the estate into ruin. It must be in the blood…'

Alice caught herself, glancing up at the ceiling.

'Oh, I'm sorry, Tamsin. Your poor ma lying up there in a state like that, and me gossiping! Jake always says I don't know when to hold my tongue, and I 'spect he's right about that.'

I smiled faintly. Alice had a heart of gold, but she was indeed known as the gossip of the hamlet.

'It's all right, Alice,' I said. 'It will do me no harm to think of nothing but poor Mammy every single minute.'

'But 'tis disrespectful! I shouldn't have gone on about it, not with poor Rose…'

'She's not dead yet,' I said spiritedly. 'And she won't be either if I have anything to do with it!'

Alice touched my arm.

'You're like her in so many ways, Tamsin, do you know that? She's always been a fighter, and you are too. Never say die, that was her motto. Never say die. I 'spect she's muttering to herself now, though so quiet you can't hear her.'

I smiled again. 'I expect she is.'

'And you – you'll find the strength to see you through, come what may. Like I say, you take after her in more ways than one. And more than either of the others. Ellie's more like your pa was, quiet-like, keeps everything inside 'er. And Ruth… well, I don't rightly know who Ruth do take after. A bit excitable, your Ruth, though I'm not saying but what she's a good girl, and a good wife and mother too. But you – you'm your mother's daughter and no mistake. There's not much in this life you'll let get the better of you.'

She broke off. 'Oh lawks, there I go again! I must get back to me own house and leave you in peace. But you know where I am if you want me.'

I nodded. 'Thank you, Alice. You're very kind.'

But I was beginning to feel wearied by her endless chatter, and I was anxious to check on Mammy again.

'Oh 'tis nothing, 'tis nothing. No more'n your ma would do if it were us…' Alice was still rabbiting on, I believe, as I closed the door; still rabbiting on to herself, no doubt, as she paddled her way back through the slush to her own cottage. It was lucky for him that he was stone deaf, I thought, with a little smile.

I went back upstairs. Mammy lay exactly as I had left her.

It was at noon that another knock came on the door, and as I went to answer it I thought there was not another neighbor left who had not yet called. Someone must be making a return visit.

I pulled the door open and started in surprise. Two fine horses stood impatiently pawing the ground, and on the doorstep stood two people I would never have expected to see there.

Nicholas Penrose and Isobel Fletcher – now, of course, Isobel Penrose!

Nicholas, tall and impossibly handsome, cut a fine figure, dressed as he was in redingote, breeches and boots, with a hat pulled low over his dark, curling hair. Isobel, even more beautiful than I remembered, wore a coat and riding skirt of deepest blue, which set off the fairness of her skin to perfection. On her corn-coloured hair a cap perched jauntily and the ride in the cold air had brought roses to her cheeks. She had always been a lovely girl, if a little fragile, but maturity had given her a more womanly roundness and a glow to her perfectly formed features.

'Isobel!' I gasped. And bobbed a quick curtsey to her husband. 'Sir!'

'Oh my poor Tamsin!' Isobel reached for my hands, pulling me close enough to give me a hug and kiss my cheek. 'The moment we heard the news we could do nothing but ride over and learn for ourselves the truth of what has happened here. How is your poor mother? Is she…?'

'She's still alive,' I said. 'Just. But she is still dead to the world, I'm afraid.'

A glance passed between them.

'So she can tell you nothing of what happened?' Isobel asked.

'Nothing.'

'What does the doctor say? You have had him to see her? Does he think...?'

'He does not know. There is a chance that she could make a full recovery, but it could as easily go the other way. There's no way of telling.' I broke off, awkward suddenly, for it occurred to me I could hardly leave them standing on the doorstep when they had ridden all this way out of kindness and concern.

'Won't you come in?' I said, standing aside and pushing the door wide.

Nicholas, I thought, hesitated briefly, but Isobel needed no second bidding.

'Thank you, Tamsin.'

She went past me into the little living room and I caught the faintest scent of roses as she passed. Isobel did not smother herself with heavy perfume to cover less pleasant smells as so many grand ladies did; always she had been fastidious about her toilet, and she was now sweet and fresh as a wild flower with the morning dew upon it. Small wonder, I thought, that both sons of her guardian had fallen for her charms.

Nicholas followed her into the tiny room and stood before the fire, fanning open his coat tails to the warmth, whilst Isobel looked around with interested eyes. Suddenly I was painfully aware of how different it all was from her own grand home, spacious and comfortable, furnished with no thought to sparing expense, and decorated with rich artefacts. I knew it well; I had spent many happy hours playing with her there whilst Mammy worked. But Isobel had never before been inside my home.

It was, to me, of course, just that – my home – and I loved every corner of it. The wooden settle where as children we had snuggled side by side on winter evenings whilst Papa sat in the rocker and read his newspaper, the fireside nook with the gleaming fire irons and pile of kindling, the chipped china dog who sat in pride of place on the mantelshelf, each of them held for me the most precious of memories.

But they would mean nothing to Isobel. She would see only furniture, worn from use, which had been plain and rough even when it was new, and threadbare drapes at the windows. Even the darkness of the room would be foreign to her, for the windows at Trevarrah were large and let in a good light on the dullest of days, and the smallness might seem claustrophobic to her.

But there it was, for all our old friendship, we came from two different worlds. And I was not about to apologize for our poverty, nor feel ashamed of it.

'Can I offer you a dish of tea?' I asked.

'Oh no, it's not our intention to make trouble for you!' Isobel said.

'It's no trouble.'

'No, really.'

'Thank you, no,' Nicholas said. It was the first time he had spoken. His voice was deep and rich. The last time I had heard it, it had been reedy, I fancied – that strange uncertain croak that boys acquire when they are on the verge of becoming men.

'I have informed the constable at Truro of this,' he went on, 'but he holds out little hope of finding out who was responsible. A desperate man on the run, he seemed to think – a convict escaped from Bodmin Gaol, perhaps, hiding out on the moors and looking for sustenance. Was food missing from your kitchen?'

'I don't know,' I said. 'It never occurred to me to look, and I wouldn't know what Mammy had in, in any case. But I did not notice that anything was unduly disturbed. A stool had been overturned in this room but there was nothing untoward in the scullery.'

'Perhaps the rascal ran empty-handed in panic when he realized what he had done to your poor mama,' Nicholas said. 'Doubtless when the snow clears they'll find him dead of exposure and hunger on the moors, or in a cave in the cliffs.'

'Perhaps,' I agreed. Though the scenario was pure supposition, there seemed no other explanation for such a desperate occurrence, and in broad daylight too. 'One does occasionally hear of such things. And Mammy had no enemies, no one who would wish her harm. Of that much I am certain.'

'No, not she,' Isobel agreed emphatically. 'She was not the woman to make enemies. I cannot believe that anyone who knew her could be responsible for something so terrible.'

'I am warning all my tenants to ensure they keep their doors securely barred day and night until the man is found, dead or alive,' Nicholas said. 'Not that that is of any help to your poor mama, of course, but it may save some other poor soul from a similar fate. You did not have your door barred, I notice, Tamsin, in spite of what has happened.'

'No. Perhaps it is a little unwise of me, but I doubt the attacker will return to the scene of his crime,' I said. 'Besides, I do not like the idea of being locked in, and my sister and the children are next door. I don't want to lock them out either.'

'Your sister and her children were not there yesterday,' Nicholas said.

I was not sure if it was a question or a statement.

'Ruth and her elder boy had come into Truro with Jed to meet me from the coach,' I said.

'Hmm.' Nicholas's eyes narrowed. 'You do not think it possible, then, that perhaps your mama's attacker saw them leave and knew he could break in here undisturbed?'

'Surely if that were the case, he would have broken into the house he knew to be unoccupied,' I said.

'Perhaps if he were watching from the moors he made a mistake,' Nicholas suggested. 'The houses are, after all, identical, and the door of your mother's house and the one next door quite close together. And the horse and trap might have obscured his vision.'

A thought occurred to me.

'It's possible,' I said, 'that Ruth and Jed *did* come out of Mammy's door. Ruth left the baby with her; she would have taken him into Mammy's house at the last moment, and perhaps Charlie went in with her. He is very fond of his grand-mama. Jed would have fetched the trap from Mr Parry and then driven along the track to pick them up. A watcher might well have thought the wrong house was unoccupied.'

'Well there you have it!' Nicholas tapped his riding crop against his thigh. 'When he broke in, thinking to find the house empty, there, instead, was your mama. He panicked and attacked her.'

'It may be so,' I agreed, 'but whatever...' I bit my lip. 'She's in a bad way now for putting up a fight.'

'Oh Tamsin!' Isobel touched my hand. Her cornflower-blue eyes were sparkling with tears of sympathy. 'I only wish there was something we could do to help. If you can think of anything – anything at all – you must not hesitate to mention it and we shall oblige.'

I nodded without speaking. The sight of her tears was making my own eyes prick and there was a lump in my throat. So far I had been too shocked and frantic with anxiety to cry a single tear; suddenly I felt that if I began now, the floodgates would open and I would never stop.

Isobel, I think, must have noticed my fight to retain my composure.

'It's good that you are home, Tamsin,' she said, changing the subject. 'I cannot tell you how good it is to see you again after so long – albeit we could both wish that it were under different circumstances. I often think of the good times we spent together. We had such fun, did we not, you and I? And it made such a pleasant change for me to have another girl for company, when most of the time I could do nothing but tag along behind the boys – making a dreadful nuisance of myself, no doubt.'

Not so much a nuisance that they did not both fall in love with you, I thought wryly.

'Yes, they were good times,' I agreed. 'I, too, have happy memories of them.'

'Have you come home for good?' Nicholas asked. 'Has your employer in Launceston released you?'

I started. I had not yet given a single thought to the fact that I was expected back in Launceston in a week's time. Mammy's condition had totally occupied my mind.

'I came for a visit only,' I said. 'Ruth had written me that Mammy was sick, and I wanted to see her. I should be on the coach back up-country next week, but now...' I broke off.

'You cannot leave your mother in such a condition,' Isobel finished for me.

'I certainly cannot,' I confirmed. 'Ruth has too many responsibilities to give her the care she needs, and even if that were not the case, I would not go.'

'So you will lose your employment to care for your mother,' Nicholas said.

'If I have to, yes,' I replied. 'Would not any daughter do the same?'

Nicholas picked up his hat, which he had laid down on the table.

'Well, we'll take our leave, Tamsin. I'm sure you have a great deal more to do than spend the day with visitors.'

'But we felt we must come over and express our concern,' Isobel said, and added, with a little smile: 'And besides, I wanted to see you, Tamsin. I have missed you, you know.'

I nodded. 'And I you.'

'Now be sure to keep us informed as to how things go.' Nicholas was moving to the door, his usual long strides modified to cater for the smallness of the room with its clutter of furniture. 'And be assured we shall leave no stone unturned in the effort to find the man who was responsible for this outrage and bring him to justice.'

'I'm very grateful,' I said, and it was no more than the truth. Any offer of assistance was welcome, and especially one from a man as influential as Nicholas Penrose. But it was also totally unexpected. Had not Alice Weaver said he was an uninterested squire? Well, it seemed she was wrong on that score. Unless, of course, it was Isobel who had brought her influence to bear on him. Yes, that must be it. Isobel had been my friend, and she had seemed genuinely pleased to see me, as I had been to see her. It must have been Isobel who had urged her husband to take a personal interest in our plight.

Now, she drew on her soft leather riding gloves, straightened her little three-cornered hat, and kissed me again on the cheek. Nicholas handed her up on to her horse – a sleek little bay mare – and mounted his own fine hunter with athleticism and grace. Even I, my mind preoccupied with worry, could not help but think what a handsome couple they made. Then they were gone, heading back, not along the track that ran the length of the row of houses, but directly on to the moors in the direction of Trevarrah.

I went immediately upstairs to check on Mammy; there was no change. And before I had even finished fussing over her bed covers, I heard Alice calling from downstairs.

'Be 'ee there, Tamsin?'

In spite of my anxiety, I could not help but smile. It was typical of Alice, I thought. She had seen the fine horses at our door and could not contain her curiosity.

The moment I descended the stairs, my suspicion was confirmed.

'You had some grand visitors and no mistake!' Her face was flushed with excitement. 'Fancy Mr Nicholas calling on you! My, you are honoured! What did he want, may I ask?'

'Word had reached them of what happened to Mammy,' I said. 'They were concerned.'

'Mr Nicholas – concerned! Well, there's a turn-up for the books! I never would've thought he'd have time for the likes of us!'

'Perhaps you do him an injustice,' I said. 'Though I expect it was Isobel who suggested they ride over.'

Alice pursed her lips. 'I always thought she was as bad as he.'

'She was my friend,' I said quietly. 'Friendship does count a great deal, you know, especially when it is forged young.'

Alice chattered on for a while, then asked if she could see Mammy. I took her up, and was glad of her offer to sit with Mammy for a while to enable me to get on with some of the necessary chores. So far the day had been an endless round of visitors; with that and sitting with Mammy myself I had not even had the chance to bring in fresh wood for the fire or think about preparing myself something to eat.

As I worked I found myself thinking about what Nicholas had said about me being forced to give up my position in Launceston. The problem was not yet imminent, for I had the best part of a week yet before I was expected back, but if there was no change in Mammy's condition by the end of that time, then I would have to inform Mrs Melhuish of the position and throw myself on her mercy. I rather thought she would be prepared to extend me some leeway, but even if she did not, I certainly could not leave Mammy in such a condition. Ruth had her hands full with her home and children; she could not easily manage to give Mammy the care she needed, and in any case, I could not have brought myself to leave her. In fact, just at the moment, I did not think I could bring myself to leave her ever again. She should not be living alone now that she was old and frail. She needed me, and my place was here, with her.

Of course – a dark chill whispered over my skin – if she took a turn for the worse, then the decision would be made for me. But I would not even think of that. So far she was holding her own. I prayed with all my heart that it was a good sign.

–

The day passed slowly by, a strange, unreal day overlaid with the peculiar feeling of living a nightmare from which I could not wake. When darkness fell I went about lighting the lamps and candles and took one up to Mammy's room. This time when I dripped water into her mouth I felt sure she made an effort to swallow it, and my heart lifted with hope.

Perhaps, I thought, I should try her with a little broth. Dr Warburton had not expressed any instruction one way or the other – perhaps he had thought she was too far gone – but it seemed to me that a little sustenance could be beneficial, so long as she did not choke on it.

I warmed some broth, taking care not to make it too hot, removed all the lumps of potato and turnip that might catch in her throat, and took it upstairs. Sure enough, I was able, with care, to get some into her, and again I had the distinct impression she was swallowing for herself, not merely allowing it to trickle down her throat.

I put the cup aside and took her hand.

'Did you enjoy that, Mammy?' I asked. 'I think you did! It tasted good, didn't it?'

To my utter amazement, I thought I felt her fingers tighten momentarily on mine.

'Mammy?' The breath was tight in my throat. 'Can you hear me?'

Again I thought I felt that faint pressure. My heart was beating so hard I felt it would burst from my chest.

'Mammy – squeeze my fingers!' I whispered urgently. 'Squeeze my fingers if you can hear what I am saying!'

I waited expectantly, scarcely daring to breathe. But this time, long for it as I might, I could detect no sign of response.

I tried again – still nothing. Had I imagined it? Or had Mammy really squeezed my fingers? Had she briefly shifted up from the depths of her coma? If she had, perhaps the effort had exhausted her and that was the reason she was not responding to me now. I really could not be sure, but the tiny spark of hope deep within me which I had struggled so hard to keep alight now burned with a steady flame.

I had wondered if I would sleep tonight in my own room. Whilst Mammy lay unmoving and unaware, there seemed no absolute necessity to keep up a constant vigil, and if I was to care for her properly, I really needed to catch at least a little sound sleep. But if she really had been aware enough, even for a few moments, to squeeze my fingers, then it put a completely different complexion on things. I did not want her to regain consciousness to find herself alone. If there was even the slightest chance of that, someone must be with her.

Jed or Ruth would be only too willing to share the vigil with me if I asked them, I knew. But I was reluctant to ask, since I knew Jed had his work tomorrow and Ruth, with the two little ones to care for, needed what sleep she could get. Besides, I did not want to tell them yet of my notion that Mammy might be coming out of her unconscious state. I was not sure enough that it had not simply been wishful thinking on my part. I did not want to raise their hopes if there was no foundation to my imaginings. No, I would spend the night again in the chair beside her bed and snatch what rest I could.

The chair was still beside the bed; all that remained was to fetch a pillow and blanket from my old room. I went to collect them, and whilst I was there, went to the window to close the drapes, more from habit than anything else.

I stood for a moment at the window, looking out. The night was clear, the low cloud that had obscured the sky for most of the day scattered by a fresh breeze that had sprung up. But for a few remaining banks, the sky was clear and studded with stars; a bright moon, almost full, was suspended in it over the sea, which, by day, was just visible from this side of the house, though tonight its blackness merged with the sky.

The breeze ruffled the scrubby trees that had been planted along a low wall the length of the row to protect the houses from the worst of the weather when gales blew in from the sea. They were misshapen and stunted from their battles with the elements and they looked for all the world like an army of short, squat men. They moved like an advancing army of men too, not soldiers, but jerky old men bent with the rheumatics. I smiled to myself at the thought, then suddenly froze.

One of the army seemed to detach itself from the rest and move, not with the wind, but to one side, creeping towards our end of the row, blending, moving again.

My heart seemed to stop beating; my hand flew to my throat.

Someone was out there, lurking in the shadows! And whoever it was, I was certain from his stealthy movement that he had no right to be there!

Four

As I watched, startled and frightened, the man disappeared around the corner of the row, making, I thought, for the front of the row of cottages.

For a moment I stood rooted to the spot, my heart beating a tattoo. Could it be Mammy's attacker, returned to finish what he had begun? I thought with trepidation of Nicholas's assertion that he had likely been a prisoner escaped from Bodmin Gaol and desperate for sustenance, and of his warning to keep the bolt on the door. I had not heeded it. We never locked our doors except at night, and it had seemed so very unlikely that the man, whoever he was, would return, given the awful thing he had done to Mammy. I had thought he would be too afraid of being apprehended and hanged for his crime. Now my knees turned weak as I realized that all he had to do was to lift the latch and he could be inside the cottage once more. And I would be scarcely more able to protect myself against him than poor Mammy had been!

And what of Ruth and Jed – had *they* bolted *their* door? There was every chance they would not, since they would want me to be able to get in if I should need them during the night. They would be in bed and asleep by now, I felt sure – Ruth had long since come in to say goodnight and, with the broken nights she still suffered with baby Billy and the fact that Jed had an early start in the morning, they tended to retire early. Suppose this time the man should try *their* door instead of Mammy's? Both they and the children could be murdered in their beds with no chance to defend themselves!

As the terrible thought occurred to me I moved like lightning, fear for my sister and her family making me forget my own fear. I ran downstairs, slithering over the narrow treads in my haste, and, stopping only to grab up the stoutest of the fire irons, ran out into the night.

The moon had hidden now behind one of the remaining banks of cloud and the track looked deserted, but it was impossible to know if someone was lurking in the shadows of the little outbuildings that lined the other side of it. Not that I waited to search closely. I ran straight to Ruth's door, hammering upon it with my fists whilst holding the fire iron aloft with my other hand and keeping a sharp eye over my shoulder.

I tried the door too; it was barred. Ruth and Jed had more sense than I. At least no one had been able to slip easily inside *their* cottage. I hammered again and called out, thought I heard an alien sound, and shouted more loudly still.

'Jed! Ruth! Wake up!'

The window above my head opened; Jed's head and shoulders emerged.

'What the devil…?'

'Quick, Jed! There's someone out here…'

Along the row, in the next-door cottage, another window flew open and Alice's face, topped by a ruched nightcap, appeared. My knocking must have disturbed her too, though Jake, her husband, who was deaf as a post, would have slept through any amount of racket.

'The attacker!' I screamed. 'He's out here! Jed…!'

Jed's head and shoulders disappeared and at the same moment I heard another sound and Alice let out a cry.

'There! There he goes!'

I swung round and saw the figure of a man break from the cover of the outhouses and make a run for it along the track.

'Oh!' I squealed, and without even thinking, set off after him. Fortunately for me, I had no hope of catching him, of course. For one thing he had a head start on me, for another, his longer legs would have easily outrun mine even if he had not. When I was but halfway along the row he had disappeared into the darkness and I thought I heard the sound of horse's hooves.

I stood for a moment, catching my breath and almost sobbing with frustration.

Jed was out of the house now, his nightshirt flapping around his knees, and before I could make my way back to meet him, Jim Weaver came running from his cottage, alerted, no doubt, by his mother. Jake, his father, was close behind him.

'What's to do?' Jed asked me, bleary with sleep. 'Whatever are you on about, Tamsin?'

'There was a man!' I said urgently. 'I saw him hiding in the bushes and then he came around to the doors side of the houses. He's gone now. I think he may have had a horse.'

'Never!' Jed sounded disbelieving. He had seen nothing, I realized, and he had no longer been at his window when the man had made a run for it. Alice, though, typically, had missed nothing.

'I seen him!' she shouted from her window. 'I seen the varmint!'

We all looked up; Alice was in her element.

'I seen him clear as day!' she shouted down. 'He went that-a-way, as fast as his legs would carry 'un! He's gone now, though, like Tamsin do say. You won't catch 'un now.'

'Did you see his face?' Jim called up to his mother. 'Did you see who it was?'

'No, worse luck, I never. 'Twas too dark, and he were too quick fer me. He were a big chap, though, tall and well made from what I could see on it. All dressed up in a thick coat, and a hat pulled down over his head...'

'What's she say?' Jake cupped a hand behind his ear, narrowing his eyes in an effort to hear. 'What's she say, eh?'

'She couldn't see,' I shouted at him. 'It's too dark.'

By now other doors were opening along the row, folk disturbed by the commotion emerging to see what was going on.

Jim was fairly dancing with frustration. 'Oh, if only we'd been a bit quicker! We could've caught him red-handed! Shall we go and look for him, boys? What d'you say?'

There was a murmur of agreement from the men.

'Ah, let's see if we can catch 'un!'

'He'll be on the end of a rope by morning if I do lay hands on 'un!'

'Come on, lads, let's have a go!'

'It's useless,' I said. 'He'll be long gone. If he did have a horse, he could be halfway to Truro by now. Or back in a hideout on the moors. Nicholas Penrose thought it likely he's a prisoner escaped from Bodmin Gaol.'

But even as I said it, I was wondering how an escaped prisoner would have come by a horse. Unless, of course, he had stolen it – maybe even murdered its poor owner to get his hands on it.

I shivered and realized it was not just from the chill night air. I was trembling all over – a reaction, I suppose, to my fright – and to the realization that the man who had attacked and half-killed my mother was not only still free, but also still in the vicinity and ready to return to the scene of his crime, for some reason I could not comprehend. It was a most disturbing thought that we were no longer safe in our own homes, by day or by night.

But there was nothing more we could do tonight. The menfolk could scour the district from now until dawn, I could not see that they would catch the man.

'I am going to Mammy,' I said to Jed, and, leaving the makeshift posse still chewing over what they should do, I went back inside the house.

Back upstairs, I collected the blanket and pillows from my old room – I had dropped them on the floor in a heap when I had realized someone was lurking in the bushes outside – and took them to Mammy's room.

The voices of the men on the track outside floated up; they were still out there chewing the fat over what they should do, though it must have been obvious even to them that it was much too late to do anything. I suppose, roused from their beds, they were now too fired up to be ready to sleep easily again, and reluctant to give up on what was most likely an adventure to them. I have no doubt they deceived themselves that their zeal was quite altruistic, a crusade for retribution on Mammy's behalf, and also partly fuelled by their determination to protect their own families from a similar fate. But men will be men, and I could not help feeling that they were secretly enjoying themselves.

'Oh, such a to-do, Mammy!' I said aloud as I stacked the pillows in the rocker. 'Such a to-do as never you saw! There's nothing to be afraid of, though. Half of Mallen is out there in their nightshirts ready to protect us.'

I heard what sounded like a dry croak. It startled me and I spun round, but Mammy lay unmoving, exactly as before. It must have been a timber settling, I thought, or even the wicker creaking as I moved the chair in the dark. Nothing but my imagination, working overtime as a result of my fright.

But it had not sounded like a timber settling, and I felt certain it had come, not from the chair beneath my hands, but the bed behind me.

'Mammy!' I said urgently. 'Mammy – was that you?'

The sound came again, and this time there was no mistaking it.

It came from Mammy's lips.

'Oh!' I stood for a moment, the bunched blanket clutched to my chest.

The death rattle! That was the first thought that came into my head and my blood turned to ice. I had never heard the sound with my own ears, for I had never been with anyone who was dying, but I'd heard it spoken of in hushed tones, tones of doom. It came, they said, when a person was breathing their last.

'Mammy!' I let the blanket fall to the floor and dropped to my knees beside the bed, shaking from head to foot. 'Mammy – are you all right? Can you hear me? Oh, Mammy, please – please don't die!'

Again the sound came, loud in the stillness of the room, though no doubt amid the hubbub of normal everyday life it would have been scarcely audible. Not so much a rattle, if rattle was indeed an accurate description of the ominous precursor of one's end, but a staccato croak. For all the world as if a parched throat was attempting to force out words.

My heart leaped, dread turning to a desperate hope I dared not yet acknowledge.

'Mammy!' I said urgently. 'Mammy, I believe you *can* hear me! I'll fetch you a drink. Don't try to speak again until I've fetched you a drink of water!'

I ran downstairs. My hands were shaking with urgency so much that I slopped water on to the counter as I attempted to pour it into the cup, and I had to force myself to slow down as I hurried back up the narrow stairs or risk spilling it all down my skirts.

I bent over the bed; put the cup to her lips. And this time, without a shadow of doubt, she swallowed. Noisily, with difficulty, but unmistakeably, she swallowed.

'Mammy!' I could scarcely believe it. 'Mammy – try a little more!' I reverted to the words she had used to me when I was a child, and sick of the fever. 'Come on, now, there's a good girl! Just a little more, for me.'

Some trickled down her chin, but most went down her throat. And in the silence and dark of her own bedroom her lips moved again and she spoke. Just a croak, still, but an identifiable word.

'Ruth?' my mammy said.

It did not bother me in the slightest that it was my sister's name, not mine, that was the first word Mammy spoke on emerging from her coma. It was, after all, scarcely surprising, since Ruth was the one who was here all the time, and although Mammy had known before her attack that I was coming home, still, after lying senseless for so long it would not be me she would expect to find at her bedside.

In any case, I was so overjoyed I would not have cared what my mother said – that she had said anything at all was all that mattered. I ran to the bedroom window and threw it open. Most of the men were still there in a gaggle, though Jake had returned to his bed, and Ruth had joined them. She looked up, half-fearful, as I called her name.

'Tamsin? What…?'

'Mammy!' I cried. 'Mammy spoke! She's asking for you!'

And I burst into tears.

By the time Ruth had come running, Mammy had drifted away again and no matter how often we cajoled her and squeezed her hand there was no response. But the hope aroused in us would not die – and it was justified.

Before the night was out she had rallied again two or three times, muttering, and returning the pressure of our fingers upon hers, and the next day, for the first time, she opened her eyes. There was a bemused look in them, as if she did not know where she was or who we were, but she took a little broth, swallowing it gratefully before sinking back again into the sleep I suppose her poor broken body needed. I changed the dressings on her wounds and with Ruth's help bound her ribs with an old piece of sheet. But not too tightly. She was surely in enough discomfort without making it worse, and breathing was still a great effort for her. I could not see that constricting her lungs would be beneficial.

Jed called for Dr Warburton on his way to work at Wheal Henry, and he arrived at around noon, huffing and puffing his way up the stairs and proclaiming it a miracle.

'To tell you the truth, Tamsin, my hopes were not high,' he said. 'A woman of her age, in poor health, and to take such punishment – no, my hopes were not high. But now… well, unless she suffers a relapse, I think we may well look to at least a partial recovery.'

'What should we do for her, Doctor?' I asked.

He scratched his head, knocking his wig a little askew.

'Follow your instincts, my dear,' he advised. 'Take things as they come. It will be a little step at a time, I expect, and sometimes a backward one. Don't expect too much. Keep her quiet, offer her a little sustenance and wait. Time is the best healer. Oh, and continue to give her the medication, of course, that I prescribed. That may well be what has brought about this rally. Yes. I would be very surprised if it were not the medication we have to thank. It's good stuff, though I say so myself.'

I had to suppress a smile. Trust a medical man to want to think Mammy's recovery was his doing! I did not tell him the medication lay untouched in the scullery. The foul smell of it had made me unwilling to subject poor Mammy to having to try to swallow so much as a mouthful!

But: 'You will be paid, Doctor, have no fear of that,' I said. 'I don't have the wherewithal just at present, but I will get it by next quarter day, and pay you in full for your trouble.'

He huffed and puffed some more, and left.

During one of Mammy's periods of awareness, Ruth brought little Charlie in to see her.

The poor little boy was clearly bemused to see his grandmother lying there so white and still, where usually she was bustling and smiling and making a great fuss of him, but Ruth brought him to the side of the bed, holding his chubby little hand out and putting it in Mammy's.

'Here's Charlie, Mammy! Charlie's come to see you!'

And Mammy's eyes flickered open for a moment and I thought I saw a glint of recognition cross the blankness of her expression.

'Charlie,' she mumbled. 'Dear Charlie!'

Her heavy eyes closed again, but I knew it was another step along the slow road to recovery.

As the days passed, the periods of Mammy's awareness grew more frequent and lasted for longer, and we began to allow ourselves to have faith that our prayers would be answered and she would, in time, make a good recovery. But she was still very sick and weak, and seemed to have difficulty in gaining a grasp of reality. Sometimes it seemed she knew me, sometimes not, and though I tried to explain the reason I was here, I was not convinced she understood me.

Still she could speak only with difficulty, the words coming singly rather than in sentences, almost like a child just learning to talk. She said nothing of what had occurred on the day she was attacked, nor did I think it right to press her. But sometimes, if I moved towards her too quickly, or raised a hand too abruptly to smooth the pillow beneath her head, she would shrink away, the fear naked in her eyes, and I thought that some part of her befuddled brain was remembering.

Her progress was so slow that at times it seemed there was no change at all; it was only by contrasting the way she was now with the way she had been that it was possible to measure it at all. And all the while the time allocated for my visit was ticking away.

I could not leave her like this, I knew. It never occurred to me for a single moment that I might be able to do so. I wrote a letter to Mrs Melhuish, explaining the circumstances and asking for a longer leave of absence, but adding that I would quite understand if she felt it necessary to terminate my employment and take on a new lady's maid, and sent it with the mail coach. I was sorry to place her in such a position, but I knew I had no choice.

Each day I reminded Mammy of who I was, and why I was here, but she simply gazed at me with puzzled eyes and, I think, promptly forgot again. Then one day a slow smile spread across her face.

'Tamsin! Why, it's Tamsin!'

'Yes, Mammy, that's right.' I took her hands in mine.

'But... Launceston...' she managed.

'I'm here now,' I said. 'And I have been all the time you have been ill.'

Tears filled her eyes and trickled down her cheeks.

'Tamsin... missed you...'

'I know, Mammy, and I have missed you. But have no fear, I am not going away again. Not as long as you need me here.'

She struggled to smile through her tears, and I had the satisfaction of knowing that by making up my mind to remain at home I had, without doubt, made the right decision.

71

We had seen neither hide nor hair of the man I had surprised outside the cottages, and as far as we had heard, no escaped prisoners had been apprehended, nor indeed any strangers sighted in the vicinity. But then, though the snow had mostly gone, the moors were still bleak and inhospitable, and no one ventured far from the beaten track if they had no business to do so. It might well be that spring would bring the discovery of a body, for if the man was hiding out there, I could not see that he could survive all winter long. There were, of course, barns and farm outbuildings which were scarcely ever opened up at this time of year, but there were no reports that we heard of that food had been stolen from outlying cottages or farms, and certainly no more unprovoked attacks on innocent folk. We began to sleep a little more easily in our beds, but we had more or less given up hope of Mammy's assailant ever being caught, and resigned ourselves to it regretfully.

So when a knock came at the door, one grey morning when the mist from the sea was so thick you could scarce see a hand before your face, and I found one of Nicholas Penrose's men standing there, my first thought was that someone had indeed been caught and Nicholas had been kind enough to send us word of it.

Toby Crankie had been with the Penrose family since he was a lad, and had progressed from stable boy to game-keeper. Now, it seemed, he was messenger too. He stood on the doorstep, blowing on his hands and stamping his feet.

'Toby!' I said. 'Won't you come into the warm?'

'No, thank'ee kindly, Tamsin. I must get back to Trevarrah – I've plenty there to keep me busy. But Miss Isobel would have me ride over to give you this.'

He pulled a letter from his pocket and held it out to me.

'A letter from Isobel!' I exclaimed, surprised, wondering why ever she would write to me and pull Toby from his duties on the estate to deliver it to me.

'Aye, and I'm to wait for a reply,' he informed me.

'Then you must come inside while I read it,' I said. 'I cannot leave you standing out here in the cold.'

He grinned. 'I'm used to it, Tamsin. And my boots are thick with mud. I don't want to track it all over your clean kitchen.'

'Well, I shall have to close the door,' I said. 'Mammy's downstairs for the first time today and I don't want her getting a draught.'

Toby, however, refused to be persuaded inside. I closed the door, noticing as I went back inside that Mammy was watching fearfully, like a fawn about to run from the hunters. As if, I thought sadly, she would be able to run anywhere in her frail state!

'It's all right, Mammy,' I said, 'it's only Toby Crankie with a letter for me from Isobel. You remember Isobel, don't you?'

'Isobel,' Mammy repeated without so much as a hint of recognition.

I opened the letter, taking it over to the rush lamp which I had kept burning, so dark was it in the house today, the better to read it.

It was but a short note.

Isobel was very glad to hear that Mammy had regained consciousness and prayed that her recovery would continue. She could still scarcely believe such a terrible thing could have happened, and on Penrose land too, which made both her and Nicholas feel they must bear some responsibility.

I smiled at that. The Penroses could scarcely be blamed for everything that happened on the far-flung estate, though it was a pity they did not pay a little more heed to the hunger and poverty of their tenants. But it was typical of Isobel that she should take it upon herself to feel guilt – or at least say that she did.

And then I came to the paragraph that was clearly the reason behind Isobel's missive.

I wonder if you could come over to Trevarrah to see me? she wrote.

> *There is something I very much want to talk to you about, with regard to a matter which may well prove of great importance to us both. I would have come to you, but circumstances prevent me. I will explain further when I see you. If, that is, you can spare an hour to call on me. I realize I am asking a great deal, but, dear Tamsin, you would do me a great favour if you would concur.*
>
> *I have asked Crankie to bring me a reply as to when I might expect you. If you are unable to commit yourself at such short notice, however, I feel sure a reply sent by way of Jed and through the foreman at the mine would safely reach me. Whichever, dear Tamsin, do please come to Trevarrah as soon as you are able.*

It was signed: *Your loving friend, Isobel.*

For a moment I stared wonderingly at the letter, rereading it. I was touched that Isobel wanted to see me,

74

but I had not the faintest idea what it might be about. 'Something which may prove of great importance to us both…' What in the world could it be?

I think curiosity would have spurred me on even had Toby not been waiting on the doorstep.

'I have to go to Ruth's house for a minute, Mammy,' I said. 'You'll be all right here, won't you?'

Mammy nodded as if it were expected of her, though I am not at all sure she really understood.

I hurried out, closing the door after me and telling Toby I would not detain him long. Then I went into Ruth's kitchen, where she was peeling potatoes with little Charlie sitting on the floor at her feet playing with the long ribbons of skin that fell from her knife.

As concisely as I could, I explained Isobel's request.

'Would you be able to sit with Mammy for a couple of hours whilst I went over to Trevarrah?' I asked. 'She's no trouble now, and I think she'd like a change of company and especially to see Charlie and Billy.'

'Of course I could, Tamsin,' Ruth said without hesitation. 'I already feel guilty that you are doing everything for her and I nothing.'

'Oh, don't be silly!' I chided her. 'I've nothing to stop me, and I'm glad to do it. But I would like to go over and see what Isobel wants.'

'Whatever can it be?' Ruth said. 'The likes of a lady such as her… But then you and she were always a pair. Snug as two bugs in a rug.'

'Hardly that,' I said, laughing.

'When do you want me?' Ruth asked.

I considered. 'What about tomorrow? If I go in the morning I can be there and back in daylight. It's not really the time for social calls, I know, but that can't be helped.'

'Tomorrow morning, yes. I'll come round as soon as I've given Charlie his breakfast,' Ruth promised.

And so it was agreed. I asked Toby to tell Isobel I would be at Trevarrah by eleven o'clock in the morning. He rode away, and I was left still puzzling over Isobel's request.

But there was nothing for it but patience. I would learn the reason in good time. Until then, I must concentrate on nursing Mammy.

––

*There was something she had to do. Something of great import-
ance that had already been delayed too long.*

*The urgency of it prickled over her skin and stirred deep within
her. But strive as she might to remember what it was, it was lost
in the thick grey fog that clouded her brain.*

*As so much was lost to her. Distant past and present were
fused, throwing her into confusion, and what lay between was a
foreign land she could not travel.*

Isobel.

*The mention of the name had struck a chord, reawakened that
vague but persistent unease, and awareness that she had somehow
failed to carry out some vital duty. But for the life of her she did
not know why.*

Isobel.

*Again and again she struggled to remember, but each time
she came close to grasping it, it slipped away out of reach as the
fragments of a dream slip beyond our recall with the light of day.*

*There was something she had to do. A promise that must be
kept. But what…? What?*

*The effort of struggling to remember was tiring her. The mists
were closing in again.*

Drift with the tide. Drift. Drift.

76

Young again. No aching bones. No creaking joints. Young and lithe and pretty. And so in love.

Handsome. Oh, how handsome he is! His lips tasting of salt from the sea wind, his hands strong and gentle, his body...

Oh Ralph, my love.

Time gone. An echo, sad and sweet and haunting. Nothing more. Ralph. Something I must do for Ralph...

No good. Sleep. Sleep. I have to sleep...

The moment of urgency had passed, leaving nothing but defeat in its wake. And a darkness which blotted out memory. She closed her eyes and drowned in it.

77

Five

Trevarrah House was four miles or so from Mallen as the crow flies, and set on higher ground, so that although it was further inland, the view of the sea was clearer. As I emerged from the valley fold and began to climb, I looked out as I always did because the sea in all its moods drew me like a magnet.

This morning it was steely grey, white-flecked where the waves broke, and looking for all the world like the ridges of snow that still lay in the lee of the hedges where the sun had not reached.

I crossed the open grazing land, passing quite close by the dilapidated buildings that were now all that remained of Wheal Trevelyan, or, as it was known locally, Old Trevarrah Mine, where my brother John had fallen to his death. Ahead of me I could see the tall skeleton of Wheal Henry's headgear silhouetted against the skyline, and soon I was passing the big stone engine house. Few men were about; the day core had begun hours ago and would last hours yet. As I walked I kept my eyes open for the shafts that had been bored at intervals to allow fresh air into the workings below, and gave them a wide berth.

Ruth, who must have been turning things over in her mind after I told her what Isobel had asked of me, had remarked, when she came in this morning, that she would have thought it would have been a great deal easier for

Isobel to ride over to see me, rather than having me walk there. But Isobel had expressly mentioned that there was a reason why she could not do this, and in any case, I did not mind at all.

I had always enjoyed walking, and today especially it was good to be out in the open air. I had scarcely left the house for the best part of two weeks, and after being cooped up in the small airless kitchen with the fire stoked high to ensure Mammy did not take a chill, it was wonderful to feel the wind on my face and taste the faint salty tang of it on my lips.

It was still cold, though no longer frosty, but I did not mind that either. Walking briskly, I was soon glowing, and by the time Trevarrah House came into sight, I was a little breathless too. Life in Launceston had made me soft! I thought.

Trevarrah was a big, rambling house built of Cornish stone. When I had visited it with Mammy as a child, we had always gone in by the tradesman's entrance at the rear of the house, and I was, through habit, making my way there when it occurred to me that perhaps as an invited guest of Isobel, who was now the lady of the house, I should go to the front.

For just a moment I hesitated, then made up my mind. I walked boldly up to the front door and rang on the bell.

After a few moments it was answered by a maid, a rather pinched-looking girl who was suffering from a cold, judging by the redness of her nose. She frowned when she saw me standing there, looking down her sore nose at my rough woollen cloak and Mammy's stout boots which I had borrowed to walk over the rough ground, and deciding I had no right to be there.

Before she could tell me to go around to the tradesman's entrance, I drew myself up.

'Miss Isobel is expecting me.'

My tone must have impressed her, for she stood aside, if a little reluctantly, for me to go in. Perhaps I had learned from Mrs Melhuish, I thought, smiling inwardly. In the years I had been her lady's maid something of her demeanour had rubbed off on me.

The girl showed me across the great hall with its mullioned windows and portraits of past generations of Penroses, which I remembered so well, past the withdrawing room on the left hand side and into the small winter parlour. On the other side of the sweeping staircase was, I knew, the large parlour and library, and at the back of the house were the kitchens and buttery.

The winter parlour was a comfortable room, positioned to make the best of any sunlight. A fire was burning brightly in the hearth and a spinning wheel was drawn up in front of one of the chairs. I had never seen it here in the old days and I guessed Isobel must have taken up spinning. Certainly she had never cared much for embroidery and she would need something to fill her days.

The maid left to tell Isobel I was here, closing the door behind her, and I sat down to wait. Given that she had asked me to call, and her warmth towards me when she had come to the cottage, I had thought she would be quicker to greet me. But of course, Isobel was no longer the young ward with no duties or responsibilities beyond amusing herself all the day long. Now she was the mistress of the house. She would have to discuss menus with the cook and oversee general housekeeping matters. Hardly onerous, compared with the day-long grind of the womenfolk of poor families, but not her former carefree life either.

I glanced at the pretty little French clock on the mantelpiece, already worrying about getting back to relieve Ruth, and as I did so, the parlour door opened. I swung round, expecting to see Isobel there, and started in surprise.

Not Isobel. A man, tall, broad-shouldered, with his own dark hair curling about his ears and tied back at the nape of his neck. He wore a narrow-waisted dark coat and buff-coloured breeches, which displayed the length and strength of his legs, and carried a riding whip. I half-recognized him and yet did not recognize him at all. But I knew in an instant who he was, for the likeness to Nicholas was unmistakeable, although his features were stronger, less classically handsome than Nicholas's, and there was a long scar on his cheek which ran from the corner of his eye down beyond his mouth.

Adam. It could be none other than Adam, grown to full manhood and hardened and disfigured by the battles he had fought in America – and elsewhere, too, for all I knew.

I opened my mouth to greet him, but before I could say a single word his eyes narrowed so that the scar tightened and stretched white.

'What are you doing here?' he demanded curtly.

I was utterly taken aback, I must admit. His tone made the question an accusation; my jaw dropped, I am sure. Then indignation at being addressed in such a manner flared in me. Why, I was a guest, and it was not even his house, if what Alice had told me was to be believed.

'I beg your pardon?' The hauteur in my tone matched the aggression I had recognized in his.

'What are you doing here?' he repeated.

'I am here at Isobel's invitation,' I returned spiritedly. 'If it is any concern of yours.'

'I thought as much.' There was no hint of apology in either his voice or his face. 'It's Tamsin, isn't it?'

'Yes,' I said. 'And you, if I am not mistaken, must be Adam Penrose. It's some years since last we met, but clearly neither of us have changed very much, since we recognize one another so easily.'

At that moment Isobel appeared in the doorway behind him. She was wearing a gown of violet; there was a faint sheen to the fabric, which fell gracefully from a high waist. Her hair was swept up from her face, though tiny golden curls escaped to frame her high forehead and heart-shaped jawline. She looked, if such a thing were possible, lovelier than ever.

'Tamsin!' She swept past Adam as if he were not there, and as I rose to greet her, she kissed me warmly on the cheek. 'Oh Tamsin, thank you so much for coming! I am so sorry I was not here to greet you.'

'I expect you had better things to do, Isobel,' I said. 'In any case, I haven't been waiting long, and you're here now.'

'You remember Adam?' She turned, smiling at her brother-in-law. 'Adam, this is Tamsin Hardy.'

'Yes, I know.' His tone was still clipped. 'I was most surprised to see her here.'

'Why should you be surprised?' she asked blithely. 'You must remember that Tamsin and I are old friends!'

'Yes, of course.' He turned on his heel. 'Well, in that case, I shall leave you to renew your friendship.'

Then he was gone.

'Oh, don't mind him, Tamsin!' Isobel said with a little shake of her head. 'Adam always had a brusque manner, as I'm sure you recall. And since he came back from the war... Well, I think fighting can leave its mark upon a man, don't you?'

'I don't know,' I replied. 'I've never had any dealings with soldiers.'

It was the truth – and I certainly had no intention of reporting Adam's odd attitude when he had found me in the parlour. But it did occur to me that it might be something quite different to fighting in a war that had made Adam's temper more uncertain since his return – namely coming home to find his brother installed as squire in his place, living as master of his old home and married to the girl who had been his sweetheart and whom he had expected to one day make his wife!

'I think his leg pains him, too,' Isobel went on. 'Especially in this weather. He took a lead shot in the knee, you know, and was lucky not to lose his leg. Hopefully it will trouble him less when the summer comes, and his temper will improve with it.'

I said nothing.

'Anyway, let's forget about Adam.' Isobel smiled at me conspiratorially. 'I didn't bring you all this way to talk about my brother-in-law. Can I offer you some refreshment? A dish of tea, perhaps – or some hot chocolate?'

'Oh, I don't want to put you to any trouble,' I protested.

'It's no trouble at all. And I'm sure you'd like something warming after your long walk. Very well, if you are too polite to choose, then I shall do it for you. We shall have hot chocolate. We always loved our hot chocolate, did we not?'

I smiled, remembering how much I had used to enjoy the special treat. Hot chocolate had never tasted as good since as it had in those far-off days – Trevarrah hot chocolate, rich, dark and creamy.

'Yes, we did. I'd love a hot chocolate. Thank you, Isobel.' She went off to order it and as I waited for her return I thought again of Adam. He must have seen a good deal of fighting, if he had been wounded in the leg as well as whatever had happened to cause that livid scar on his face. No wonder the family had thought it quite possible he was dead.

A little shiver ran through me which I could not quite identify. The horror of war, made suddenly real for me, I supposed. And yet I had the strangest feeling it was more than that...

Isobel came back in.

'The chocolate will be here very soon,' she said, taking a seat opposite mine. 'Now tell me, Tamsin, how is your dear mama? Word came to Nicholas through William Hastings, the Captain at Wheal Henry, that she is much improved. Is that true?'

'She is improving day on day,' I confirmed. 'But she is still very frail and she has difficulty remembering things.'

'She remembers nothing at all?' Isobel's eyes were wide and concerned.

'I think her memory is returning little by little,' I said. 'A week ago she scarcely knew who I was – even when I told her, she kept forgetting. But she knows us now – Ruth and Jed and me and the children – though sometimes she mistakes Charlie and Billy for John and Luke, her own sons, who as you know are both long dead. Especially she mistakes them for Luke, who was not much older than Charlie is now when he was taken by the fever.

The long-gone past is clearer to her than the recent, I think.'

'So she has said nothing of her assailant?' Isobel asked.

'Nothing. Nor would I wish to remind her of the attack,' I said. 'To remember what happened that day would very likely upset her badly and perhaps cause a relapse. I couldn't risk that. Not whilst she is still so frail.'

'Too frail to be left?' Isobel asked.

'At present, yes. Ruth is sitting with her now.'

'But you think that is changing? She will not have to have constant care for ever?'

'I certainly hope not!' I said emphatically, then added quickly: 'Not that I begrudge it, of course. But being unable to leave her unattended does make things difficult.'

'And what of your position in Launceston?' Isobel asked. 'When last we spoke, you thought you might be forced to give notice.'

'At present it is being kept open for me,' I said. 'But truth to tell, I don't think I shall ever return. Though Ruth is just next door, it is not the same thing as having someone else in the house, and I don't think I could bear to leave her alone again. I think I shall write to Mrs Melhuish and tell her she must look for someone to take my place, then find some sort of employment hereabouts that will enable me to continue living at home.'

'As I thought,' Isobel said.

I looked at her sharply.

'I couldn't see you leaving your mama entirely,' she went on. 'That's the reason I asked you to come here today.'

'I don't follow...'

'It's very simple,' Isobel said. 'I should like to offer you a position, Tamsin. When your mama is well enough to be left for part of the time at least, I should like you to come here, to Trevarrah, as my companion.'

'Oh!'

Frankly, I was completely taken by surprise, and my first reaction was that she was making this offer out of charity, something which offended my pride and went as much against the grain with me as it had done with my mother.

'But you don't need a companion, surely? You have a husband, a brother-in-law, a houseful of servants, and a full social life too, I am sure. Why should you need a companion?'

Her smile faded. 'Don't you like the idea, Tamsin?'

I was saved for the moment from answering by the arrival of the maid with the hot chocolate. When she had set it down on the low table and left again, Isobel turned to me urgently.

'You do not know just how much I need a companion, dear Tamsin. Nicholas is far too busy with running the estate and the mine and… other things… to be able to spare me much time, and I confess I find it very lonely. I have no lady's maid, and never have, and I know you are most experienced in that capacity. But I would never ask you to take a job with such a description. It would be an insult to our friendship – though I hope as my companion you might feel able to help me out as a lady's maid would. And with the running of the house too, perhaps. There's always so much to do, so much to think about, that my head spins! I'm really not a very practical person.'

'I suppose you've never had to be,' I said, though I would have thought that, as the only female in the house for so long, Isobel might well have grown naturally into the role a woman was expected to play.

86

'There's another reason, too.' Isobel's hands went instinctively to her stomach, and as she hesitated, I knew what it was she was going to say. 'I am expecting a child.'

'That's wonderful news!' I exclaimed.

Her clear features clouded. 'Is it? Oh Tamsin, I'm not sure! I have to confess I am terrified...'

'But it's the most natural thing in the world!' I pointed out. 'Plenty of women have strings of children as easily as shelling peas.'

Isobel flushed scarlet, and I bit my lip. There was the difference in our breeding, clear for all to see. I had grown up in a world where families all lived in close proximity to each other and to nature. We had few inhibitions about such things. Isobel, on the other hand, had led a sheltered life, and one where ladies did not say such things.

'My own sister, Ruth, has two lovely babies, and I'm sure there'll be another soon,' I went on hastily. 'And my other sister, Ellie, already has four. I'm sure that once you hold your baby in your arms, you'll think that any pain or discomfort was well worth it, and quickly forget.'

'You may be right,' Isobel said doubtfully. 'But it's not just the thought of childbirth that frightens me. I can't imagine how I will be able to cope with looking after a baby either! They're so little, so demanding – and so fragile!'

I smiled. 'Mostly, they are a great deal tougher than you might think.'

'Oh perhaps. You must think me a terrible coward, Tamsin, and I expect I am. But truly I cannot face the thought of going through it all alone. If I had another woman with me... especially a friend such as you...'

She met my eyes imploringly. 'Oh, please say you'll do as I ask! You'll be well rewarded, I promise! Only please say you'll come to Trevarrah as my companion.'

For all her explanations, I was still puzzled. Was there something else she was not telling me? But the pleading in her eyes was real enough and I could not resist it.

'Of course I will,' I said. 'There's nothing I would like better, and it would be the answer to all my problems. Only I can't leave Mammy just yet. It may be a few weeks before she's fit enough, and even then I wouldn't want her to be alone for too long. I'd certainly need to go home every evening. I couldn't agree to live in at present.'

'Oh, that wouldn't matter!' Isobel said, shining now with relief. 'Nicholas is here in the evenings, so I'm not alone then. We can take things step by step. And the date for my confinement is still a long way off. I've only just discovered my condition in the last few days – it's the reason I didn't want to ride over to see you. I'm sure your situation will improve very soon.'

'I certainly hope so,' I said. 'Just as long as you understand I can make no promises.'

'No, of course, I wouldn't expect you to.' Isobel crossed and took my hands in hers. 'Oh Tamsin, I can't tell you how happy you've made me! It will be the two of us again, just like it used to be.'

'And the baby,' I reminded her, smiling.

'Oh – not for months and months!' Isobel said gaily. 'Perhaps you could come over for just a few hours once or twice a week to begin with. Just seeing you has made me feel so much better!'

We sipped our hot chocolate, which was every bit as delicious as I remembered it, whilst we discussed arrangements and remuneration. I felt a little uncomfortable, being paid for my company by a friend, but I could not afford to be squeamish. In fact, truth to tell, it was a great relief to know that I would have a little money coming in, for I had been desperately worried about how Mammy and I were going to manage.

At length I rose. 'I must go now, Isobel. Ruth will be wondering what has become of me.'

'Yes, I suppose you must. And it won't be long before you're back again, will it? That's what I must tell myself.' To my surprise I saw tears sparkling suddenly in her clear blue eyes and she took my hand again, squeezing it tightly, as if she would never let me go.

'Yes, I'll be back very soon,' I assured her. But when we went out into the hall, she found yet another excuse to detain me.

'Can you wait just another minute, Tamsin? There's something I want you to have.'

Impatient though I was to get back to relieve Ruth of Mammy's care, I could scarcely be so churlish as to refuse, and in any case, Isobel had already started for the staircase, barely waiting for my reply.

It was as I stood there in the great hall, tapping my booted foot on the tiled floor whilst I waited for her to return, that the sound of raised voices reached me. They came, I realized, from the library, the door of which was not quite closed, and at once I recognized Adam's angry voice.

'By God, Nicholas, you're a fool — and a dangerous one at that!'

I could not hear Nicholas's reply, just a low snarl, then Adam shouted back: 'I won't allow it, do you hear?'

This time, Nicholas raised his own voice. 'And how do you propose to stop me, might I ask? In any case, you're too late. It's all arranged.'

Adam swore. 'You always were an unprincipled bastard, Nicholas, with no thought beyond your immediate gratification. But this – I would scarcely have believed even you…'

'Do you want us to face ruin, Adam? Is that what you want? Because that is the alternative, make no mistake of it. The prices of copper and tin are down again, and likely to fall still further. Wheal Henry is becoming a liability, and we've no other way of supplementing our income, let alone paying our debts…'

'*Your* debts, you mean!' Adam returned. 'Debts you have run up with your extravagances – and your gambling. Dear God, Papa must be turning in his grave at the mess you've got us into!'

'You're a fine one to talk!' Nicholas flashed back. 'No one has lost more on the turn of a card than you! If Papa had not stepped in and bought you a commission you'd be rotting in gaol now – or sweating your guts out in chains as convict labour in Australia. And you have the brass nerve to come back after four years' absence and tell me you disapprove of my way of doing things! Look to the beam in your own eye, Adam, before you criticize the speck in mine!'

Embarrassed beyond belief, I moved further from the library door. But I could not escape those angry voices.

'There is no excuse for what you have done!' Adam raged. 'You sicken me, Nicholas!'

'And you sicken me, Adam.'

'Then at least we have one point of agreement.'

The library door was thrown open and Adam came storming out. His face was dark with fury; the scar stood out livid on his cheek. When he saw me there, his expression darkened even further, if such a thing were possible, and he vented the remains of his bad temper on me.

'You're still here then! I thought you would have had more sense!'

I was, quite literally, speechless, and before I could ask what in the world he meant, Isobel appeared at the head of the staircase. Adam gave an impatient shake of his head, swore, then strode, with a noticeable limp, to the front door. He yanked it open and went out, leaving it swinging open behind him.

At that moment, Isobel came running down the stairs. 'Here we are, Tamsin, I'm sorry it took me so long...' She broke off, perhaps noticing that I was severely discomfited. 'Is something wrong?'

I shook my head, not wanting to tell her what had occurred. 'Nothing. What is it you have for me?'

'Oh.' She smiled at me and held out her hand. There, lying in her open palm, was a small pendant in the shape of a fleur-de-lys, which I recognized at once.

'Do you remember when we were children how you admired this? I want you to have it.'

'Oh Isobel, no, you mustn't!' I protested.

'Yes, I want you to have it,' she repeated. 'As a token of our friendship. Every time I wear it I think of you. And I hope that when you wear it, you will think of me. Perhaps it will serve to keep you from changing your mind about being my companion.'

'I wouldn't change my mind,' I said, 'but you can't give it to me. You told me once it belonged to your mama.'

'I have all my mama's jewellery,' she said. 'This is but one small thing, and not worth very much. Come now, Tamsin, humour me please. It would mean so much to me, knowing that you were wearing it.'

'Well, thank you then,' I said awkwardly. I still felt uncomfortable accepting such a gift, but touched by the sentiment that made her want to part with the pendant.

'Let me put it on for you.'

She put it about my neck and I turned so she could fasten it for me, then she kissed me on the cheek.

'Dear Tamsin, I am counting on you,' she said.

She touched the fleur-de-lys where it lay on the bodice of my plain wool gown, as if for luck, and smiled. But the smile was a little tremulous.

'Don't be afraid, Isobel. I'll be there for you,' I said.

And, as I moved to the door, which Adam had left standing open after his angry departure, it occurred to me again to wonder if it was not only because she was with child that she was in need of a friend.

—

As I walked the four miles or so back to Mallen, my thoughts were racing. To have been offered such a position was the most enormous piece of good fortune, for it held out the promise of employment closer to home than I had dared hope for, and with the added advantage that I had not had to commit myself to any arrangement that would impinge on my continued care of Mammy. I could, for the present at any rate, tailor my duties to her needs and Ruth's ability to help out. And I would be working for a girl who had been my friend, and who clearly still believed that I was hers.

But my whole visit, and the pleasure I would otherwise have gained from it, had been overshadowed by the quarrel I had overheard, the embarrassment it had caused me, and by Adam's antagonism.

I should not let the latter upset me, I knew. Clearly he was a bad-tempered and quarrelsome man, and perhaps in part that was, as Isobel suggested, because he was in constant pain. Pain, if it went on day after day, could grind men down and bring out the worst in their natures. Why, when he suffered with recurrent bouts of gout, Mr Melhuish, usually one of the gentlest men I had ever met, would snap and grumble at anyone who crossed his path. Whatever, Adam did not live in the big house, he lived in the lodge, and hopefully I would see little of him. But it *did* upset me, all the same, in a way I could not understand.

Worse, however, was the inescapable feeling I had that something was very wrong at Trevarrah.

I smiled wryly to myself at the thought. A quarrel such as the one I had witnessed between the brothers was surely proof of that. From what I had heard, there were serious problems, either with the estate, or the mine, or both, and clearly they differed violently in their opinion of the way the problems should be dealt with. There was a good deal of bad blood between them, that much was clear, and it was hardly surprising, given the circumstances.

Yet I could not help feeling that it was more than that.

To begin with, Isobel's eagerness to have me there had not, I felt, been properly explained. That she was frightened, I had no doubt, but I did not think it was just because of the coming baby. There was something else – something she had not mentioned. Could it be, perhaps, that she was afraid of *Adam*? He was possessed of a vicious temper, that much I had seen for myself, and he very likely felt that Isobel had betrayed him by marrying his brother. But surely he was no real threat to her? And if his presence was upsetting her, then why did Nicholas not ban him from the house? There was, after all, no love lost between the brothers and surely Isobel's feelings would be taken into account.

Nicholas. My puzzling thoughts went to him. He, from what I had heard, was as capable of losing his temper as his brother, and the things Adam had said suggested he was no saint in other ways. But he had shown a kind side to his nature by riding over to enquire after Mammy when news had reached Trevarrah of her attack. Even though I thought Isobel had probably instigated the visit, he had come with her, whether from concern for Mammy or concern for her riding over alone scarcely mattered. Either way it showed a good heart. Yet something was bothering me concerning him – and not just the accusations of ruthlessness that Adam had thrown at him.

As I walked, I puzzled over it – and then it came to me.

He had known I was there at Trevarrah. He must surely have known Isobel was asking me to be her companion – she would never do such a thing without first gaining his approval, since it would be he who would pay my wages. And he certainly must have been aware that I was there in the hall. When Adam had spoken angrily to me, the library door had been wide open, and the parting conversation between Isobel and me had scarcely been conducted in whispers.

Yet not once had he shown his face. Surely the natural thing would have been for him to come out and exchange a few words at least with me? But he had not done so. Perhaps he was mortified, of course, to realize that

I had overheard the quarrel. But that seemed unlikely. Gentlemen did not usually give a fig for what servants thought of them, and that was what I would be in his eyes, simply a servant, though Isobel regarded me as her friend. No, more likely he was still too angry to be able to bring himself to exchange pleasantries. But even that did not fully explain the omission.

Isobel had not heard the quarrel. She had been upstairs when it had erupted. Yet she had not gone into the library as I might have expected, to tell Nicholas I had accepted her offer of employment. She had not asked him to confirm the arrangement and give it his blessing. She had behaved as if he were not there at all.

And last but not least, what seemed to be the reason behind the quarrel was giving me some cause for concern. Money — or the lack of it. Why, Nicholas had actually spoken of ruin. Yet here was Isobel offering me employment that would mean another wage to be paid.

Oh, I didn't understand it. I didn't understand any of it. But that feeling of foreboding that I had learned to trust — and fear — was there in the pit of my stomach. And though my anxiety to take the position made me tell myself I was simply being foolish and fanciful, and looking a gift horse too closely in the mouth, I could not dismiss it entirely, and neither could the wind off the sea blow it away.

Six

Mammy was recovering now by leaps and bounds. Her head wounds had healed over beautifully, though remnants of scab still clung to the bits her hairbrush had not agitated away, and the healthy food I made sure she ate was restoring her vitality. I had to speak to her quite firmly, in fact, to stop her from trying to carry out household chores, for I was worried for her ribs, which were still painful and clearly not yet mended, and I was anxious that she should conserve her strength.

But still she had no recollection of what had happened on the day of the attack. Though she could remember with clarity things that had occurred years before, when she was a young woman and we were children, more recent events were lost to her beneath a dense dark fog.

'I didn't do that!' she would say of something we knew perfectly well she had, indeed, done, or: 'I didn't know that!' about some event which had occurred in the village in the past few years which had been common knowledge.

When I told her I was to take up employment with Isobel at Trevarrah, she was delighted — she remembered Isobel well as a child, but found it hard to believe she was now a grown woman who was going to have a child herself, even though she knew that Isobel and I were of an age.

'She's married to Nicholas,' I explained.

'You mean Adam.'

'No, Nicholas,' I repeated patiently. 'He's squire now that his father is dead.'

Mammy turned white. 'Ralph? Dead? Oh no, no!'

'He's been dead a long while, Mammy,' I said gently. 'And you did know. You must have.'

'Ralph – dead!' she repeated, shaking her head. Her lip was trembling, her eyes anguished. 'Oh dear, dear. How could I forget something like that?'

'Don't upset yourself, Mammy,' I said, trying to placate her. 'You'll make yourself ill again if you do.'

But there was no doubt she was indeed dreadfully upset, for several times during the day I heard her muttering to herself: 'Ralph dead! Oh dearie dear!'

It was, I supposed, the end of an era to her, and she, who had suffered so many losses during her lifetime, had seen yet another anchor-hold slip.

To my great relief, however, the shock of coming face to face with stark, forgotten realities did not bring about the relapse I had feared. If anything, it seemed to strengthen Mammy's determination to recover the memories that were lost to her. As always, I was in awe of her strength and resilience in the face of adversity.

A week later Ruth and I together decided that I could take up my new employment for at least a few hours a day.

'I think it will do Mammy good to have a little independence,' Ruth said, 'and I am just next door to keep an eye on her. Besides, you don't want to keep Isobel waiting too long, or she may change her mind.'

Given Isobel's seeming desperation to have me as her companion, I thought that unlikely, but I could see the sense in her arguments, and besides, I was quite looking forward to Isobel's company as well as the little income the position would give me, for managing to put food on the table was becoming something of a worry and I could not rely on Ruth and Jed's generosity for ever. Their circumstances were stretched enough without having to provide for Mammy and me as well.

I sent word by way of Jed that I would begin next day, and after I had seen Mammy washed and dressed and had prepared some breakfast for her, I set out.

The day was damp and overcast, one of those bleak days when it seems that spring and summer will never come. I walked briskly, my chin buried in the warm folds of my cloak.

As I approached Wheal Henry, there seemed to be a good deal of activity taking place. A team of mules had been lined up ready to transport a load of copper ore, and men were busy loading it into panniers swung over the animals' backs. A tall figure in coat and breeches stood watching – whether it was Nicholas or Adam, I could not tell from this distance, but from his stance and attire it was clearly one of them, and before I reached the mine he had disappeared.

As I passed, giving the workers as wide a berth as possible, I heard a cry. I wheeled round, alarmed, for the cry was one of shock and pain, and saw to my horror that an accident had occurred. A man lay on the ground, and the other men had abandoned their labours and were crowded around him.

I suppose in truth it was no business of mine. I should have turned away and kept on walking. But in the country we had a tradition of helping our neighbours where we could, and in any case it was not in my nature to ignore another human in distress. I was a woman – perhaps there was something I could do that a man could not by way of nursing.

Picking up my skirts, I ran between the huddled mine buildings to where the man lay.

I could see at once what had occurred. Blood was pouring from a long gash on the man's temple and he was half senseless – clearly he had taken a nasty kick from one of the mules. One of his friends was kneeling beside him and attempting to staunch the flow of blood with a piece of cloth, but it was filthy with black dust and would, I thought, be likely to do more harm than good, since it might very well introduce infection into the wound.

Careless of the men's astonishment, I pulled up my skirts and tore a length of fabric from my white cotton petticoat.

'Here – let me!'

I dropped to my knees beside the man. I did not recognize him, but that was of no importance to me. I pressed the length of clean cloth to the wound and asked one man to go for a can of water. The poor injured man looked to me to be lying in a most uncomfortable position, though someone had taken off their coat and placed it beneath his head, and I thought that lying on the cold damp ground would do him no good at all.

'Can you find something to lay him on?' I said, barely glancing up from my appointed task of stemming the bleeding.

'There's canvas in the storehouse. Do as the lady says and fetch some at once. And lead those mules away before someone else is kicked in the head.'

The voice was low but authoritative. I looked up and saw Adam Penrose towering above me. It must have been him I had seen earlier; now he had re-emerged from the cluster of buildings to see what was going on to disrupt the morning's work.

At Adam's barked command, one of the men scurried off, and two more led the half-loaded mules away to a safe distance. The first man returned with a bowl of water and I did my best to cleanse and tend the wound. He was coming round now, and by the time the second man came back with a length of canvas, he was able to sit up rather than lie on it.

'Damned beast don't like me!' he muttered. 'Oh, my poor head!'

'You'm too rough with 'un, Joe,' one of the men said. 'A mule's a mule when all's said and done...'

'Be still!' I told him. 'You've taken a very nasty blow to the head.' I thought of Mammy, and what Dr Warburton had said about bleeding on the inside as well as where it could be seen. 'You need to rest, not excite yourself, or goodness knows what damage you'll do.'

'I be all right!' Joe, the injured man, tried to rise, but, clearly still groggy, he tumbled down again.

'You see?' I said sternly. 'You see what happens when you try to move?'

'I can't afford to lose a day's work,' Joe protested. 'I got a wife and children to feed.'

'And you'll not do it by making things worse!' Adam interposed. 'You'll go home for the rest of the day at least, and rest.' He turned to Captain Hastings, the mine foreman, who had appeared on the scene. 'Is there a cart, William, that can take him?'

'I can find one, yes.' Captain Hastings did not sound overly enthusiastic. His cart, no doubt, had been earmarked for other duties.

'Then have it made ready.'

'I tell you, I can't afford…' Joe began groggily, but Adam cut short his protestations.

'I'll personally see that you do not go the loser of a day's wages,' he said. 'Now, let's have no more argument about it.'

His tone was abrupt and impatient, but I was surprised by the generosity of his offer. If a man was off sick he could not usually expect to be paid wages, even if it was as a result of some kind of accident at his place of employment. And it was not as if Wheal Henry was making vast profits, either. From the quarrel I had overheard between Adam and Nicholas, indeed, it seemed that it was running at a loss.

The cart was brought and Joe helped into it. I tore yet another strip from my petticoat to make a pad and a makeshift bandage, then stood watching for a moment as the cart pulled away.

The group of men were doing likewise, until Adam's sharp tone addressed them.

'The rest of you – get back to work. There's no more to be seen here, and if your jobs are not done – and properly – it will be you paying Joe Needs' wages.'

His words brought me up short, reminding me it was not just the mine workers who were shirking their duties. Isobel would be expecting me to be at Trevarrah by now – she would be wondering what on earth had become of me.

And what a state I was in! My cuffs were splattered with blood, and there were damp muddy patches on the front of my skirts where I had kneeled, unthinking, on the filthy ground. They felt rough against my bare legs, too, for I had used half my petticoat in order to care for the injured man. *My very best petticoat!* I thought ruefully. But at least it had been ruined in a good cause.

I turned to set off for Trevarrah House, but I had gone but a few steps when Adam's voice arrested me.

'Tamsin!'

I stopped, turned, and he limped towards me.

'It was very kind of you to stop and offer your assistance,' he said.

For some reason I could not fathom, I felt my cheeks grow hot.

'It was nothing.'

'On the contrary, many folk would have passed by on the other side, telling themselves it was none of their business.' He paused. 'Are you going to Trevarrah?'

I nodded.

'Then I must not delay you. Isobel is very anxious for your company, it seems.' He paused again, then went on: 'I feel I owe you an apology. I believe I may have offended you the other day. Sometimes my ill temper gets the better of me and I take it out on those who do not deserve it.'

My colour deepened. I really did not know what to say. I was quite unused to receiving apologies from members of the upper classes, and especially from one who had been as rude to me as Adam had been! Suddenly I was dreadfully flustered.

'I took no offence...' I stammered.

'I hope not.' He smiled suddenly, and the smile seemed to transform his rather stern face, with its livid scar.

Something sweet and sharp twisted deep inside me, compounding my confusion.

'I really must be on my way,' I said. 'Isobel will think I am not coming.'

'I am going home to Trevarrah shortly myself,' he said. 'I could offer you a ride up behind me.' He caught my quick, startled look, and added: 'Lancelot is a strong horse; he is well able to bear the weight of two.'

'Oh, thank you, but no! I am very used to walking,' I said hastily.

'As you please.' A corner of his mouth twisted; I could not help but think he was amused by my discomfiture. 'No doubt I shall see you at Trevarrah.'

'No doubt.' I tried to smile; my lips felt stiff.

I turned and resumed the path I had been taking to Trevarrah.

—

As I walked, my cheeks cooled, but the confusion that had overcome me remained.

I could scarcely believe that the Adam I had seen this morning was the same arrogant, ill-tempered man I had encountered at Trevarrah a week or so ago. That man had not only spoken rudely to me for no apparent reason, he had also shouted insults at his own brother and cut Isobel dead before storming out of the house.

This morning, besides the attempt to make amends to me, I had witnessed his consideration towards a lowly employee – an act of kindness he had seemed almost to wish to deny. Though that was understandable – no employer of large numbers of men would wish to be thought soft-hearted, lest their workers take advantage of the weakness.

But it was my own reaction to this new Adam which puzzled and disturbed me most. I thought again of the heat that had burned in my cheeks and the strange fluttering I had experienced deep within when he had smiled.

I pictured the way his mouth had twisted against that long scar, and his eyes crinkled, and felt the excitement twist again, an echo of what I had experienced before, but every bit as sharp.

As it subsided, I caught myself up short. I must be taking leave of my senses! And to entertain such feelings for even a moment was to court trouble. Not only was Adam out of my class, he was the brother-in-law – and former sweetheart – of my friend and employer. But, for all that, I suddenly felt like singing.

It was so long since I had experienced such a giddy response. I had begun to wonder if I was incapable of feeling attraction to a man – for that, without doubt, was what I was experiencing now. And even knowing that nothing could come of it, even if I wanted it to, did not have the power to mar my pleasure.

I *was* human, after all! For the moment that was quite enough.

When I approached Trevarrah, I saw Isobel looking out of an upstairs window, watching for me, no doubt, for by the time I reached it, the front door was thrown open and she ran out, smiling, to meet me.

'Tamsin! I was beginning to think you were not coming! Is everything well with you? Your mother isn't worse again?'

'No,' I said. 'The reason I am late has nothing to do with Mammy. I'll tell you all about it when we get inside. You shouldn't be out in the cold and damp in that thin gown in your condition.'

'Oh, you're not going to fuss over me, I hope!' she said. 'I'm perfectly well. I don't seem to be suffering any of the dreadful sickness some women complain of.' But she shivered, all the same, as the cold wind blew a gust of damp air all around her, and, taking my arm, she led me inside.

As I took off my cloak, she looked at me, frowning.

'Whatever...? Tamsin, your clothes! Whatever has happened to you? Did you catch your foot and fall?'

'No, there was an accident at the mine and...'

'An accident?' she repeated, alarmed. 'What sort of an accident?'

'Nothing serious,' I hastened to reassure her. 'A man was kicked by a mule, that's all.'

'Oh, thank goodness!' Her relief was obvious. 'I know that Nicholas is dreadfully concerned about the safety of some of the levels, and Adam is forever berating him about it too. But Nicholas says he hasn't the money to spare to put things right...' She broke off. 'Oh, we don't want to talk about the mine, do we? I have quite enough of that from the men. Just tell me how you come to be in such a state!'

I related events, making as little as possible of my part in it, whilst wondering if conditions at Wheal Henry and what Nicholas intended to do about them were behind the quarrel I had overheard.

'Anyway, Adam has sent the poor man home now in a horse-drawn cart,' I finished.

Isobel seemed almost to wince at the mention of his name.

'Adam? Adam was there?'

'Yes,' I said. 'He seemed to be in a much better humour than he was the other day. He promised the man would not go the loser of his wages.'

Isobel puckered her lips. 'Nicholas will have something to say about that! Adam trying to make himself popular at his expense.'

'He even apologized to me for his ill temper the other day,' I finished.

Isobel's blue eyes widened, and she sighed. 'It sounds to me as if he has been drinking.'

'At this time of day?' I exclaimed, amazed. 'I have to say he didn't appear at all drunk to me.'

'He hides it well.' Isobel gave a small shake of her head, then tucked a golden curl behind her ear. 'When men drink a good deal, they are often able to carry it well enough to deceive the casual onlooker. As for the time of day... I am afraid Adam takes little account of that since he returned from America.'

Her assertion surprised me a great deal – and rather spoiled my illusions. Perhaps he had been drunk when he had spoken so rudely to me and quarrelled with Nicholas. But certainly he had seemed perfectly sober this morning.

'Do you think I could wash my hands?' I asked. 'I'm really not fit for anything until I have.'

'Of course! Just go to the kitchen and ask Aggie for some water. And tell her we would like some hot chocolate while you are about it. You must be half frozen!'

'As well as dirty!' I said ruefully.

'I shall let you have a clean dress to wear,' Isobel offered. 'We'll go and choose one while we're waiting for the chocolate. I'm sure my things will fit you – we're much of a size, aren't we? And if you are able to look after me, you'll need to be familiar with my rooms and my wardrobe, so we shall be killing two birds with one stone.'

I smiled. It was the first time Isobel had made mention of my duties, and I was glad she had done so. It brought me down to earth and made me remember that in reality I was no more than a servant here at Trevarrah, however much Isobel might try to pretend otherwise.

—

And pretend she certainly did! A beautiful blue velvet gown was pressed upon me, with the offer that I could keep it for my own, since Isobel said she would soon be too plump to wear it, and petticoats too, when she saw the state mine had been reduced to. She even insisted I choose a pair of slippers.

'Isobel, I can't take them!' I protested. 'Your feet aren't going to get bigger, though I suppose they may swell a little later on.'

'I want you to have them,' Isobel insisted. 'You can't possibly wear those old boots in the house. You can leave the slippers here to wear when you're with me if that makes you feel better. Think of them as part of your uniform.'

A very nice uniform! I thought wryly as I caught sight of myself in her dressing mirror. In the blue velvet gown, with Isobel's pendant around my neck and her slippers on my feet, I was hardly recognizable as the sensibly but plainly dressed girl who had left home less than two hours earlier!

I still felt a little uncomfortable in accepting what felt to me like charity, but Isobel was so excited by my transformation, it seemed churlish not to show a modicum of pleasure myself. At midday, however, when Nicholas came home for a light meal of cold meats and cheese, I saw him looking at me a little askance, knew he had recognized the gown as belonging to Isobel, and felt awkward all over again.

He made no mention of it, however, and neither did Isobel. And at least Adam was not with him. I have to confess to experiencing a frisson of disappointment, but I told myself that, given my foolish reaction to him this morning, it was for the best.

'Tamsin tells me a man was kicked by a mule today at Wheal Henry,' Isobel said, delicately picking at a slice of ham.

'I believe so.' Nicholas seemed utterly unconcerned. 'These things happen all the time. I don't involve myself unless it's serious.'

'Tamsin says Adam had him sent home by horse-drawn cart and promised his wages would be paid.'

Nicholas speared a piece of pork angrily. 'So I understand. He takes too much upon himself, that one. Coming home after all this time, thinking he knows better than I how things should be run! I've had a few sharp words with him about it, I can tell you.'

I kept my eyes firmly on my plate. Clearly the brothers had quarrelled again. It explained, I supposed, why Adam had not come home with Nicholas for the midday meal. But I could not help thinking that, if I had been Isobel, I would not have raised the subject, since she must have known it was likely to annoy Nicholas.

'It's all very well for Adam to be magnanimous,' he went on now. 'We simply do not have the wherewithal to pay men when they are not doing their work, whatever the reason. Adam does not seem to understand the difficulties we are experiencing and he stands in my way at every turn. And as if that isn't enough, he wants to play the bountiful squire too. He's impossible!'

'I dare say he was only thinking of the poor man,' Isobel said.

Nicholas banged down his knife and glared at her. 'I might have known you would take his part, though I would have thought it was your duty, if not your inclination, to take mine!'

Colour rose in Isobel's cheeks. 'Of course I take your part, Nicholas! How could you suggest I would do otherwise?'

'From long experience, my dear.'

The bitterness in his voice shocked me, and glancing at Isobel I saw something defensive in her expression – defensive and almost furtive. Was it possible, I found myself wondering, that she did indeed still care for Adam? She had believed him dead when she had agreed to be Nicholas's wife. Was it possible she was now regretting her decision – and Nicholas knew it? Small wonder, if that were the case, that there was so much bad feeling between the brothers.

'Well, we have no choice but to put up with him – for the moment,' Nicholas said. 'I only hope we can be rid of him before too much longer.' He seemed suddenly to become aware of me, sitting just across the table with my eyes lowered to my plate. 'Let's forget about my damned brother. All this talk of him is doing no good whatever to my digestion.'

He attacked his cold meats with vigour and no more was said about Adam. But the shadow remained and I knew without doubt that, whatever the rights and wrongs of it, this was indeed a very troubled house.

–

Thoughtful as ever, Isobel insisted I leave in time to get home before nightfall, but the dull, dank day brought an early dusk, and by the time I was back in Mallen, lamps were lighted in the cottage windows and I was scarce able to see my hand before my face.

I found Ruth and the children in Mammy's house. Charlie was sitting on Mammy's lap and she was allowing him to play with her hair, which he had unpinned and was trying to fix again – with little success, of course. My heart lifted. Mammy must indeed be feeling more herself to allow Charlie to carry on so!

As I greeted them, Ruth came bustling in from the kitchen and at once I could see she was in a state of agitation.

'Oh Tamsin, thank goodness you're back! I've been so worried!'

'Why? Whatever is the matter?' I asked, alarmed.

'Oh, such news! You won't have heard it, I suppose. That's why I've been so worried. In case you came across him on your way home...'

'Ruth, what are you talking about?' I asked.

Ruth took me by the arm and pulled me into the scullery.

'Mammy's attacker, of course!' she hissed, keeping her voice low so Mammy would not hear. 'I think I know who it was.'

'What...?'

'Just listen to me!' Ruth was gripping my arms so hard she was hurting me. 'A man broke into a cottage in Mount Hawk last night, looking for food, or so they think. The householder surprised him and he ran off. But not before he was recognized.'

'He was *recognized*?' I repeated.

'Yes. And it explains everything! Do you know who it was? Joshua Tripp!'

'Joshua?' It seemed I had been reduced to merely repeating Ruth's words like some sea captain's parrot, but this was the last thing I had expected to hear. 'But Joshua Tripp was sent to the penal colony in Australia years ago! How could it be him?'

'The talk is, he must have gained his freedom one way or another and worked his passage home. Oh, they seem sure enough it was him. The man worked with him once, in one of the mines. He said though Joshua was older and thicker-set, he'd have known him anywhere.'

'Joshua Tripp!' I said again. 'Then...'

'Yes!' The anxiety was clearly written on Ruth's smooth, plump face. 'You see what it means, don't you? He must have been the prowler you saw outside, that night. He must have been the one who attacked Mammy! Joshua is back, desperate and perhaps vengeful too. And he's still in the district, and on the loose! I tell you, I'm scared to death, Tamsin!'

I stared at Ruth in total stunned disbelief.

'Oh surely – not Joshua!' I said. 'He wouldn't...'

'He always was a bad lad,' Ruth ran on. 'Always in some kind of trouble. Thieving, poaching, fighting... you must remember, Tamsin! And after his experiences, being transported, living the life of a convict, he's no doubt hardened and worse than ever.'

I shook my head wordlessly. Joshua *had* been a bad lad, it was true. He had always been known as a troublemaker who took too much to drink and got into fights. Once he had led a gang of young tearaways against a group of lads from the village of Dovey who were considered foreigners in our hamlet, and half killed a couple of them, so it was said. And when the barn of a farmer who had chased them off went up in flames the very next night, Joshua and his cronies had been blamed, though nothing was ever proved.

He had been a thief too, and a poacher – many was the dark night we had seen him creeping off with a gun and a sack. But we had always thought that the hares and pheasants that appeared mysteriously on our doorstep had been left there by him, though he had never admitted it, and he had never been anything but respectful towards Mammy. I simply could not believe he could have done something so terrible as to beat her senseless and break her ribs – an old woman he had known all his life.

'Joshua wouldn't harm Mammy,' I protested again.

'Who's to say what he would do if he was desperate?' Ruth argued. 'Life in the penal colony will have taught him wicked ways, and may even have driven him a little mad. They do say the convicts there are no better than animals. If he came looking for food and shelter and Mammy refused him, he may well have lost his temper with her.'

'I can't see Mammy refusing him basic needs,' I said frankly. 'And anyway, why would he come here – to Mallen? His mother and brother are both in the ground long since.'

'He wouldn't know that though, would he?' Ruth pointed out. 'If he has only just arrived back in England, he wouldn't know they were dead. He came here looking for them and found the house all locked up, and if he looked through the windows he could see that his mother's things were gone and everything changed. So he went next door, to Mammy's house, and attacked her in a rage. You must see, it all pieces together!'

'Have you mentioned this to her?' I asked.

She shook her head. 'I didn't want to upset her.'

'We have to ask her, Ruth,' I said.

I went back into the living room. Mammy was still playing contentedly with Charlie. I crossed to her chair, dropping down on my haunches beside her and speaking in a gentle tone.

'Mammy, do you remember Joshua Tripp?'

She looked up. Her hair was all tangled about her sweet face so that she looked as if she had been pulled through a bush backward. She smiled at my question, her eyes faraway, as if she were surveying the distant land that was the past.

'Joshua? Yes, of course. Such a naughty boy! But I liked him. You couldn't help but like Joshua.'

'Did Joshua come here on the day you were attacked?' I asked gently.

She laughed softly. 'Joshua was sent to Australia, my dear. The magistrate sent him to Australia.'

'Yes, Mammy, but Ruth says he's come back.'

'Oh good!' Mammy smiled. 'His mother will be so pleased. She's never got over it, you know, losing him like that...'

I shook my head and rose, straightening my skirts.

'It's no good. She remembers only things that happened years ago. She's even forgotten old Mother Tripp is dead and buried, though she went to her funeral. And though she knows you live next door, in the Tripps' old house...'

I broke off suddenly, a small chill whispering over my skin. 'You live in the Tripps' old house,' I repeated.

'Yes.' Ruth's voice was low and urgent. 'That's what I've been trying to say, Tamsin. We live in what Joshua no doubt still thinks of as his home.' She pressed her hands together in the folds of her skirt but I could see they were trembling. 'I'm frightened, Tamsin. I'm frightened he'll come back.'

'I'm sure he won't,' I said, trying to reassure her. 'If it was him who attacked Mammy he'd be far too afraid of being apprehended. He'd know that this time he wouldn't just be transported. He'd know he'd be swinging on the end of a rope.'

'But he did come back, didn't he?' Ruth persisted. 'He was lurking outside that night when you saw him from the window and raised the alarm. It couldn't have been anyone else. But why did he risk it? That's what I'd like to know! He must be crazy with rage is all I can think. And I tell you straight, I'm worried to death.'

'Oh Ruth...' I did not know what to say. If she was right and it had been Joshua who had attacked Mammy, if it had been him lurking outside that night with some sort of perverted revenge on his mind, and if he was indeed still in the district, perhaps living rough, then it could be that we were in danger. But what could we do about it except keep a sharp eye out and take care to bolt our doors behind us?

'Jed will be home soon,' I said, trying to comfort her. 'He will know what's to do for the best.'

But I could not, in truth, see that Jed would have any more idea than I did as to what could be done.

—

My nerves were on edge as we ate our evening meal and I cleared away the pots and dishes, and several times I went to the window, looking out and straining my eyes into the darkness for any sign of movement or indeed anything untoward. But everything was as it always was.

As I worked, I searched my memory, trying desperately to conjure up a picture in my mind's eye of the man I had seen lurking in the shadow of the bushes, and trying too to picture Joshua as I had known him. But matching the two was beyond me. Joshua had been a gangling lad, with a thin face and wicked dark eyes, but if Ruth's story was to be believed, he had filled out now, grown, I could well imagine, to a powerful figure of a man.

The prowler had appeared quite big to me, but I had had nothing to measure him by and it had been far too dark for me to see his face. I had no way of knowing for sure that it had been Joshua, though I had to admit, if he was back in the district, it could very well have been. Yet still I found it hard to believe that Joshua Tripp could have been responsible for the attack on Mammy. A bad lot in some ways he might be. Violent even. But to kick and beat a defenceless woman he had known all his life... no, I still could not bring myself to believe it of him. Either the harsh lot of a convict in the penal colony had changed him for the worse, or I had never known him at all.

'You have been to Trevarrah today,' Mammy said unexpectedly when I went back into the living room. She was looking pleased with herself, proud, no doubt, that she had remembered.

'Yes,' I said.

'How is Ralph?'

I sighed inwardly. 'Mammy,' I said patiently, 'Ralph is dead. I told you that.'

'Oh yes.' Her smile faded and once again I saw the distress flicker over her face. 'Oh dear, yes. I forgot. I forget so many things, Tamsin.'

'But soon you'll begin to remember again.'

'Oh, I do hope so!' She chewed her lip, an expression of fierce concentration making her eyes go faraway. 'There's something I have to do. Something of great importance. For Ralph. And no matter how I try, I cannot remember what it is.'

Frustration niggled at me. Mammy was making no sense at all. 'All you have to do, Mammy,' I said gently, 'is to concentrate on getting well.'

Time was short. He had been patient for too long; now his patience was fast running out.

It was ill luck indeed that the woman he felt sure held the key to the Treasure had — or so those close to her maintained — lost all recent memory. He was not totally convinced that was the case. People could be devious when it suited them to be. Greed was a powerful motivator. But whether it was the whole truth or not made little difference. The information he so desperately needed was withheld from him. There must be a way to access it. By fair means or foul he would find that way and regain the Treasure. Without it he was lost.

His skin crawled now with impatience.

Why had the old man decided upon such a devious course? He had always been a secretive soul; old age and illness must have made him more so. But to entrust the secret of the whereabouts of the inheritance to someone outside the family circle had been a bizarre decision.

The inheritance belonged with him. Not only did he desire it fiercely, with every fibre of his being, it was of vital importance to him that he gained possession of it – and quickly. Everything depended upon it.

And in the end he would. Whatever it cost, whoever was hurt in the process, nothing else mattered.

Very soon the inheritance would be his. He was determined upon it.

Seven

I did not go to Trevarrah again for several days. We held a family council when Jed returned from his 'core' at the mine, and decided it would be for the best if I remained at home with Mammy. Ruth had been quite unnerved by the thought that Joshua might be lurking in the vicinity, and though I still found it difficult to believe that he was the one who had attacked Mammy, yet I was dreadfully afraid I might be wrong. Who could tell how his years of exile might have affected him? Embittered, hardened, perhaps driven a little mad by his experiences, it was possible that some kind of twisted logic might be persuading him that the cottage where he had been born and raised was still his by right, and that Ruth and Jed had somehow stolen it from him. And he could be blaming all of us for the death of his mother and brother and seeking some kind of perverted revenge.

Someone had beaten Mammy senseless for no apparent reason. Someone had been stealing about outside our cottages and run off when he was surprised. And if Joshua had tried to steal food from a house in Mount Hawk, then very likely he was living rough – and had tried to do the same elsewhere. Everything pointed to it being him who had attacked Mammy, and until he was apprehended we could not feel safe.

I knew I could not stay at home for ever, of course, and I felt dreadful about letting Isobel down so soon, and after she had been so kind. But my first duty was to my family. If they needed me, then I must be here for them. And truth to tell, I still harboured feelings of guilt that if Jed and Ruth had not come into Truro to meet me on the day I had come home, Mammy would not have been attacked. Foolish, perhaps, but I could not help feeling in some way responsible.

And so I sent word that family matters were preventing me from coming to Trevarrah and busied myself with caring for Mammy and keeping a sharp lookout for anything untoward that might indicate Joshua was nearby.

On the third day I was upstairs making up the beds with clean linen when I heard a rap at the door. 'Tamsin!' Mammy called, and I hastily straightened the sheet and started down the stairs. Mammy was at the door, unbarring it herself.

'Mammy – don't!' I warned sharply, but too late. She had the bolt off and the door opened before I could stop her, and I saw her take a startled step backward, her hand going to her throat.

'Ralph!'

I ran down the last couple of steps and was across the room in a flash. What in the world was Mammy saying?

Then I stopped in surprise. The visitor, standing outside our door, was none other than Adam Penrose.

'Oh – I'm sorry – I thought...' I could feel the foolish colour flooding my cheeks.

'No, if I frightened you, then I am the one who should apologize.' His mouth quirked a little. 'And I frightened your mother too. I believe she thought I was a ghost. I had not realized how much I resemble my dead father.'

I had not realized it either. But then, I had never known Ralph Penrose as anything but an elderly man.

'Mammy is still very confused,' I explained, and took her arm. 'Mammy, this is Adam.'

'Adam?' She shook her head, laughed a little. 'No, Tamsin, you're mistaken! Adam is a little boy!'

'No, he's grown up, as I have. We were children together, don't you remember?' I looked back at Adam, standing there in the doorway, riding whip in hand, and felt the same disturbing flutter deep inside as I had felt before.

'Won't you come in?' I said, and hoped my voice did not betray the confusion I was feeling.

I stood aside and Adam came into the little room, filling it, or so it seemed to me, with his presence. Mammy followed him in, crossing to sit in her chair by the fire. She was still looking at him strangely, a dazed expression on her face.

'I called by to pass on to you the thanks of Joe Needs and his wife for the assistance you gave him the other day,' Adam said. 'They are most touched by the care and consideration you showed him, and since I knew I would be passing close by Mallen today, I promised that I would convey their gratitude to you.'

'Oh, there was no need!' My words came awkwardly, in a rush, to be followed by a moment's silence when my tongue seemed to lose its function entirely and I felt the hot colour in my cheeks again. Why, Adam would think me a perfect fool! 'How is the poor man?' I asked, partly to cover my confusion and partly because I truly was concerned for his health, considering his livelihood depended on it.

'He's back at his work,' Adam replied. 'A little shaken and pale, but the wound has not been infected – thanks to your timely ministrations. In my opinion he should still be at home, resting, but I suppose needs must where the devil drives.'

His tone was clipped; I remembered Nicholas's hard views on paying the man even a day's wages when he was not able to carry out his duties, and thought that in this case it was *he* who was the devil.

'I must be on my way, then.' Adam moved toward the door once more. 'I have business to attend to that will not wait.'

Sharp disappointment ached in me that his visit had been so brief, yet it was tempered with relief. Adam's presence was disconcerting, and it was a terrible struggle to conceal the foolish response it elicited in me.

At the door he paused. 'What is the real reason you have not been to Trevarrah?' he asked in a low voice. 'Isobel was under the impression your mother had taken a turn for the worse, but that doesn't seem to be the case.'

I stepped outside, pulling the door to behind me.

'We had something of a scare the other day,' I explained, and went on to tell him about Joshua. He listened intently, tapping his riding whip against his thigh.

'I can well understand your concern,' he said when I had finished. 'I would think if he was almost apprehended in Mount Hawk, he would have the sense to put some distance between himself and anyone he knows, but I can see that it's troubling for you none the less.'

He stood silently for a moment, looking around, then his gaze seemed to fasten on the low stone wall that backed the outhouses.

'It looks to me as if that wall is crumbling and could do with some attention.'

I frowned. I had thought he was paying attention to our problem and here he was talking about crumbling walls!

'I think it might be an idea if I were to send over a couple of men tomorrow to repair it,' he said, then glanced at me, a half-smile quirking the corner of his mouth. 'Do you think you might feel a little safer with two burly labourers hard at work outside your door?'

'Oh!' Realization dawned. 'Yes,' I said, a little flustered. 'Yes, I'm sure we would.'

'Good. So I can tell Isobel you will be back at Trevarrah, perhaps? She is anxious, I know, for your company. We could always send transport over for you if you are nervous about being alone on the moors.'

'Oh, there's no need for that!' I said quickly. 'I'm sure I'll be perfectly safe and... you've already promised more than enough...'

'Good.' He smiled, and my heart gave that disturbing leap. 'That's settled then.' With surprising ease for one with a shattered knee, he mounted his horse. 'Good day to you, Tamsin.'

'Good day – and thank you.'

As he rode away I stared after him, bemused but curiously exhilarated. Was that the real reason Adam had come here today – to arrange for me to return to Trevarrah? Why were they so anxious to have me there that they went to such lengths? Or had Adam offered the workmen who would be in effect guards out of concern for our safety and the goodness of his heart?

My pulses skipped again, all my misgivings disappeared as if by magic, and, as I went back into the cottage, I found myself smiling.

Adam's labourers arrived almost with the dawn to start work on the repair of the outhouse wall, and when I had offered them a little refreshment, I set out for Trevarrah. Isobel was delighted to see me, and smiled smugly when I explained that Adam's offer had made us feel that it was safe enough for me to leave Ruth and Mammy.

'Ah, yes. We thought it was time some work was done to bring the properties up to scratch,' she said, and, unreasonably, I felt a twinge of disappointment. I had thought it had all been Adam's idea, on the spur of the moment; now I was not so sure. I gave myself a little shake, and told myself not to be so foolish. What did it matter whose idea it was, so long as two burly workmen were on hand to make sure Mammy had no unwelcome visitors?

Soon I had fallen into my new routine, spending the days with Isobel and going home at night to sleep in my own bed. When the work on the outhouse wall was completed, the men found other jobs to do on the maintenance of the cottages, but we were beginning to forget our fright, in any case, and one day I told Isobel that really there was no need for the Penroses to continue to make work in order to provide protection. 'Well, if you're sure, Tamsin,' she said. 'I expect Nicholas has plenty of other work lined up for them.'

'Of course he has,' I said. I was only surprised that he had allowed them away from their other duties for so long, given his attitude towards getting value for money where his workforce was concerned!

Another milestone was reached when the remainder of my belongings, all packed up in a trunk, arrived from Launceston, together with a letter from Mrs Melhuish saying how sorry she was to have to let me go, and that a new girl had started in my place. I could not help feeling a little sad, the years I had spent in Launceston had played a big part in my life, but they were over now. My future was here now, at home in Mallen, and with Isobel at Trevarrah.

A week or so later, Isobel took me quite by surprise with a curious request.

'Since you seem much easier in your mind now about leaving your mother alone, Tamsin, I am wondering if I can persuade you to spend a whole night away from them.'

She saw my uncertain frown, and went quickly on: 'Oh, don't think I am going back on our arrangement. I know you don't want to live in here at Trevarrah at present, and I wouldn't want you to. This is a special occasion – for one evening only. A charity ball is being held next week at the Assembly Rooms in Truro and I really would like you to accompany me.'

My frown became a look of astonishment.

'But whatever for?' I asked. 'You'll be with Nicholas, won't you, and all your friends will be there.'

'Friends!' She gave a small, rather sad laugh. 'They are not *true* friends, Tamsin, as you are. And Nicholas… well, he doesn't really understand either.'

'Understand what?' I pressed her.

She lowered her eyelashes, pink colour tingeing her cheeks.

'The way I am at present. The effect this pregnancy is having on me.'

'But you're blooming!' I said. 'You look so well!'

'I may look well, but… I haven't said anything before, but I've been having very strange turns, Tamsin, when I feel dreadfully faint. Yesterday, after dinner, I truly thought

I was going to swoon clear away. If that should happen at the ball…'

I was shocked. Certainly if Isobel was feeling poorly she was hiding it very well.

'Surely if you are having fainting fits it would be best if you didn't go to the ball at all!' I said.

She shook her head. 'No, I must go. Everyone would think it very strange if I did not. My condition is not public knowledge yet, and won't be for some while if I can help it. And Nicholas says there will be important people there who may be able to help with his financial difficulties. It's always best to approach them in a social environment. He is insistent we should go.'

'Perhaps he should put your well-being before his financial affairs,' I said, a little tartly.

'Don't be too hard on him, Tamsin,' Isobel said. 'He's under a great deal of pressure at the moment. And Adam is not helping. Since he came home, he seems to criticize and interfere in everything Nicholas tries to do.'

For some reason I found myself flying to Adam's defence.

'As is his right, surely,' I said, before I could stop myself.

'Nicholas had to take control of everything in his absence!' Isobel returned passionately. 'Adam may be the elder, but he was not here when he was needed. He doesn't want the responsibility in any case. If it wasn't for having been wounded he would still be off with his regiment enjoying himself fighting, and leaving us to take care of the estate and everything else! It's very unfair of him to question Nicholas at every turn.'

I bit my lip. Whatever my private feelings, I would be foolish indeed to appear to be taking sides in their ongoing power struggle.

'Anyway!' Isobel seemed as keen to change the subject as I was that she should. 'Let's talk about the ball. I was rather looking forward to it until I had these strange turns. I shall enjoy it, I know, just so long as you are with me in case I become unwell. And you would enjoy it too. It would do you good to have a little fun, Tamsin. Oh, please say you will attend with me! For friendship's sake...'

I sighed inwardly. I had not the least desire to be forced to mingle with Isobel's grand friends and acquaintances, and neither did I want to spend a night away from home. But I had been glad enough to accept her offer of employment as her companion, and she had been very understanding of my situation. I owed it to her to make a little effort on her behalf.

'Very well, I'll see if I can arrange things at home so that I can accompany you,' I said reluctantly.

And found myself wondering still what was the real reason behind her insistent invitation.

–

Though I had lived in Cornwall all of my life and visited Truro for one reason or another many times, I had never before seen the interior of the Assembly Rooms. Nor had I ever been to a formal ball, though I had learned to dance a little at far less illustrious dances in barns when village folk had occasion for celebration, which was rare enough. So I was utterly spellbound by the scene which greeted me when I arrived with Isobel and Nicholas.

The great room was alight with hundreds of candles arranged along the walls, and on a platform a band had already begun to play. Never in all my life had I seen such finery as the ladies were attired in – shimmering silks and brocades of gold and silver and every colour of the rainbow, and the sparkling jewels at their throats must have been worth a king's ransom.

I was glad, indeed, that Isobel had persuaded me to borrow one of her dresses – a gown of deep pink – and though my only adornment was the simple pendant she had given me, I felt that at least I was not conspicuous for my poor dowdy appearance. Yet still I could not help feeling uncomfortable and out of place. It was not that I was in awe of these grand folk, the cream of Cornish society. I had met plenty of grand folk whilst in the employ of Mrs Melhuish, and always held to the rather defiant belief that, for all the gulf that lay between their station in life and mine, I was as good as any of them.

No, it was rather that I felt I had no place here. For all that she had begged for my company, the fact was that Isobel was partnered by her husband, and I made a rather strange addition to the party. Several times, as she introduced me to her friends, I could not help but notice they gave me sidelong, curious glances.

I was not, of course, the only unattached girl by any means. There were gaggles of them, watched over by their proud and vigilant mamas, who were, no doubt, hoping they might find suitable beaus or even husbands amongst the handful of eligible men. Certainly dance cards were being completed all around me with a great many bows from the gentlemen and simpering and blushing on the part of the girls.

I had no expectation of being solicited for a dance, and no desire either – until the scraping of the band set my toes tapping. But I told myself I was here for the sole purpose of being on hand should Isobel need me, and no one was likely to wish to take to the floor with a hired companion. I was, then, quite taken by surprise when a short, pot-bellied man in silk breeches and powdered wig asked me rather pompously if he might have the pleasure of the next dance.

I glanced helplessly at Isobel; she, suppressing a gleam of amusement, squeezed my hand.

'Dance, Tamsin! Enjoy yourself! It's the whole reason I persuaded you to join us tonight.'

So, I thought, as I had suspected, Isobel had been finding excuses when she had asked me to accompany her. I could not imagine why she should have gone to such lengths except that she genuinely thought I was in need of a little fun, and I was touched by her thoughtfulness. She had known very well that I would never have accepted an invitation to the ball unless I thought it was in my line of duty.

'Well, I won't be far away if you should want me,' I said, a little wickedly, perhaps, and her blue eyes sparkled a conspiratorial response.

The moment the dance began, however, I forgot all the guilt I was feeling at the thought of Ruth and Jed having to take care of Mammy whilst I frittered the evening away. I forgot that my partner was a fat little man with perspiration dripping down his forehead from beneath his wig, forgot all my cares and anxieties. The pleasure of whirling to the music with my feet keeping time was so great that for the duration of the dance I thought of nothing else.

As it came to an end and the little man thanked me and returned me to the edge of the floor, I looked around for Isobel and Nicholas, but they were nowhere to be seen.

It was, I thought, a little odd, and hoped that Isobel had not really been taken poorly. Mammy always used to say that telling a lie was tempting the devil, and someone who feigned illness would surely be struck down by it. But Isobel's 'lie' had been for my benefit, and well intentioned. And she seemed in sparkling form this evening, as well as looking beautiful in her gown of washed ivory silk, with creamy pearls in her ears and at her throat.

'Well, Tamsin, you are light on your feet and no mistake!'

I whirled round at the sound of a familiar voice, that ready colour rising in cheeks already flushed from the dance. Adam was standing there, smiling that crooked smile that pulled at the slash of his scar, and teasing me with his eyes. I had not seen him come in – if I had I might have been a good deal more self-conscious and less willing to abandon myself to the pleasure of the dance. Now, I composed myself and tried to still my pulse, which had begun to race.

'I'm no dancer, I'm afraid,' I said. 'I've not had enough practice.'

'Then perhaps we should rectify that. Will you do me the honour of a dance?'

'But… Isobel…' I stammered.

'Isobel won't even miss you,' Adam said. 'I have just seen her and Nicholas go to the refreshment room, where at this very moment they are drinking good wine in the company of Lord Wisbech.'

'But…'

'I shall be mortally offended to think that you will dance with an old fool like Kington and yet refuse me.' Adam's eyes teased me again, and I felt that treacherous flutter of response deep inside. 'Come on, now, Tamsin, don't hurt my feelings so. You've no excuse – and excuses are all that you can hope to offer.'

'Oh – very well,' I said recklessly.

The band scraped up again and he led me to the dance floor, one hand placed lightly on my waist. His touch made my skin prickle; it was as if his fingers were burning me through the thin silk of Isobel's gown.

Where before, with Mr Kington, I had thought of nothing but my dancing, with Adam I could think of nothing but him. Where before my feet had seemed to know exactly where to go without me telling them, now they fumbled awkwardly.

'I'm sorry...' I murmured as I made yet another false step.

'Don't apologize!' he said lightly. 'Never apologize for anything, Tamsin – especially to me.'

'But I'm such a fool...'

'The world is quick enough to blame us for our failings without us drawing attention to them.'

The thought occurred to me that he was talking of something other than dancing, but was as quickly gone. My head was spinning, my heart beating very fast. When at last the music stopped, he looked down at me gravely.

'Are you willing to give it another try?'

I looked around. There was still no sign of Isobel. An imp of recklessness danced in me, making me careless of my duty.

'Why not?'

And so we danced again, and this time my feet were better behaved, though my heart was not.

And: 'I really must find Isobel,' I said when the music stopped again. 'She'll think I have deserted her.'

'If you must, you must. But I shall claim another dance before the night is over. Our practice is not yet complete.' There was a wicked twinkle in his eyes.

'You mock me!' I chided. But I did not mind. Oh, I did not mind in the least!

—

Isobel and Nicholas were still in the refreshment room, still talking with a man I recognized as Lord Wisbech, a wealthy local landowner whose estate bordered Penrose land on the south side.

Isobel glanced round as we approached, looking almost startled, and I wondered if she had quite forgotten that she had brought me to the ball.

'Tamsin has refused me another dance because she is concerned you will think she is neglecting you,' Adam said, and suddenly it occurred to me that there might be quite another reason for Isobel's startled look.

'You have been dancing with Tamsin?' she asked, and I fancied there was a brittle note beneath the lightness of her tone. 'Why, I declare I am most jealous, Adam! And surprised, too, since you told me your knee prevented you from taking to the floor.'

'Dancing with Tamsin is pleasure enough to make one forget such things,' Adam said, and the spark between them was so unmistakeable it pierced my heady glow.

These were two people who had once been in love and, it was said, promised to one another. Was there still something between them? Was I just a pawn in some game they were playing?

'Would you object to me taking Tamsin for a glass of wine?' Adam asked Isobel now, and: 'Of course not!' she replied. But still the edge was there in her voice, so real you could almost touch it.

And so he steered me to a corner of the refreshment room that was screened by potted ferns and pressed a glass of wine into my hand, and watched, amused, over the rim of his glass as I tasted it. And before long the warmth of the claret and the way his eyes held mine made me forget the unpleasant thought that had occurred to me – or put it on one side at any rate.

I had never had such an evening as this before. I should, in all likelihood, never have one such again. It comprised a few magic hours stolen out of time. Perfume and music and heady wine – and Adam.

I determined to forget everything else and concentrate on enjoying it.

I slept that night – or rather did *not* sleep – in a great box bed in a guest room at Trevarrah, as had been arranged for the sake of convenience.

On the way home in the carriage, Isobel was in a strange, brittle mood, one moment feigning sleepiness, the next questioning me avidly as to what had passed between me and Adam, who had barely left my side all evening. He had ridden his own horse home, but before we parted he had kissed my hand and thanked me for my company, his lips saying he hoped he would see me again very soon, his eyes promising much more, though of course I did not tell Isobel that. For the moment I hugged it to myself and, a little intoxicated by both wine and happiness, I chose not to question his intentions.

But later, as I lay in the unfamiliar bed, staring wide-eyed into the darkness, with the effects of the alcohol beginning to wear off, I warned myself I must not read anything into it, for I would surely be disappointed if I did.

I thought again of the tension I had sensed between Isobel and Adam, and wondered if one or the other or both had been using me for their own ends. But in the last resort, what did it matter anyway? Isobel or no Isobel, there could never be anything between Adam and me but a brief flirtation. Oh, perhaps he would be ready enough to give me a quick tumble if I were willing – gentlemen were not above taking advantage of the favours of girls who were their social inferiors – but they most certainly did not become romantically involved with them. I was not the sort of girl to follow that certain path to shame and disgrace. No matter how foolishly infatuated – and flattered – by his attentions I might be, I had too much sense, and too much pride.

At least, I certainly hoped I had!

Eight

Over the next days, however, I began to wonder.

Adam seemed to be spending more time at Trevarrah than he had done previously, and though there was no opportunity for us to be alone, I had the distinct impression he was trying to create one. And still there was that frisson of something between us, as tangible and disturbing as the force of nature that charges the air before a thunderstorm.

He would be talking to Nicholas or Isobel of something quite inconsequential and I would feel his eyes upon me; he would fill my glass at the midday meal and let his fingers brush mine, a touch so light it might have been accidental. But I knew it was not, and the sharp response it elicited in me was undimmed.

I told myself I was courting danger, yet I could not change the way he made me feel. Nor did I want to. After all the years when I had felt not the slightest stirring of interest in a man, this excitement was intoxicating and sweet as forbidden fruit.

I had at least thought I was managing to hide my foolish feelings, but it seemed I was not achieving the success for which I hoped, for one day Isobel gently made mention of it.

'Adam is a charmer, Tamsin,' she said. 'But don't be deceived by him.'

Colour flooded my cheeks. 'A charmer?' I said with a little laugh. 'With his black moods and sharp tongue?'

Isobel refused to be sidetracked. 'He is a powerfully attractive man, none the less,' she said. 'And a dangerous one. There are things I could tell you about Adam that would shock you to the core. Be careful, Tamsin.'

'What do you mean?' I asked.

Isobel merely shook her head and refused to elaborate, changing the subject to ask after Mammy, her general health and whether her memory was returning, but her warning regarding Adam had resurrected my caution.

I had long thought there might still be some spark between her and Adam, and now I remembered the thought that had occurred to me on the night of the ball, that I might be a pawn in some game they were playing. Could it be that Isobel was jealous of his attention to me – or that she thought he was paying attention to me in order to make her jealous? Or was she genuinely concerned that I was in danger of allowing my infatuation to run away with me? There was little doubt that Adam did represent a danger. Yet again I told myself I must put a stop to this insanity that had overtaken me or risk making a fool of myself – or worse.

I began to avoid Adam's eyes – to avoid *him* wherever possible, and when I could not, I was cool and distant. It was the hardest thing I had ever had to do, and it made no difference to the way my heart hammered and my pulses raced, but at least I was retaining some dignity.

One day when Isobel was resting I took a walk in the grounds.

It was much warmer than of late, a day when the sky was lighter and a watery sun was breaking through; a day when it seemed that spring was just around the corner after all. I walked around the side of the house, exploring the vegetable plots where gardeners would soon be hard at work planting early potatoes, onions and root vegetables, and then back through the rose garden.

It was bare of flowers now of course, but the first young green shoots were bursting from the old brown wood and I pictured how it would look in summer when the arches dripped petals of yellow and pink, and bees stole pollen from overblown heads. The perfume would be a joy wafting on the warm air, and I wondered if I would be still here to see it. I passed beneath the last arch and drew up short as I came face to face with Adam.

I had known he was at Trevarrah today, of course, but I had seen little of him. He and Nicholas had both seemed preoccupied with the difficulties, whatever they might be, that were plaguing them. There had been tension between them at the midday meal, and afterwards, when they had repaired to the library, raised voices could be heard from behind the closed door. I had tried to close my ears to them. I preferred not to know about their differences.

Now I felt that familiar twist of excitement as I saw Adam there, blocking my path, tempered by something close to panic at the realization that we were quite alone.

'Why, Adam, you startled me!' I said with a little laugh.

He did not return my smile. His eyes were narrow, his expression taut.

'Why are you avoiding me, Tamsin?' he asked bluntly.

Instantly I was all confusion. 'I am not!' I lied.

'Oh, but I think you are! Is it me you are afraid of? Or is it yourself?'

'I don't know what you mean!' I countered. 'And I must go to Isobel. She will be wondering what has become of me.'

I tried to slip past him; his hand shot out, grasping my arm and arresting me.

'Damn Isobel!' he grated.

'You're hurting me!' I said, a little alarmed by the passion in his low voice. 'Let me go at once!'

He made no move to release me. 'Not until you tell me what has changed. You were happy enough with my company on the night of the ball. You know that as well as I. So why…?'

'That was a night for foolishness,' I interrupted quickly. 'I had too much claret. I've never had claret before and—'

Quite suddenly he laughed. 'Oh Tamsin, you are priceless! I am quite sure you did not drink too much, even if you are unused to it. And in any case, if I remember rightly, not a drop had passed your lips when first we danced.'

I could not think of a single thing to say; he was quite right, of course, but I had not the slightest intention of admitting it.

'I freely admit *I* was intoxicated that night – by something I am unused to, but very much hope to experience again,' he went on. 'The company of a young lady such as I have never met before. No airs and graces, no silly chitter-chatter, no affectations…'

'No breeding,' I said sharply. 'And no mother trying to matchmake either.'

He smiled slightly. 'That, I'm afraid I must admit, is very much in your favour. The absence of a mother trying to reel in a prospective son-in-law, I mean.'

So – I had been right. It was just a dalliance he was after. I had done well to nip it in the bud.

'I'm sorry, Adam, but I am afraid I am going to have to disappoint you. I'm not the kind of girl you clearly believe me to be. I did enjoy myself on the night of the ball, I admit. It was a different world for me and I was a little carried away by it all. But now things have returned to their proper place, I can see what folly it was. I am Isobel's companion – that's the whole reason for me being here at Trevarrah. I am not your plaything, whatever you might think.'

He frowned. 'I don't want you for a plaything, Tamsin. Where did you get such an idea?'

Had I read him wrongly? Was I making a fool of myself all over again by presuming he had an interest in me when in reality he had none? High spots of colour rose in my cheeks.

'Perhaps not a *plaything* then! A weapon to make Isobel jealous, perhaps.'

His face darkened; his grip on my arm tightened.

'Is that what you really think? That I still care for Isobel?'

I lifted my chin, meeting his eyes defiantly.

'Don't you?'

'What was between me and Isobel was over long ago,' he said harshly.

'Because she chose to marry your brother. Your pride is hurt, I expect, if not your heart, and you want to make her pay.'

Anger flashed across his face; for a moment I thought I had gone too far. Why was I saying such things?

Then: 'Isobel has nothing whatever to do with it,' Adam said in a low voice. 'It's you. You fascinate me, Tamsin. You have fascinated me from the moment I laid eyes on you.'

Again I experienced the treacherous inner turmoil; again I reacted with the only defence I could muster.

'And you think that gives you the right to accost me, hold me prisoner... I won't be bullied into giving you what you want. It won't work, Adam.'

'Then maybe this will.'

Before I knew what was happening, before I could make a single move to prevent it, he pulled me towards him and his lips were on mine.

Briefly I resisted. But the pressure of those lips, brutal almost, not gentle at all, was having the most devastating effect on me. My muscles, it seemed, were turning to jelly, and my will dissolving with them. My skin prickled, my heart pounded, and somewhere deep within me a great need yawned and ached, a need that was emotional, but physical too, and more powerful than anything I had ever experienced before.

After a moment the pressure of his mouth softened and as his lips caressed mine I felt my own lips moving in response and my free hand going to his arm, his strong arm, the muscles clearly defined beneath the woollen sleeve of his coat.

It was, I think, the realization that I was returning his kiss that shocked me back to reality. With a small sob I pulled away.

'Oh!'

'Does that tell you how I feel about you, Tamsin? And about how you feel about me?' His face was still dangerously close to mine, his hand still gripped my arm. There was grim satisfaction and barely controlled desire in his voice.

I think even then I might have succumbed. With that one kiss he had shown me how very easy – and how very pleasurable – it would be. But at that moment a voice cut the stillness of the air. A voice heavy with scorn.

'So, your plan is working, brother! Tamsin is taken in by you, is she? Well, not for long, I think.'

It was Nicholas. He was not wearing a coat; I imagined he had come straight from the house looking for Adam. Instantly I was all confusion, horrified that he should have happened upon such a scene, puzzled by his strange choice of words.

'What are you talking about?' Adam growled.

'You know very well. And don't think I am so stupid that I don't know either. You are a low bastard, Adam. You'll stop at nothing, will you, to get what you want? Shall I tell her? Shall I explain to Tamsin why you are trying to seduce her? Oh yes, I think—'

He got no further, for it was then that Adam hit him. His fist flew out and caught Nicholas's jaw with such a crack I thought it must be broken. Nicholas staggered and went down, sinking to his knees in the wet grass. His expression was more startled than hurt. Adam, meanwhile, stood over him threateningly.

'You have been inviting that, Nicholas, ever since I came home. I have taken about as much of you as any man can be expected to take. I'll thank you to remember this is my house and my land and you remain here by my good grace. I have no wish to see you and Isobel homeless, but believe you me, if you try my patience much further, that is the position you will find yourself in. I shall take what is rightfully mine and—'

'And set Tamsin up as lady of the house as payment for what she will do for you!' Nicholas sneered.

I do believe, if he had not still been on his knees, Adam would have knocked him down again. His face was dark with fury, his scar standing out livid above the tight lines of his mouth, and his whole stance taut with aggression. Frightened, I wondered if I should attempt to come between them, but even as the thought crossed my mind, Adam seemed to take control of himself with an effort.

'I could kill you, Nicholas, and one day, if you don't mend your ways, I'll do just that. But not in front of the lady.'

With that he turned on his heel and strode away, his back straight and tight, his hands still balled to fists, his limp more evident than ever.

I realized I was trembling from head to foot. The fight had frightened me badly – to see the brothers' hatred of one another erupt so was shocking, and if Adam had not managed to regain control of his temper, it could have been still worse. And I was mortified, too, that I had been the catalyst. That Adam had kissed me and Nicholas had witnessed it and thought... Oh!... my face flamed at the memory.

Nicholas was getting to his feet a little groggily, brushing dirt from the knees of his breeches. Blood was trickling down his chin; he had bitten his own lip, I supposed, or maybe his tongue, when Adam had struck him. I stood, undecided whether I should go, or stay to assist Nicholas.

'That's my brother for you!' Nicholas pulled out a kerchief and began mopping his chin. 'Violence is the only argument he understands – and always has been. I'm sorry you had to see it though – and sorry too that he should treat you in such an inexcusable fashion.'

What could I say? That I had been as much to blame as Adam? That if our situations had been different I would have welcomed his attention? That even as things were I had actually, for a moment, responded to it? I could say none of these things. So I remained silent.

'That's another of his vices, I am afraid,' Nicholas went on bitterly. 'Womanizing. And he is very practised at it. When Adam chooses to make use of his charm, no woman is safe. It's fortunate for you that I came along when I did. In future I would advise that you steer well clear of him. You wouldn't be the first girl he has ruined.'

Though I was still shaking, I lifted my chin, trying very hard to regain some of my lost dignity.

'Thank you for your concern, but I really do not have the slightest interest in Adam, or in anything you have to tell me about him,' I said.

And left him there, nursing his sore nose.

—

I found Isobel up and about in her room and sorting a box of earbobs and feathers.

'Where have you been?' she greeted me. 'I called when I woke, but you didn't answer.'

I hesitated, wondering if I should tell her of the fight, but I did not think it was my place to do so, and in any case, I was ashamed of my own part in it. Oh, they were perfectly capable of quarrelling all by themselves over everything and anything, of course, and finding Adam with me might simply have been the trigger for a gun that was already loaded. But all the same I did not want to admit what had happened. I didn't even want to think about it!

'I was in the garden,' I said vaguely.

Isobel seemed not to notice that I was suffering dreadfully from lack of composure. She was far too engrossed in sorting out her fripperies.

'You can help me with these, Tamsin. Tell me the colours you think suit me best. As you know, the dressmaker is coming tomorrow with bolts of cloth and sketches for my new dresses, and there will be so much to choose from, I thought it would be a good idea to have some idea beforehand of what I would like. Now, do you think this blue? Or the pink…?'

I made a tremendous effort to put what had happened from my mind and concentrate on doing what I was supposed to do – help Isobel with her wardrobe. But it was a near impossibility. As we held first one pair of earbobs against her face and then another, as we tied ribbons and feathers in her hair, I could think of nothing but Adam's kiss, my response to it, and Nicholas's warning.

It was not the first time, it seemed, that Adam had behaved so. From Nicholas's anger and disgust, I would scarcely be surprised if he did not have a history of ruining girls, and servants of any kind were always especially vulnerable. It was not uncommon for maids and the like to be landed with a permanent reminder of the attentions of their employer – for all I knew, the district could be littered with Adam's bastards. He had set about trying to win me over to be the next in his line of conquests and I had been naive enough, and flattered enough, to allow myself to be compromised. Heaven alone knew what would have happened if Nicholas had not come upon us when he did…

And at that thought my cheeks flamed anew, and yet at the same time my treacherous body was remembering just how it had felt to be held and kissed by Adam, and to my shame I knew I wanted to experience it again.

143

At last it was time for me to leave, and I was very, very glad of it, for I wanted nothing more than to be alone with my shame and my confusion.

'Now, you will be here in good time tomorrow, won't you?' Isobel said. 'The dressmaker will be early, I expect, and I shall rely upon your help to make my decisions. After all, I've never had to choose clothes that will suit a growing stomach before!'

And quite suddenly I knew that I simply could not face another day here. I could not face Isobel, who would almost certainly know by tomorrow about my indiscretion, for Nicholas would certainly tell her; I could not face Nicholas, who had seen it with his own eyes, and most of all I could not face Adam.

Even worse, I knew now that I could not trust myself not to behave so recklessly and shamelessly again. And that, more than anything, set the seal on what I had to do.

'I'm sorry, Isobel, but I don't think I shall be here tomorrow,' I said. 'Or indeed, ever again.'

'What? What are you saying?' Her face was the picture of puzzlement.

'It was very kind of you to offer me the position,' I said, 'but you don't really need me. It was done, I know, out of friendship and the goodness of your heart. But it was a mistake.'

She spread her hands helplessly. 'But why? I thought that you and I were getting along famously! What has changed?'

I couldn't bring myself to go into it. Tears were gathering in my throat, tears of shame and regret. If only I had not been so stupid as to let myself be carried away by Adam's charms! I had been a total fool. Everything was ruined, and it was all my own fault.

'I am sure your husband will explain,' I said.

'Nicholas? But… what has Nicholas done?'

I knew then I could not escape so lightly.

'Nothing,' I said. 'Nothing but witness a highly embarrassing scene. I'm sorry, Isobel, I should have told you at once when I came in from the garden. Nicholas came upon Adam kissing me.'

'Oh!' Isobel exclaimed, her mouth tightening and her eyes widening with outrage. 'Oh, that man! He is the cause of every trouble in this house! Yes, you should have told me, Tamsin. I *knew* something was wrong – you've been so quiet and withdrawn, not yourself at all this afternoon. But it's not your fault! I don't want to lose you because Adam thinks he is God's gift to every woman who walks this earth! Well, he won't bother you again, I'll see to that. I'll have Nicholas throw him out, which is no more than he deserves.'

'Except that you can't do that, can you?' I smiled wanly. 'The house and the estate belong, in law, to him. He made that perfectly clear to Nicholas.'

Isobel turned pale and her hands made tight little fists.

'He actually threatened that the two of you would be the ones who would have to go if Nicholas interfered with his right to do as he pleased,' I went on. 'And it was because Nicholas was trying to defend my honour that it came about. I am truly sorry, but I have done nothing but cause more trouble here. I really think it would be best if I…'

'No!' Tears sprang to her eyes; she caught my hand. 'Tamsin – no please – I can't bear it without you! Those two men quarrelling all the time, me pregnant with…' she broke off, biting her lip hard.

'I'm sorry, Isobel,' I said again. 'I really wish it could have been different. But I know I am doing the right thing.'

I squeezed her hand, turned, and walked out of Trevarrah House.

My own eyes were full of tears.

Nine

I was perhaps a little more than halfway home when I heard the pounding of horse's hooves behind me. I did not look around; it had, as I thought, nothing to do with me. I just continued to walk blindly, depression weighing down my steps, foolish tears threatening.

The horse and rider drew alongside me, the hoof beats slowing to a walk, and my heart seemed to stop beating.

Adam, on Lancelot. For a crazy moment hope flared in me. But I dared not allow myself to believe for even a moment what I so desperately wanted to believe. I lowered my head and kept walking.

'Tamsin!' His voice was urgent.

'Leave me be!'

'You can't go like this, Tamsin! You've upset Isobel dreadfully. She is in a terrible state.'

Isobel. He had come because Isobel was upset. He *did* still care for her, whatever he might pretend. Cared enough to come riding after me to persuade me to change my mind. I glanced up at him furiously.

'And whose fault is that? If you hadn't… done what you did this afternoon…'

'I'm sorry!' But it did not sound like an apology, more an explosion of frustration.

147

'So you should be!' I returned sharply. 'Oh, I dare say it was not entirely your fault. I dare say you think I invited it, like the trollop I am...'

He exclaimed loudly in what sounded like exasperation. 'You are not a trollop, Tamsin! Far from it!'

'I have been behaving like one, though, ever since the night of the ball. And if you thought that I was game for a quick tumble, I dare say no one could blame you. But however it may have seemed to you, I am not that sort of girl.'

'I never for one moment thought you were! And if I have offended you, then I am truly sorry.'

I could not look at him. I walked on, my head bent.

'Oh, for goodness' sake!' he exploded. 'I seem to have done nothing but apologize to you since I met you!'

I flashed anger. 'If that was all you had done, then we'd have no argument!'

'Well, it won't happen again. What more do I have to say to make you change your mind about giving notice as you have?'

The tears pricked my eyes again; that really was not what I had wanted to hear. Not looking where I was going, I trod on a loose stone. My ankle turned and I stumbled, almost falling.

'Tamsin!' He was off Lancelot in a flash. 'Are you all right?'

'Yes, I'm all right,' I snapped, shaking his hand from my arm. But the moment I took a step, my injured ankle gave way beneath me and I squealed in pain.

'You are not all right!' There was no sympathy whatever in his tone – he sounded almost accusing. 'You've hurt your ankle!'

'And what do you care if I have?' I took another defiant step, but again cried out in pain as the weight went on to my ankle.

'You know damned well I care!' His tone was still angry, his face, in the fading light, was grim. 'Oh, for the love of God, Tamsin! Why am I pretending I came after you for Isobel's sake? *I* don't want you to go! It was myself I was thinking of when I came after you, not Isobel!'

My heart seemed to stop beating and the world around me stopped with it. For a moment in time I believed him. But wasn't that exactly what I wanted to do? What my foolish, treacherous heart was urging me towards?

'But you and she...' My voice tailed away.

'I already told you – that was over long ago,' he said harshly. 'Yes, I cared for her once – too much. And I do still care in a way. When one has loved... well, it's not possible to deny that altogether. But my affection now is the affection one has for a sister. She chose to wed Nicholas – I have accepted that. And in any case, even if she were not Nicholas's wife, it would make no difference. My feelings toward her had changed even before I came home. And now they are well and truly in the past. Because I met you, Tamsin.'

'Oh!' I was confused now, standing there in the twilight with my ankle throbbing and my pulses racing. But a fierce joy was beginning somewhere deep inside me, a joy I could scarcely put a name to as yet, but which was lighting my world nonetheless.

'You know as well as I do the attraction that is between us,' he said urgently. 'Why do you continue to deny it?'

'Because... because it cannot be,' I faltered.

'Why not?' he demanded.

'You're a gentleman! I'm just... well...'

'You think I care that you were born and brought up in a miner's cottage on my father's estate? Dear God, Tamsin, you are worth ten of any girl born with a silver spoon in her mouth! Come back to Trevarrah. Give us another chance.'

I could not speak.

'If you cannot bring yourself to do that, then at least give *me* another chance,' he went on. 'Give *us* a chance. Don't turn your back on what there is between us because of what you see as the difference in our stations in life, and some foolish notion of pride. For what we feel for each other is something that comes but rarely – maybe only once in a lifetime, if at all.'

I found my voice.

'Yes,' I said, for I knew that what he said was true. Certainly I had never felt this way before and I could not imagine ever feeling so again. And if a small doubt as to the wisdom of it remained, I was suddenly too happy to care.

'Yes, you will come back to Trevarrah? Or yes, you will give me the opportunity to woo you?'

'Both,' I said.

In the fading light, his face was all planes and shadows, but his mouth curved into that half-smile that could make my stomach twist and my pulses race.

'And if I were to kiss you again, you would not try to run away?'

I laughed then, the swell of joy making my heart light. 'With my ankle ricked, I don't think I could run very far!'

'Then you have done us both a service.'

He pulled me to him. This time his lips were gentle on mine, not hard and demanding as they had been in the rose garden. But the effect was just the same. I felt as if

I were melting into him, until our bodies were not two at all, but one. I put my arms about him and the muscles in his back were hard and long beneath my eager hands. His mouth tasted good; my lips moved beneath his and the whole of my being seemed to be drawn into that kiss. I wanted nothing more than it should go on for ever – except perhaps to be closer yet to him. But all too soon for me he drew back, looking down at me.

'It's time you were getting home, Tamsin. Very soon it will be dark and your family will be worried about you. And if I do not let you go now, this minute, I swear I never shall.'

I nodded regretfully.

'There will be other times and other places,' he said, 'more conducive to making love.'

But none sweeter, I thought.

'I offered you a ride up behind me on Lancelot once before,' he said. 'You refused then, but I hardly think you are in a position to refuse now.'

'No, I don't think I am!' I said ruefully.

Adam hoisted me up on to Lancelot's broad back. I had ridden before, but not often, and then only on an old nag, never on a fine-mettled gelding like Lancelot. But, of course, I did not have to ride now. All that was required of me was to grip with my knees and wind my arms around Adam's waist so that I did not fall off.

Adam rode gently, with consideration for me, perched there behind him, but I was still exhilarated by the feel of the wind in my hair and the smooth movement of the horse beneath me. And by my closeness to Adam! It was all I could do to keep myself from laying my face against his shoulder, and I believe I fastened my arms more tightly around his waist than was strictly necessary!

All too soon the row of cottages that was Mallen came into sight, silhouetted against the darkening sky.

'I had better come for you tomorrow,' Adam said. 'You shouldn't be walking so far on that ankle of yours, even if you are able – which I doubt.'

He put me down and kissed me again, very briefly. I wondered what our neighbours would think if they should see, and smiled to myself.

Likely they would think, as I had, that my virtue was in danger. Likely they would think I was foolishly allowing liberties on the part of the squire, which would lead me into trouble.

And perhaps I was. Perhaps I had believed the things he said because I wanted to. Perhaps I would live to regret my naive trust. But in that moment, as I watched him ride away into the gloom, I was far too happy to care.

Ten

When I look back upon those days, I remember them as a time of innocent magic. I see them through a rosy haze, touched as they were with wonder and filled with promise.

Spring was at last beginning to soften the harsh winter landscape with a sprinkling of green and the air was softer too, and sweet with the scent of raindrops on new growth. Now, looking back, that time of year always rekindles for me an echo of those lovely silver days, the bittersweet aura of youth and freshness and happy anticipation that can never come again.

I lived them with every fibre of my being, my senses alive to the glory of the wonder being wrought around me by Mother Nature, I heard the sounds of the birds as they built their nests, I sniffed the air, I smiled to see the catkins spilling in greeny-gold cascades from the hazel in the hedges, and the furry little buds of the pussy willow. I picked a bunch of yellow cowslips from a grass bank and put them in a jar beside the chair where Mammy sat for much of the day, and took another to Trevarrah for Isobel.

And the freshness and the promise was an echo of my love for Adam. My caution was gone, evaporated as if it never had been, though we had decided, for the time being, to be discreet about our relationship. We wanted to hug it to ourselves, allow it to blossom as the new fresh spring growth, unsullied by the tensions that might be unleashed at Trevarrah if we acknowledged it openly. And I was happy, so happy, in that secret, enchanted time.

I was less worried about Mammy now, too. Her memory had still not completely returned, she was still confused. But, apart from the times when she muttered anxiously about some mysterious 'something she had to do', she seemed content enough, as if she had come to terms with her condition.

As I recall it, there was just one incident which jarred on the magic of those halcyon days and gave me pause for thought as to the state of affairs at Trevarrah.

Adam had taken to fetching me and taking me home in the pony and trap, for my ankle, though much better, was still not well enough for me to walk the four miles over rough ground and, truth to tell, we were using it as an excuse to spend some time together without arousing too much suspicion.

One evening as we headed back towards Mallen we encountered three men on horseback. Two of them blocked our path, and the third rode alongside shouting to Adam to stop.

I was, I confess, alarmed. From their attire and their fine horses, it appeared that they were gentlemen, but their manner was threatening and their faces cold and unfriendly.

'We're looking for your brother,' the one who had ridden alongside Adam said abruptly. 'Where can we find him?' Adam clearly took exception to their lack of ceremony.

'I have no idea,' he returned coldly, though I knew that was not true. Nicholas was in the library at Trevarrah working on the estate books.

154

The man swore.

'Pah! You're as bad as he! But he can't creep into a hole and avoid me for ever!'

'What is this about?' Adam asked shortly.

'You mean you don't know?'

'If I did,' Adam said, 'I would hardly be asking.'

The man pointed his riding whip accusingly at Adam. 'Your brother owes me a great deal of money. I won it from him fair and square and his payment of it is long overdue. Well, I am not prepared to wait for it any longer.'

'I see.' Adam's features were set, now, in stone.

'Tresillick is the name. Walter Tresillick. Of Goontowan. And if I don't find your brother this day, you can tell him this from me.' The man jabbed at Adam with his riding whip, emphasizing every word. 'If I don't have repayment of my debt by the end of the month, I'll come to Trevarrah, not just with two friends, but a dozen, and less good-tempered than these two, and take what I'm owed in kind.'

I could see that Adam's temper was barely under control.

'Perhaps you do not realize, Tresillick, that Trevarrah belongs to me, not to my brother, and if you touch so much as one stone on my land, I shall have you arrested as a trespasser and a thief.'

Tresillick's lip curled.

'Is that so? Do you hear that, my friends? Penrose is threatening me. Like I say, they're as bad as one another! Well, you can tell your brother this. He'll settle his debt to me and quickly, or he'll rue the day. I won't be made a fool of by the likes of him, and one way or another he'll pay the price. I'll see to that, have no fear.'

Adam had had enough. He raised his own whip threateningly.

'Get out of my way!'

For a moment Tresillick held his position, and his friends moved in threateningly. Of the upper classes they might be; just now they looked like nothing so much as thugs. But Adam was not to be intimidated, and after a moment Tresillick jerked his horse's head around.

'We'll leave it for now. But be sure to tell your brother: my money, or you'll both be sorry. Just look out for my calling card. You are not the only one who can make threats, Penrose.'

He gesticulated to his friends and reluctantly they did his bidding and moved out of our way.

Adam flicked the reins sharply and we set off at a brisk trot, leaving the men behind us. His face was a set mask of fury.

'My brother is a fool!' he muttered angrily. 'If I had not returned when I did...' he broke off, turning to me. 'Are you all right, Tamsin?'

'Yes,' I said. 'I'm perfectly fine.'

But I was not. I was trembling all over from the unpleasant confrontation, which could so easily have become violent. But I did not want to make things worse than they already were. Another quarrel between the brothers was looming, I rather thought. I did not want to contribute towards it.

I had not witnessed any confrontation between them of late and had hoped things were perhaps easier between them. Now I realized that there were still problems aplenty, and felt anxious on Adam's behalf. I did not now think, of course, that any of them might be of Adam's making. I was far too deeply in love to consider for a moment that he might be anything but a paragon of virtue, and any accusations made against him merely Nicholas's way of retaliating.

Whatever was said between the brothers about the incident must have taken place that evening, however, for I heard nothing of it, and I tried to put it out of my mind. I did not want anything to mar the happiness I was living with every fibre of my being in those lovely days.

One morning, however, I woke from my night's sleep with an overwhelming sense of foreboding. I simply could not understand it. I had gone to bed perfectly happy, yet just before dawn unpleasant and confused dreams had come, and the distress I had experienced in them had followed me into wakefulness. As I got myself dressed and prepared breakfast for myself and Mammy, the feeling persisted and made me more and more uneasy. I tried to tell myself the pervasive sense of impending disaster was due to nothing more than the cheese I had eaten last night for supper, but lifelong experience of my inexplicable premonitions kept whispering to me that it was more.

When Adam arrived to fetch me, I wanted nothing more than for him to take me in his arms, hold me very close and tell me there was nothing whatever to worry about. But, of course, I made no mention of it to him. I would have felt foolish indeed trying to explain my strange mood. And as we drove, he imparted some information which could not fail to lift my spirits.

'I think we shall have the opportunity to spend more time together today than usual,' he said with a crooked smile. 'I have to go into Truro today for some provisions, and when I said as much last night, Isobel asked if I would take you with me.'

'Oh, and I can guess the reason!' I said. 'Word came yesterday that the first of her new dresses is ready. She wants me to visit the dressmaker and collect it. Am I right?'

'Yes. She's most anxious to have it – and a few bits and pieces besides.' He smiled again. 'She asked very humbly if I would mind taking you along, as if she thought it would be an imposition. And I grudgingly agreed. So, unless she has changed her mind, as she is wont to do, it looks as if I shall be saddled with your company.'

I smiled at his teasing, and determined I would not worry any more. Instead I would relish the prospect of the best part of a whole day with Adam.

When we arrived at Trevarrah, Adam went off to prepare for the trip and I went into the house.

Isobel was usually in the parlour at this time of day, attending to her correspondence and going through the menus which Pol, the cook, had prepared, though she never made a final decision on them until she had discussed them with me. But this morning there was no sign of her.

I took off my cloak and hung it up, changed my boots for the slippers I kept at Trevarrah, and went in search of her.

I found her in her room, sitting on the little brocade stool in front of her dressing table. Her silver-backed hair-brush was in her hand and she was fiddling with her hair. She did not look around as I came into the room.

'Isobel?' I said.

Still she made no move.

'Are you unwell?' I asked. 'Is morning sickness catching up with you at last?'

It was a constant source of wonder to me that whilst so many women suffered dreadfully from vomiting in the early stages of their pregnancy, Isobel seemed quite unaffected by it.

'No... no...'

She turned around, and to my horror I saw an angry bruise high on her cheek, just below her eye. Clearly she was trying to rearrange her hair to hide it, just as clearly she was not achieving her objective.

'Isobel!' I said, shocked. 'What on earth has happened to you?'

'Oh...' She gave a little laugh, but it sounded brittle and tremulous. 'Oh, I am so foolish! I caught it on the closet door. Do I look a dreadful fright, Tamsin?'

'You couldn't look a fright if you tried,' I said, trying to make light of it. But there was no doubt the bruise was marring her perfect little face, and she was not in the least deceived by my protestation.

'You are being kind, as usual, Tamsin. It's very unsightly, I know.' She examined it with her fingers and winced. 'And sore too,' she added ruefully.

'I'm sure it is!'

She looked back at herself in the mirror; standing behind her, looking at her reflection, I saw her eyes fill with tears.

'I can't see anybody looking like this,' she said.

'I think the looking glass is accentuating it,' I said, in an attempt to make her feel better. 'It's the way the light is falling on it – it makes it look worse. I'm sure if we were to powder over it...'

'No!' Isobel interrupted fiercely. 'No, I won't see anyone! I can't!'

I bit my lip. Though in the very first instance I had not thought to doubt her story, now I was beginning to have my suspicions. I simply could not see how she could have caused an injury such as this by colliding with her closet door. Her forehead, yes, the whole side of her face, perhaps, her nose even. But her *cheek*, in that hollow that should be naturally protected? I felt a sudden flash of protective anger for the girl who was my friend as well as my employer.

'Who did this to you, Isobel?' I asked before I could stop myself.

Her face crumpled; there was panic now in her tear-filled eyes.

'No one! I told you, I caught it...'

'I don't believe you,' I said bluntly. 'You've been struck – but not by a closet door. Who did it? Not Nicholas, surely?'

'No! No, of course not!' she cried fiercely. 'Nicholas would never...'

'Then who?'

'No one,' she repeated mulishly. 'I caught it on the door! Why don't you believe me? Why are you suggesting such terrible things? If you are going to make wild accusations and practically call me a liar...' She slammed the brush down on to the dressing table and spun round on the stool to face me. 'I don't want a companion who thinks such things, and certainly not one who says them!'

'Oh, I'm sorry, Isobel. Of course I believe you,' I said quickly.

It was not the truth. I did not believe her. Not only could I not see how she could possibly have injured herself in the way she described, her defensiveness, her whole demeanour, was enlightening. She was making up a story to preserve her pride, I felt sure. But I also realized it was not my place to question it. Clearly she was not going to admit the truth of what had happened, and all I could do was play along with the pretence.

But I was totally puzzled as to who it was that she was protecting. Surely it could not be Nicholas? I could scarcely believe he would have harmed her in this way, especially when she was carrying his child.

'Oh Tamsin, I don't want to quarrel!' She got up, holding out her hands to me. 'But you must not tell a single living soul what a fool I've been, or they might jump to the same wrong conclusion that you did. I shall stay in my room and pretend I am unwell. Then no one but you need see me until the bruise is faded.'

'If that's what you want,' I agreed. 'Would you like me to stay with you? Adam did say you had asked him to take me to Truro with him to collect your new dress, but if you've changed your mind...'

'No – no!' She ran her hands across her waist. 'I'm getting far too fat for anything in my wardrobe, and a new dress to wear is exactly what I need – the best possible medicine!'

I could not help smiling to myself. To me, Isobel looked as slender as she always had done.

'I think I would quite like to be alone in any case,' she went on. 'It's not an outright lie to say I am unwell. My head is throbbing dreadfully and I do feel a little shaky. I shall stay here and rest.'

'Very well, if you're sure,' I agreed.

'Yes. But will you deal with Pol for me? Go over the menus with her? The last thing I want is the servants seeing me like this. They do talk so.'

And they know everything too, I thought. It was impossible to keep anything from the servants for long. But I did not want to upset Isobel again by saying so.

'I'll do what needs to be done before we leave for Truro,' I promised. 'And we'll be back before you know it with a new dress to cheer you up.'

It was a good hour before I was ready to accompany Adam to Truro, and when I was, he was nowhere to be found. I was a little puzzled, but presumed he had things of his own to do, and sure enough, before too long he was outside the door with the trap.

'Are you ready then?' he asked. His tone was impatient, as if it were me who had been keeping him waiting, rather than the other way around.

'I've been ready for a long while,' I returned tartly.

'Oh, I thought you were in the kitchen, wasting time with Pol Saunders.'

I frowned, puzzled by the apparent change of mood from his earlier good humour to this rather ill-tempered one.

'I did have things to sort out with her, yes. Isobel is indisposed today...' I glanced at him, wondering if he already knew this and if so whether it was the reason for his change of temper. Did he think, as I did, that her bruised face was no accident? And was he angry on her behalf?

But if he did know, he gave no indication of it, busying himself with tightening a buckle on the harness, and I was left wondering if I should say more or not.

Adam's mood did nothing to lighten as we set out for Truro. He was not, and never had been, a talkative man, and it was usually me who did all the chattering whilst he listened, but today he was positively morose. And since I had Isobel on my mind, and was also still annoyed at the way he had spoken to me, I was not in the mood to chatter either.

Perversely, Adam noticed this.

'What's the matter with you?' he asked rather shortly after a long spell of silence.

'I might well ask you the same question,' I retorted with spirit.

He did not reply.

'You've been snapping my nose off for the last half-hour,' I said. 'I'd rather like to know the reason why.'

'We're very late leaving for Truro. We shall be lucky to get everything done now...'

The thunder of a horse's hooves behind us made him break off, and I thought I heard someone shout Adam's name. I looked over my shoulder and saw a figure I recognized as William Hastings, the mine captain, bearing down on us. Adam checked our pony.

'Will Hastings! What now?'

Captain Hastings drew alongside us. He looked dishevelled from his gallop and his face was grim.

'Adam! Thank God I've caught up with you!'

'What's the matter, man?' Adam demanded tetchily. 'I pay you to look after the mine, not come chasing after me.'

'It's not the mine,' Will Hastings snapped back. 'You must come home at once. Something terrible...'

My heart seemed to come into my throat with a thud. Isobel! I thought. I should never have left her today!

'What are you talking about?' Adam's face had grown dark, his eyes narrowed, his mouth a tight line.

163

'It's Nicholas.' Will Hastings was a little breathless, but the urgency in his voice was unmistakeable.

'What about Nicholas? What the devil has he done now?'

'We just found him,' Hastings replied grimly. 'He's been shot.'

Whatever I had expected to hear, it was not this. My heart thudded again, painfully, and my mind seemed to go blank. Nicholas – shot? Did Captain Hastings mean he was *dead*! The self-same thought must have occurred to Adam at the self-same moment.

'What is his condition?' he asked abruptly.

'I can't answer you. They've taken him to the house and Milsom has ridden for the doctor. I haven't seen him for myself. I knew you were on your way to Truro, so the moment I heard the news I set out post-haste to catch up with you.'

'Then we had better make post-haste home and find out,' Adam said grimly.

Eleven

When we reached Trevarrah, a pony and trap I recognized as Dr Warburton's was already there, pulled up to the front door, which stood ajar. I was surprised that he was so quickly on the scene, and could only assume that he had been in the neighbourhood visiting another patient when Milsom, the stable lad, had gone looking for him.

I followed Adam into the house, sick with trepidation. Voices reached us from the small parlour as we made our way across the hall.

Nicholas lay on the chaise, mostly obscured from my view by Dr Warburton, who was bending over him, and two estate workers, presumably the ones who had brought him into the house.

My first reaction was profound relief; Nicholas was not dead, thank God! Then I noticed Isobel. She had drawn back into the corner behind the door and stood, her arms wrapped around herself, clearly in a state of shock. I went to her, putting my arm around her.

'Isobel?'

She seemed scarcely to notice me. She was aware of only one person. Pushing me aside, she ran to Adam, pummelling him with her fists.

'What have you done? *What have you done?*'

'For the love of God, control yourself, Isobel!' he snapped, brushing her off and turning to Dr Warburton. 'How is he, doctor? What's the damage?'

To my amazement, it was Nicholas himself who replied.

'Lead shot in the shoulder, brother. As if you didn't know.' His voice was taut with pain.

'*What?*' Adam demanded.

'The doctor says I'll live, though. Not quite what you had in mind, I dare say.'

'You are accusing *me*…?'

'Who else wants me out of the way? Who else would shoot me in the back in my own tack room? Your aim is not so good though, brother.'

Adam swore, turning away furiously.

'Calm yourself, Nicholas,' Dr Warburton said. 'You'll exacerbate the damage if you do not.' He straightened; I saw the knife in his hand and the bowl of bloodstained water on the table at his side, and realized he had been removing the bullet. Then he turned to Adam. 'You had better leave, sir. You are only upsetting your brother by your presence.'

'I am to let him accuse me and say nothing?'

'Just leave!' Dr Warburton's tone was authoritative. Adam glared at him for a moment, then he turned and limped angrily from the room.

'And you, madam, should not be upsetting yourself either,' Dr Warburton said to Isobel.

Somehow I found my voice. 'No, Isobel, you should not,' I said gently. Though my thoughts were racing, I knew my duty was to my friend. Heaven alone knew how something like this would affect her in her condition.

'Oh, will you all stop treating me like a child!' Isobel cried.

'Isobel, please!' I took her arm; this time she did not shake me off, though she did take a step towards her husband.

'Nicholas…'

He sank back against the chaise, his eyes closing in a face white and drawn with pain. Blood ran down his bare chest from beneath a pad the doctor had pressed against the wound.

'Go with Tamsin, Isobel,' he said wearily. 'She will take care of you.'

It was only later that I remembered his strange words and wondered at them.

Gently I urged Isobel to the door. As we emerged into the hall, I saw the curious and anxious faces of Pol and the other servants framed in the kitchen doorway. Of Adam there was no sign.

'Make a hot posset for Mrs Penrose,' I called to Pol. 'Quickly now. She's very upset.'

I guided her towards the drawing room, then changed my mind. In winter the drawing room was little used; the fire would not be lit and it would be chilly there, if not downright cold.

'Nicholas is going to be fine,' I soothed her. 'And I am taking you to your own room. Come on now, no more arguments.'

She was acquiescent now, all the fight gone out of her, and when the door of her own room closed after us, she looked at me for a long, stricken moment, then burst into tears.

Helpless for the moment to do anything else, I held her whilst she wept. Then, when her sobs subsided, I offered her a handkerchief to dry her poor bruised face.

'Oh, why do they hate each other so, Tamsin?' she whispered, blowing her nose. 'I can't bear it, really! And if Adam...'

'He would never shoot his brother in the back, I'm sure of it,' I said.

'You would take his part!' She blew her nose. 'You are besotted with him, Tamsin. You think I don't know, but I do. I've warned you about him before, but you just won't listen!'

I had no intention of getting into a discussion about my feelings for Adam just now.

'What makes Nicholas think it was Adam who shot him?' I asked instead. 'Did he see him?'

'No. He was shot from behind, wasn't he? He was sorting tack, heard a sound behind him, and luckily twisted out of the way. If he hadn't...' Her voice tailed away.

'Then there's no reason for him to suppose it was Adam,' I said reasonably.

'Adam was furious with Nicholas,' Isobel said mutinously. 'He came up to see me shortly after you did this morning. He wanted to discuss with me some of the things he needed to buy in Truro. He saw my face, and jumped to the same wrong conclusion that you did. He accused Nicholas of striking me. And he stormed off to have it out with him.'

'But not to shoot him!' I said.

Isobel crumpled the handkerchief between her hands.

'He'd do anything for me, Tamsin. Oh, I don't mean to upset you when I know you care for him, but he is obsessed with me, and always has been.'

Pain knifed through me. Although I did not care to admit it, I could not help suspecting there was some truth in what she said. I could imagine that he would indeed have been furious if he thought Nicholas had struck Isobel, and when he was furious he almost always lost control of himself.

'Who else could it have been?' Isobel demanded.

'I don't know...' I broke off, suddenly remembering the men who had accosted Adam and myself that day with threats as to what they would do to Nicholas if his gambling debts were not paid. 'Nicholas does have enemies, doesn't he?' I said softly.

'No! No!'

'I think he does, whether you know about them or not,' I persisted, anxious to convince myself as much as Isobel that Adam was not responsible for this outrage. 'I think he owes a great deal of money that he lost gambling. Men can become violent when they believe they are being robbed of what is rightfully theirs.'

She looked up at me, a spark of hope lighting her small, ravaged face.

'You really think...?'

Although I was glad to have provided an alternative solution as to who could have shot Nicholas, another twinge of pain prickled inside me.

Isobel did not want to believe Adam was responsible either. She still cared for him, too. I had long suspected as much. The bond was still there between them, although she was Nicholas's wife.

Was it the reason she made derogatory comments about him to me – because she could not bear the thought of me becoming involved with him? And was the reason he had instigated a relationship with me that he had sought to dull the pain he felt at having lost her to his brother? Had I been so blinded by the attraction I felt for him, and called love, that I had deceived myself into believing he felt it too?

Mary, the kitchen maid, came tapping at the door with Isobel's posset, and I tried to put all such thoughts from my mind. I had a job to do – looking after Isobel.

But I knew that all the doubts that had suddenly risen like a flock of crows in my mind were not going to go away readily. The first flush of innocent joy had gone from my heart like the dew on a rose when the sun burns too hot or the wind blows it away. I was not sure whether I would experience its glory in quite the same way ever again.

–

I did not see Adam for the rest of the day. Unsurprisingly, he did not come in for the midday meal and I wondered if he was riding out his temper on Lancelot, or whether he had gone alone to Truro to collect the supplies. If he had, Isobel would have to wait until another day for her new dress, for I could not see him putting himself out for her after the wild accusations she had thrown at him.

Either way, what should have been our pleasant day out together had been ruined. Instead of enjoying Adam's company alone for a change, I spent it consoling Isobel and nursing Nicholas, who Dr Warburton had insisted should retire to bed to rest.

And still the bad feeling hung over me, making me doubt everything that only yesterday I had been so certain of.

Was Adam merely using me in an attempt to heal the pain of his broken heart? To hide the fact that he still cared for Isobel – or to make her jealous even? And worse, was it possible that it really had been him who had shot Nicholas, as both Nicholas and Isobel had claimed? Certainly he had had the opportunity. There had been an hour or more when I had been in the kitchens with Pol and when I had emerged, ready to leave, there had been no sign of him. If, as Isobel said, he had gone to her room to discuss supplies soon after I had left her, and been enraged to see her bruised face, there would have been plenty of time for him to go in search of Nicholas and put a lead shot into his shoulder.

I could scarcely credit that he could be capable of doing something so cowardly as shooting his brother in the back, however angry he might have been with him – but what did I really know of him? Certainly I knew he was subject to blind rages where his brother was concerned and if he was sorely provoked and maddened with protective love for Isobel, who could say what he might do? Certainly he had been in a very strange mood when we had set out for Truro. Was that simply because he was upset at the thought that Nicholas might be abusing Isobel – or because he knew he had fired a shot in anger at his brother and left him wounded – perhaps dying – in the tack room.

I did not know, and my doubts tormented me.

When the time came for me to go home, I was a little concerned at the thought of leaving Isobel, but she assured me she and Nicholas would be well cared for by the servants.

'You have kept your side of our bargain, Tamsin,' she said. 'And I shall keep mine. You have other responsibilities — and your poor mother cannot be left alone.'

'She's a great deal better,' I said, 'and Ruth and Jed are just next door.'

'But she is still very confused, you tell me,' Isobel said. 'She still cannot remember the recent past. Or has that changed, and you've forgotten to mention it?'

'No,' I said. 'She is still confused and forgetful.'

'Then you must not even think of leaving her alone at night.' Isobel pressed my hand. 'We shall be fine, Nicholas and I. Though it has been a dreadful day!'

'It certainly has!' I agreed.

I had thought that tonight I would have to walk home, and was glad that at least the weather had improved as the day had gone on. But to my surprise, when I came downstairs, Adam was there.

'You are going to leave the patients, then?' he said with some sarcasm.

'Isobel insists they will be all right.' My tone was cool; the thoughts I had been subject to all day making me wish to keep my distance from Adam.

'I'm surprised they have not sent for a constable to protect them, since they seem to think I am such a danger to them,' he said in the same sarcastic tone. 'Well, if you are ready, we will go.'

'Oh, are you driving me then?' I do not know why I said it; I suppose I thought with all that had happened today he would have better things to do.

'I usually do, don't I?' he said coolly. 'Or perhaps you don't trust me either. Is that it? You don't feel safe riding with me?'

I was already on edge from all the events of the day; his attitude served only to make me snap.

'To be truthful, I don't know that I *do* want to ride with you in your present mood,' I said tartly.

He turned away. 'The decision is yours.'

Suddenly I could bear it no more. 'Oh, for heaven's sake! I'd be a fool to walk when I can ride. And the way I feel at the moment, the sooner I can get home the better!'

That teasing corner of his mouth lifted, but this afternoon there was little real humour in it, more weary irony.

'A gracious acceptance indeed!'

The trap was outside the door. Adam helped me up and we set off. For a while we drove in silence, then, as the moorland opened up before us, I felt his eyes on me.

'Do you really believe I am a man who would shoot his own brother in the back?'

'I certainly hope not,' I said. 'But there's little love lost between you.'

'That's true enough.' His tone was grim. 'My brother, I am afraid, is a terrible liability in every way. Life would be a great deal easier if his assailant this morning had been possessed of a better aim.'

My eyes widened in horror. 'That's a terrible thing to say! You cannot wish your own brother dead!'

'Can't I?' That twist of his mouth again; the scar stood out livid and I was shocked by the coldness I suddenly saw in his face. 'I assure you that, since I came home, many is the time I have wished just that. In any case, a moment ago I thought you believed me capable of firing the shot, not simply regretting it did not find its mark.'

'I never really thought that!' I protested. 'I told Isobel I thought it likely it could have been those men to whom

Nicholas owes money, and who threatened him if he did not pay. *Did* he ever pay, do you know?'

'I shouldn't think so,' Adam said. 'As far as I am aware, Nicholas does not have the wherewithal, and thanks to the way he managed the mine and the estate in my absence, neither do I.'

'Then don't you think… ?'

He shrugged. In the fading afternoon light his profile was craggy against the pale sky.

'I do not know. I am not sure I even care any longer. I have been home less than a year, Tamsin, and sometimes I swear I wish I had stayed away and left my brother to stew in his own juice. There are times, I promise you, when I feel like turning my back on it all and simply riding away. But I have a duty here. A duty to all the people who are dependent on the mine and the estate for their livelihood and their homes – though how much longer I can continue to provide them with either is in some doubt, given Nicholas's continued profligacy and the reluctance of backers to put money into further development whilst he remains involved.'

'Further development?' I echoed, not understanding what he meant.

He nodded. 'I believe there is money to be made if we were to open up the abandoned workings at Old Trevarrah. I have taken advice, and I am convinced there is copper there, which could save us if only we had the wherewithal to finance the digging for it. But we would need new equipment, vast new excavation, adits to drain the levels… it will all cost a great deal of money, and prospective backers shy away, believing – with some justification – that Nicholas would fritter away their investment before we finished the necessary work, let alone began to mine marketable copper. I had a meeting with Porthtowan, whose family founded the best-respected bank for miles around, and he said as much quite frankly. He would head a consortium of investors if it were just me putting the proposition on the table; with Nicholas bound to be involved, he says half of those he would like to bring in would never commit. Is it any wonder I say Nicholas is a liability?'

I was silent. I knew nothing of business matters and did not want to show my ignorance. But at the same time, the gist of what he was saying was clear enough.

'There are other reasons I cannot simply turn my back and walk away,' he went on after a moment. 'Duties to my father, and to our forebears.'

'Oh.' I was a little hurt. I would have liked him to have said that *I* was one of the reasons he remained at Trevarrah.

'And I can't turn him out, either, no matter that I've threatened it,' he continued. 'My sense of duty again. This time to Isobel.'

A muscle in my stomach tightened into a hard knot.

'Oh yes, Isobel,' I said.

He shot me a narrow look.

'Of course I have a duty to her! She has no family of her own, and Trevarrah is the only home she has known since she was five years old. If I turned Nicholas out, she would lose everything. My father took responsibility for her as his ward, and I believe that it would be his wish that she should have security for life, notwithstanding which of us she chose to wed. He would not wish me to make her homeless as well as penniless. He would turn in his grave at the very idea. Besides, Isobel has a very fragile nature. She would never survive the shame, let alone the hardship. I could not have her on my conscience.'

'Because you still care for her,' I said in a low voice.

His eyes narrowed. 'Haven't we had this conversation before?' he asked shortly. 'I told you then – I do care for her, but only as I would care for a sister. What was between us once is over and has been for a very long time.'

'Is it?' I could not stop myself now; all my doubts were flooding to the surface. 'I'm not sure that I believe you, Adam; though, believe me, I've tried. I think she still has feelings for you. And that you still have feelings for her, no matter how you try to deny it.'

Abruptly Adam reined in the pony and turned to face me.

'What do I have to do, Tamsin, to make you see that you are wrong?'

I could not answer. *Tell the world it is me you love*, I could have said, but since I had been the one to press for discretion in the first place, that would be most unfair. *Forget your so-called duty to Isobel and let her husband provide for her* – but I did not want that either. Nicholas would *not* be able to provide for her, I knew, and after the evidence of her bruised face this morning, I rather suspected he was capable of cruelty towards her too. Perhaps it was the reason she had been so anxious for me to become her companion.

Isobel was my friend; I did not want to see her suffer. And yet…

And yet I could not get it out of my head that she still held Adam's heart. I could not get it out of my head that she played a part in some way in his wooing of me. Insecurity was eating away at me like corrosive acid; there was no escaping the pain deep inside – nor the jealousy I was ashamed of, yet could not help feeling.

Foolish tears started to my eyes. For a little while stolen out of time, I had allowed myself to be swept along by emotions I had never before experienced. The excitement had intoxicated me; I had believed, because I wanted to believe it, that Adam felt as I did. But the events of this terrible day had sobered me and torn the blinkers from my eyes.

I turned away so that Adam should not see my tears. A buzzard hovered high above the springing gorse; I wished that I, too, could spread my wings and fly away.

'Tamsin?' Adam's tone was gentler than at any time the whole of this dreadful day. He took my shoulder, turning me back towards him and I jerked my face further around so that my neck strained against the sinews, not wanting to look him in the eyes.

'Tamsin!' His fingers touched my chin, turning it so that I could no longer avoid facing him. 'You little fool,' he said softly.

And then his lips were on mine. For a moment I held back, afraid of the torrent of desire for him that I knew lay there beneath the shield of resistance my doubts had raised. But the current of my longing for him ran too strong, the touch of his lips on mine was too sweet. A small sob choked in my throat, the desire twisted deep in the heart of me, and I wound my arms around his neck, giving myself up to the tide of passion that was overwhelming me. He kissed me and I kissed him back, my lips moving beneath his and parting under the pressure of his tongue.

I was lost and I knew it. I was lost, and I did not care. I could no longer concern myself with his motives or his intentions. If he was using me for some reason of his own, then so be it. I *wanted* to be used. Nothing in the world mattered but that I should be in his arms.

He kissed me until I was breathless, my head swimming, my flesh sensitized. He kissed my eyes as well as my mouth, he kissed my nose and my throat. His lips moved down to the valley between the swell of my breasts at the neckline of my dress, his hands slid beneath the fabric, exploring, and still I did not care.

I threw my head back, my eyes open to the deep violet sky, where lately the buzzard had soared, and gloried in the touch of his hands. And I parted my lips and breathed in the warm male scent of him along with the sweet evening air.

He lifted me in his arms and it was not just his strength that made me feel weightless, but the desire that ran through my veins with every beat of my heart.

He laid his cloak on the springy rough turf and I was scarcely aware of what he had done until he laid me down upon it. The cloth was rough against my cheek as I turned my head ecstatically that way then this, and as he bunched up my skirts it was rough against my bare legs too.

His body was hard against mine; I lifted my hips as the desire twisted nerves deep within me that I had never known existed. And I sobbed again as he went inside me, but it was a sob not of the sharp burning pain I felt, but of complete abandonment.

Why would I care for such a little thing as pain when my whole body was alive with delight? Why should I care for anything but the rhythmic movement of our two bodies? The past had ceased to matter, the future was a foreign land of no importance whatsoever. And the present… the present was a fusion of emotion and sensation, of desire with need.

I gave myself up to it. And when it was over and Adam was spent and I floated in a haze of contentment and longing satisfied, I looked up and saw the buzzard, still hovering above us for a moment before moving its wings with powerful yet effortless grace and wheeling away.

—

'Now do you believe me?' Adam asked. 'Now do you believe it is you that I want?'

His words jarred a little on the languorous contentment. I had just given myself to him, we had been as close as a man and a woman can be – I would have liked to hear words of love.

But Adam was not one for flowery talk. Perhaps that question was the closest he could come to a declaration of his feelings for me.

I gave a little laugh. 'I suppose I must. It's certainly what I hope.'

He raised himself on one elbow. 'Do I detect a little note of regret?'

'No! Oh, Adam, I don't know… I'm sorry…'

'I am the one who should be sorry.' He brushed a lock of hair away from my face with one finger; there was more tenderness in that gesture than he ever expressed in words. 'I've compromised you, Tamsin. I've taken advantage of you, and hurt you too, and all because I allowed my desire for you to be my master.'

'I wanted it too,' I said. 'I was just as much to blame. What must you think of me?'

'I think,' he said, 'that you are the loveliest, sweetest, most loyal girl I have ever met.'

'Oh!' I was silent for a moment, enjoying his words. Then: 'Loyal?' I said. 'Why do you call me loyal?'

He took the lock of my hair again, twisting it between finger and thumb.

'Well, to begin with, your loyalty to your family is beyond doubt. You gave up your life in Launceston to care for your mother without a moment's hesitation. And then there is your loyalty to Isobel. You fear that she is coming between us, yet you will think no wrong of her. It hasn't occurred to you for a single moment, has it, that *she* might have been the one to put a shot into Nicholas?'

'*Isobel?*' I exclaimed, shocked. 'Oh no! She wouldn't! And in any case, she was confined to her room…'

'With a bruise upon her face that was certainly not inflicted by a closet door. And whilst you are mistaken in thinking there is anything between us, I believe you are right in one respect. Things are far from right between her and Nicholas. He takes out his frustration and bad temper on her, I'm sure of it. Yes, I'm afraid it did occur to me that Isobel may well have been the one to injure Nicholas. She could easily have slipped out unnoticed, she knows how to use a gun, and she can be very… unpredictable.'

'No!' I said emphatically. 'I can't believe it!'

'You are very loyal and trusting, just as I said. But you don't know her as I do. Her background is not as you might imagine. The first five years of her life were… not the best grounding for a child, and her mother… Isobel has, I fear, inherited some of her traits. She is devious and emotionally fragile. There are things…' He paused. 'But we don't want to talk about Isobel just now, do we?'

My thoughts were racing. What could he mean? It was almost as if he were warning me against Isobel. But why?

And then Adam said something that made me forget all about Isobel.

'I think,' he said, 'that, after what has just happened between us, we should make some changes in our relationship.'

A chill whispered over my skin; my heart sank like a stone.

'Changes?' My voice faltered. 'What changes? You mean you want to end it?'

'On the contrary,' Adam said. 'I think it is time we stopped conducting our affair in this hole and corner way. I want you on my arm, Tamsin, for all the world to see. More. I want you for my wife.'

I was totally, utterly, taken by surprise. My heart leaped; I began to tremble violently; joy pulsed in my veins. And yet, for all that, there was still the small nagging edge of doubt that I could not fully explain, and something that might almost have been panic.

I was possessed by desire for Adam, yes. I had been obsessed with him for weeks, to the point of madness. I believed I was in love with him. I had allowed him to make love to me on a cloak laid out on the rough turf. But marriage...

Marriage out of my class. Marriage, when a few minutes ago I had wondered if he were capable of shooting his own brother. Marriage which would plunge me head-long into all the boiling tensions and undercurrents of Trevarrah, with no escape back to my home... the whole idea suddenly overwhelmed me.

'I have no dowry,' I said weakly.

'I don't care about dowries.'

'Mammy then... I couldn't leave Mammy...'

'Your mother could come and live with us,' he said. 'It would only be the lodge, I know, not the house itself – unless I change my mind about letting Nicholas stay. But there's room enough. The lodge is still bigger than the cottage you call home.'

'Ruth and the babies...'

'I'm certainly not offering to take them in as well,' he said wryly. 'They managed perfectly well without you before; they'll do so again.'

Isobel… I almost said it, but did not. Isobel, still there between us. What would she say if Adam and I announced that we were to be wed?

'I think,' Adam said, 'that you have run out of excuses. Well, don't give me an answer now. I don't want a rushed refusal. I've been patient thus far, I can be patient a little longer. And now, I think, it is time I took you home.'

He got to his feet, helped me up. I sat beside him in a happy daze as he drove me the rest of the way home to Mallen. The fact that I had not agreed yet to his proposal was neither here nor there. My lips might not have spoken the words that would signify my agreement but my heart knew what my answer would be. And I stilled the nagging doubts that had assailed me, for the moment anyway.

He left me at the end of the track. I smoothed my skirts and arranged my bodice as I walked along the row of cottages, wondering if I looked respectable and if I looked different than I had before. Surely I must? Surely what had occurred between us was there for all to see?

For the first time I blessed Mammy's vagueness. And I blessed too the fact that the shutters had been drawn at the windows of the cottages I passed, and the lamps lit ready for the encroaching night.

The shutters at Ruth's windows were not closed; I could see her seated on the settle with little Billy on her lap and Charlie hanging round her neck. A cosy, domestic scene the like of which I had grown up with. What would my life be if I accepted Adam's offer of marriage? Without doubt the difference in my station would drive a wedge between me and the humble families who had always been our neighbours. And Adam's grand friends would doubtless think me an upstart, too, and cut me for it. I would be caught for ever between two worlds.

But if I had Adam's love, what more could I want?

It was only then that I realized what it was that had nagged at me, marring my delight in his proposal and making me hesitate. It was a barb pricking at my flesh as if I had carelessly plucked a beautiful rose and drawn in the scent of it only to feel a thorn digging into my thumb.

Adam had asked me to be his wife.

But he had not said he loved me.

—

I hesitated for just a moment with my hand on the latch of Mammy's cottage, then I lifted it and pushed the door open.

And stopped short, breath catching in my throat, shock draining the blood from my face.

Mammy was not alone. There was someone in the kitchen with her.

A man. Big, burly, unkempt. His coat ragged, his face half-covered by an untrimmed growth of beard.

But I knew him in an instant and alarm washed over me in a cold tide.

Joshua Tripp. Joshua Tripp, whom everyone said was the man who had attacked Mammy and beaten her half to death, was here in our kitchen.

Twelve

How long I stood there frozen by shock I do not know. To me it felt like hours, yet I know it can have been no more than seconds. Then I turned, pulling the door open again, about to run for assistance.

'Tamsin!' His voice arrested me. 'Don't be frightened!'

It was much as I remembered it, that voice, rough, with a thick Cornish burr, yet now overlaid with some other, unfamiliar twang, acquired, I suppose, from the years spent in the company of men from other parts, all with their own distinctive dialects.

I spun round.

'What are you doing here?' I demanded. 'If you don't go this minute I shall raise the alarm and have you arrested.'

'You wouldn't do that, Tamsin,' he said.

'I would too! Why, Jed is just next door...' But I knew that he was not. He was not yet home from his core. Ruth was alone there with two defenceless children. In the house that Joshua no doubt still thought of as his home.

I had been loath to think ill of him, yet now, faced with his presence in my kitchen, all my fears surfaced, and as Joshua took a step towards me, I yelled at him shrilly: 'Keep away from me! Stay where you are!'

He stopped, a big, powerful figure, spreading his hands as imploringly as a helpless child. 'I won't hurt you, Tamsin. I only want to talk to you.'

And from her chair by the fire where she sat, seemingly totally unconcerned, Mammy chipped in: 'It's Joshua, Tamsin! Joshua – after all these years!'

'I know it's Joshua, Mammy,' I said, and perhaps it was the fact that she displayed no fear that prevented me, even now, from running out of the house to raise the alarm.

Her memory of the attack and of the months preceding it might still be hazy, but it seemed to me that if it had been Joshua who had beaten her senseless, she would be afraid of him now, even if the details were lost to her.

And besides… once again I told myself that it was not possible Joshua had changed so much that he could have attacked a woman at whose door he had once left poached rabbits and pheasants. Though, looking now at his burly form, I thought he could well have been the man I had seen lurking outside, that night not long after I had come home…

'This isn't the first time you've come here, is it?' I asked, my voice taut.

He did not answer me directly, but his failure to deny it was good enough for me.

'I have to talk to you, Tamsin.'

'So why did you run away when you came before?' I demanded.

He snorted. 'I'd have been a fool to stay, with you screaming blue murder. I've learned that when folk feel threatened they act first and ask questions afterwards.'

'Especially when God-fearing people have been attacked and left for dead in their own homes,' I said shortly.

His eyes above the busy beard narrowed. 'What are you saying, Tamsin?'

'Someone beat Mammy half to death,' I said. 'Here, in her kitchen, in broad daylight, and for no apparent reason. It was generally accepted a prisoner on the run from Bodmin Gaol, living rough and looking for food, was responsible.' I paused, then risked adding: 'Or a convict returned from Australia. We knew you were back – you were seen in Mount Hawk when *you* tried to steal food from a house there.'

'Sweet Jesus!' The eyes narrowed further to a scowl. 'It's true I was hungry enough to try to help myself to a little nourishment, but surely you don't think…?'

I held my ground. 'It's what was said.'

'Oh no, no!' Mammy interrupted. ''Twasn't *Joshua* hurted me! Why, if he was so much as disrespectful, I'd box his ears for him!'

'You would that,' Joshua said ruefully to Mammy. 'And it wouldn't be the first time, neither!' He turned back to me. 'It seems I did the right thing then, taking to my heels that night when you raised the roof. Either the menfolk would have hung me from the old scaffold theirselves, or they'd have handed me over to the magistrates, who'd have been glad enough to do it for them. Still would, no doubt. I'm a convicted criminal – and bound to be guilty. So I won't hang around here. I'll say what I came to say and be on my way.'

'What did you come to say?' I asked. 'If it's about your old house, Ruth and Jed have every right to live there. After your poor mother and brother died, the house lay empty until they took it, and they pay their rent to the Penrose family, who, as you well know, are the rightful owners. Everything is legal and above board.'

'Oh, I know it belongs to the Penroses all right!' Joshua's voice was scornful. 'What don't they own around here? The bastards! No – it's not the house I've come to talk about, though I grant you it was a heavy blow to me when I got home to find my family dead and gone. But it does concern the Penroses.'

'The Penroses?' I repeated, puzzled.

'Aye. The bloody Penroses. It's something that's played on my mind for years. I should have said at the time, but I didn't want to get on their wrong side, what with them owning the roof over our heads and me likely to be brought up before old Ralph if ever the gamekeepers catched hold of me. So I kept quiet, and a fat lot of good it did me. Old Ralph still had me sent to the assizes, and sat there again to order my transportation. I should've told the truth and shamed the devil.'

'You're talking in riddles,' I said. 'What was it that you should have said?'

He looked at me squarely. 'That they knew more than ever they let on about the so-called accident that killed your John,' he said.

Whatever I had expected, it was not this.

'John?' I echoed faintly. 'My *brother* John?' And Mammy, too, murmured his name very softly, very sadly.

'John. My boy.'

Joshua nodded. 'Yes. Look – I'm sorry if this is going to cause you pain, Missus Hardy, bringing up the past after all these years. I did ask meself whether it was best now to let sleeping dogs lie. And then I heard that you be all mixed up with 'em, Tamsin. Those boys, and Isobel. And I thought to meself, no, it's got to be said. You've got to be warned, like, what sort of folk it is you'm dealing with.'

A flicker of discomfort ran through my veins. 'Go on,' I said tersely.

'Well, 'twas like this.' Joshua positioned himself before the fire so that both Mammy and I could see him. 'Your John used to come and chat a lot to me. He were only a lad, o' course, and I a young man. But he used to like to watch me making my traps and...'

'That he did!' Mammy interposed, with more vivacity than I had heard in her voice at any time since her attack. 'I had strong words for him about it, and I boxed *his* ears for him! I was worried, Joshua, that you were leading him into bad ways.'

Joshua looked sheepish. 'Well, I got to admit, Mrs Hardy, he did come along with me once or twice. Crept out of the house when you was asleep. Like I say, he had a leaning for it...'

'I knew it!' Mammy said. 'You're a varmint, Joshua Tripp, and you always were! Oh, I'd have tanned the backside off him if I'd known about it! Going poaching – at his age! You should've told him so. You were older than him and should've known better. He always looked up to you.'

'I should've, I suppose,' Joshua said. 'But I liked him. He was good company – and young and lithe enough to be able to draw off the gamekeepers and outrun them every time. There was no chance of your John getting caught. And I couldn't stop him, anyway, now could I? He'd watch for me from the window, and the minute he saw me come out the house with me bag, there he'd be, right on me heels.'

'Oh, the varmint!' Mammy was working herself up into quite a state, as if it were last week or last night that

John had slipped out in the dead of night to follow Josh on his illegal foray, instead of all those years ago.

'What has this to do with his death?' I pressed Joshua.

'Well, nothing really – I'm just a-saying I spent a fair bit o' time with him one way or another, and he used to talk to me about things. That's how I come to hear about this so-called Treasure.'

'Treasure?' I echoed, totally bemused – at a loss. This conversation was becoming wilder and more unlikely by the minute.

But Joshua was not to be sidetracked. He was telling his story in his own way – presumably he had gone over it many times in his mind during the years of his exile, and he was not going to deviate from it now.

'As I say, he liked an adventure, did your John. Well, what boy don't? And he had as much spirit as any. So I reckon the very idea of it excited him. When he first told me about it, I thought he was making it up like. I mean – it do sound like a boy's tale, don't it? But he promised me it was the truth. I still don't know if it was just something silly they'd cooked up between them, but...'

'Who? Who did you think he'd cooked it up with?' I asked.

'Well, the Penrose boys, o' course! He were friendly with them, like he were friendly with Isobel. If *friendly* is the word for it. I never could understand it meself, him and those two... Old Ralph would've had a fit and died, I should think, if he'd known they was running around with one o' the peasants, if I know anything about him...'

'Whatever are you talking about?' Mammy interrupted. 'Ralph was...'

I silenced her with a sharp look. 'Let Joshua go on, Mammy.'

Joshua, in any case, seemed scarcely to have heard her. He was too immersed now in his story.

Anyway, he told me there was Penrose family treasure. Something to do with King Arthur and his Knights of the Round Table is what he told me. I just laughed at him, o' course. Told him not to be so silly, asked if he thought I was born yesterday. But he would have it he was telling the truth. There was some treasure, and he and the Penrose boys were trying to find it. "You'll be lucky," I said, and he said: "Yes, I will. And if I find it before they do, we won't be living in a hovel. We'll be in a fine house, that's where we'll be." "Oh ah," says I, "and I'm the Lord Mayor of London." Well, I thought no more on it, really. And then one day he comes to see me, all excited, and he says: "Joshua, I know where the Treasure is."'

Joshua paused for breath, but before either of us could say a word, he was off again.

'Well, "I wouldn't mind some o' that," I says to him. An' he says: "I can't get at it. I haven't got the key." "Never mind the key," says I, "I don't need no key." And he says: "'Twouldn't do you no good without the key," an' he'll say no more.'

A small strangled gasp came from Mammy. I glanced at her anxiously, thinking that perhaps all this was too much for her.

'Mammy?'

There was a strange look on her face and her eyes had gone very faraway. But she motioned impatiently for Joshua to continue.

'Well,' he went on, 'I didn't see John for some days, and when I next did, it looked to me like he'd been in a fight. His eye was black and his nose a-bleeding. "What have you been a-doin'?" I says, and all he says is: "I thought they was my friends." He didn't name no names, but I knew who he meant, all right. The Penrose boys. "Is this about this so-called Treasure?" says I, and he says: "I wouldn't say where it is, and I'm not going to now." "Well," says I, "it looks like you got the worst of it, young Johnny." An' he says: "This is nothing to what I've been threatened with if I don't tell. They say they'm going to do for me if I don't tell. They say they'll put me down the old mineshaft and leave me there until I do." "You'd best keep out o' their way then," says I, and he says: "I'm going to, don't you worry." But he was scared, I could tell. Real scared – and your John was no coward. He could hold his own with anybody in a fair fight. I still didn't take it too serious, though. I thought 'twas just boys being boys, and all this talk of treasure seemed like so much claptrap. And threats of putting him down the old mine… well, I never thought for a minute they ever would.'

'When was this?' I asked – but I already knew. I remembered John coming home with a bloody nose and a black eye. I remembered Mammy giving him a sore bottom to go with it for fighting. And I remembered his face was still a state when he was lying in his coffin.

When Joshua spoke again, he confirmed that my memory was not playing me false.

''Twas just a week or so before he died,' he said. 'I see'd him that morning, going off over the moor. And later on, I see'd him with one of the Penrose boys. I can't say for sure which of them it were, they were too far off for that, and both of 'em about the same height and build, but I could tell from the fine clothes it were one of 'em. John must've forgot about the fight, I thought to meself. 'Twas all a childish thing. And I thought no more about it. And then, next thing I knew, he hadn't come home, and you

191

was out of your mind with worry. An' I started to wonder. 'Twas me suggested we ought to search the old mine, if you remember.' He shook his head and rasped a big hand through the forest of hair on his chin. 'An' that's where he were found. Drownded.'

For a moment I could not speak. I was too filled with horror, my mind racing. We had always thought that John had gone there alone and decided to explore, though Mammy had always warned him to keep away; that the place was a death trap. But, as Joshua had said, John was a wilful lad with a taste for adventure, and we had accepted what seemed to be the only explanation – that he had been descending the ladder when a rotten rung gave way, or inching his way along one of the narrow ledges, had lost his balance, and plunged down into the dirty, stagnant water beneath.

Now Joshua was telling us there could be another explanation. That John had not been alone that day, and his death had been no accident.

'You are saying one of the Penrose boys killed John?' My lips were dry and stiff; it was all I could do to form the words.

'That I don't know. I've thought about it and thought about it, and what I reckon is it was a boys' lark gone wrong. They only meant to frighten him into telling what he reckoned he knew, and he'd made that up, like as not, to make himself important. But then again, maybe tempers were lost. A lot of stupid things are done when a man – or a boy – loses his temper. And if more blows were exchanged before your John went down the shaft, no one would ever know, seeing as how his face was still in a state from that other fight. Or you'd'a thought he'd hit it when he fell. Well, that's what I think, anyhows – and I've had plenty o' time to think, these last years, believe you me.'

'Dear God!' I said. 'All this time we've believed John fell because of his own silly fault, and now you're saying…!'

'It was his own silly fault he didn't stay away from them two,' Joshua said. 'They'm nothing but trouble, and always was. But they was an attraction to him, I reckon. And Isobel, too, with her pretty ways. He had a fancy for her, if I'm not mistaken. Any road. All these years I've been a-thinking you oughta know the truth. And when I came back and heared you was all mixed up with 'em, Tamsin, well, I made up me mind I'd risk coming back again so I could warn you what they'm like, even though I'm wanted for stealing food from houses to keep meself alive, and if I get caught they'll have me on a boat back to Australia, like as not – or worse.'

He hesitated. 'I'm still wanted there, too, if you want the truth. I hadn't yet served my sentence out, but a few on us made a break for it one night, and a guard got the worst of it. The ones they caught got hung for their pains, but I was lucky. I got meself taken on as crew for a clipper and worked my way home. But if I do get caught now – well, I don't give much for me chances.'

'Oh, Joshua!' I said. 'You've risked your liberty for our sake!'

He shrugged. 'I reckon I owed it to you. You was always good to me, Missus Hardy.'

'What will you do now?' I asked.

'Now that I've seen you, I reckon I'll get the hell out of these parts,' Joshua said. 'There's nothing to keep me here, with my family dead and gone. Reckon I'll try to make my way up to Bristol, look for work on another ship or in the docks. Nobody knows me there, nor cares less.'

'Well, you'll have a square meal before you go,' I said. 'And food to take with you on your journey.'

'Oh, I wouldn't want...' But I could see the hunger in his eyes and the gauntness of his cheeks beneath the growth of beard.

'Don't argue, Joshua. It's the least we can do.'

As I set out bread, cheese and some chutney Ruth had somehow found the time to make between caring for the children, my mind was racing. Just an hour ago I had lain in the gorse with Adam. Now Joshua was claiming that either he, or Nicholas, or both of them, had been responsible for the death of my brother.

Oh, it had happened a long time ago, of course, when they were just boys. But even boys, wild and irresponsible as they sometimes were, knew right from wrong. Young as they were, if they had threatened and tortured John as Joshua suspected, in order to make him tell the whereabouts of some supposed 'Treasure', then it said much about their characters. And they had kept silent about their part in his death all these years. Not so surprising then, I supposed – they had most likely been terrified of the repercussions if they admitted to what they had done. But now – how could they see me every day and not remember? How could Nicholas have me in his home, knowing he had been responsible for the death of my brother? How could Adam ask me to be his wife and say nothing, not even give the slightest indication that there was anything to be said?

Had John's death been an accident – a prank gone wrong, as Joshua had put it? Or had it been more than that? Certainly it seemed they had been responsible for the beating John had taken a few days before his death. Could it be that one or the other or both of them had set upon him again, angry that he refused to share with them what he claimed to know? Certainly they were both possessed of violent tempers – that much I had witnessed for myself. But to push him down the old mineshaft…!

In my mind's eye I saw my brother falling into the fetid darkness, his poor body bouncing off the rough walls, plunging into the murky black water far below. It was a terrible picture; even now, after all these years, I could hardly bear it. And the thought that Adam might have been responsible was quite unsupportable.

No! Not Adam! I could not believe it. I would not believe it!

Nicholas I did not care for. For all his aura of breeding, there was something sly about him, and I felt sure he had struck Isobel this morning for some reason. For all I knew, he had done so before – certainly, when she had asked me to be her companion, I had had the distinct impression she was afraid of something – or someone – and her pregnancy was just an excuse to persuade me to become her companion. That someone was most likely to be Nicholas, since, if it were anyone else, he would protect her from them. And Nicholas could inspire enough hatred that someone had put a lead shot into his back, perhaps with the intention of killing him. Yes, shocked as I was by Joshua's revelations, yet I could believe it of Nicholas. But Adam… no! Oh, surely I could not fall in love with a man who could do such a thing!

As we ate, I noticed that Mammy was very quiet, and I hoped desperately that all this was not causing her to suffer a relapse. But though her eyes were faraway, the expression in them was not vacant, as it had been these last weeks. Almost, it seemed to me, it was thoughtful.

I was anxious too that Ruth might come around for some reason and find Joshua seated at the table with us. For one thing, I thought she would likely go running out in a state of hysteria to fetch Jem, who would be home by now from his core, and alert the neighbourhood to the fact that Joshua was here. And for another, I really did not want to discuss with her yet the things he had told me.

I would eventually, of course. And it was likely Mammy would mention his visit, which would leave me no alternative − unless, of course, Ruth assumed that Mammy was hallucinating. But for the moment I did not want to talk about it with anyone. The implications affected me too personally.

At last Joshua had eaten his fill and we judged it was dark enough for him to be able to leave without danger of being seen. What a risk he had taken, coming here in broad daylight, I thought, worried still for his safety. If he should be captured, brought up before the magistrates and deported again, and all on account of what he had felt to be his duty to us, I would feel totally responsible. Worse, if the men of Mallen got hold of him, they might deal with him themselves, considering many still believed him to be the intruder who had attacked Mammy. A lynch mob did not stop to listen to explanations, and I might even be unaware of what was going on until it was too late. I shivered at the thought.

'You will take care, Joshua, won't you?' I urged him. 'If you were caught because of us…'

Joshua smiled wryly. 'I were always good at making meself invisible, Tamsin. You'd be surprised at how I've crept about this district these last weeks without being seen. No, don't you worry about me.'

'Not so good that I didn't see you outside that night when you came before!' I said. 'Not so good you weren't nearly apprehended at Mount Hawk. And not so good that the gamekeeper didn't catch you all those years ago, either.'

'I got careless,' he said. 'I won't get careless again.'

I gave him the food I had put ready for him, tied up in a kerchief.

'If you need anything more, and it's safe for you to do so, you know where to come,' I said. 'In fact, if there's anything at all we can do to help, you know we'll do it. And I'm very touched you risked so much to come to us with the truth about poor John.'

'I'm only sorry I didn't have the courage to speak out years ago,' Joshua said. 'Just you watch out for those Penroses, Tamsin, that's all I ask. Don't make the same mistake your brother did, trusting them to be his friends. One of these days somebody will do for them, mark my words. And do it good and proper. But until that do happen...' He broke off.

I was still too preoccupied to wonder at his words. It was only when I had watched him disappear like a shadow into the darkness that it occurred to me.

Could it have been *Joshua* who had shot Nicholas this morning? He wasn't carrying a gun now, I was fairly certain. But he wouldn't come calling on us with a gun. He had been in the district today. And he hated the Penroses with a fierce hatred that had smouldered, no doubt, throughout his years as a convict in a strange, far-off land. Hated them enough to kill them if the opportunity arose, I had no doubt.

I stood at the door staring into the darkness and hoping with all my heart that he would not be apprehended this night. If he was, then it was all too possible that this new charge, too, would be laid at his door, whether he was guilty or not. I did not want to see Joshua strung up by his neck on a gibbet.

All was quiet. There was no sound but the sighing of the wind in the gorse. I went back inside the house. Mammy was still staring into space.

'Mammy,' I said gently, 'you must not let what Joshua said upset you. It was a terrible thing, but it was all a very long time ago and none of it will bring John back.'

She did not seem to be listening to me.

'The key,' she said. 'John did not have the key. If he'd had the key…'

I gave a little laugh. 'What are you talking about, Mammy?'

'Why, the key, Tamsin!' she repeated, impatient almost, as if she thought I was being deliberately obtuse. She stood up, moving with more alacrity than I had seen since her attack, and started towards the dresser.

'What are you doing, Mammy?' I asked.

Again her voice was slow and deliberate. 'Getting the key, of course!'

To my astonishment she dragged a low stool to the dresser, climbed upon it and reached up to the top shelf for the cup that we used to store odds and ends – the self-same cup into which I had dropped the button that I had found on the floor on the day she had been attacked, and since quite forgotten about.

I saw it now as she tipped the contents of the cup on to the table among the used dishes, a small silver button which she must have torn from her attacker's coat in the

198

struggle. But it was not the button that Mammy picked out now from the little heap of oddments, but a key I had never to my knowledge seen before – a heavy key, a little rusty and pitted with age. She held it in her hand, staring down at it, and her face was taut with concentration.

'This is it,' she said. 'This is the key to the Treasure. When Joshua said, I knew it was there. But...' She broke off, the intense concentration on her face turned to a look of distress, and the eyes she raised to mine were filled with tears of frustration. 'But, oh, Tamsin, I'm in such a muddle! There's something I'm supposed to do with it. And for the life of me, I don't know what!'

–

Briefly the mists had lifted somewhat. For a little while she had felt that all she had forgotten was within her reach.

The Treasure. The key to the Treasure. Ralph, giving it into her keeping. Dear Ralph, whom she had loved so much.

She should not have loved him, of course. It was wrong, all wrong. He had a wife. She was just a lowly seamstress. But how could it be wrong to feel as they had felt? He had simply been kind in the beginning, kind to a woman who had lost her husband, a woman struggling to make ends meet, to put food on the table for her children and keep a roof over their heads.

But something had happened that neither of them had expected. Something beyond the control of either of them. An attraction that drew them together, body and soul.

Such a cold woman, Ralph's wife. Proud and disdainful and cold. He was as lonely as she. With all that he had, he was as lonely as she. But the fire that had raged between them – oh, how it had warmed them both!

And when that physical passion had cooled, the warmth of friendship had taken its place, growing deeper with the passing years.

It was to her he had turned on his deathbed. Her he had asked to do one last thing for him.

It concerned a key and a treasure beyond price. The key lay now in the palm of her hand. But, for the life of her, she could not remember what it was she was supposed to do with it.

She had failed him. He had trusted her to do what he could not, and she had failed him. Despair filled her. She clasped the key between her hands, bowed her head, and prayed.

I must remember what it is I have to do. I must remember!

But the harder she tried, the more it slipped away from her.

Thirteen

I looked on with anxiety and compassion as Mammy held the key between her hands and close to her heart. It was as I had feared. Joshua's visit and the things he had said had worsened her mental condition. Hardly surprising, really. My own brain was running in crazy circles, and I was not old, sick and confused. What strange tricks her foggy mind was playing I could only guess at, but I supposed she had fastened on to Joshua's mention of a key to the so-called Treasure and linked it in some way to an old key she had once put into the pot for safe keeping.

She was talking nonsense, of course, but I could not confuse her further by saying so.

'You're very tired, Mammy,' I said gently. 'Joshua has upset you, and you need to rest.'

'No!' She looked up at me with troubled eyes, and there was urgency in her voice. 'There's something I have to do!'

I put my arm about her thin frame.

'All you have to do, Mammy, is go to bed. I'm going to take you there myself, and then I'll make you a nice warm posset – though I shouldn't wonder if you are asleep by the time I bring it to you. Shall we put that key back inside the pot and put it back on the shelf? It will be safe there.'

She sighed, and reluctantly allowed me to take the key from her hands. I scooped up the other oddments from the table, pausing for a moment to look at the button. Someone, somewhere, was missing that button. If I knew who it was I would also know who it was that had attacked Mammy. But it was unlikely I would ever find out now. Too much time had passed, and in any case I had never known how to begin. One thing at least was certain, it was not Joshua who had beaten her senseless. His ragged clothes had never been graced by such frippery. Not that I had ever really thought that it was, whatever others might say.

I replaced the pot on the top shelf of the dresser, urged Mammy upstairs, and got her out of her day dress and into her nightgown.

As I had expected, by the time I took her up a cup of warm milk, she was too sleepy to drink more than a little of it, but I placed what was left on the small table beside her bed in case she should wake in the night and feel thirsty. Then I went back downstairs.

I should go next door and tell Ruth what had happened, I knew. But still I was reluctant to do so. First I needed time to think. First I needed a little while on my own to decide what I was going to do.

I knew that, unlike Mammy, it would be a very long time before I was able to fall asleep.

By the time Adam came for me next morning my mind was made up. I could not possibly go on as if nothing had happened, and I certainly could not accept his offer of marriage until my mind was set at rest. I must tell him of Joshua's allegations and hear what he had to say about them. But somehow I must do it without letting him know Joshua was in the district. I must not put Joshua's liberty at risk. Why, already he was being sought for housebreaking, and, if there was any truth in what he had said, it would give Adam and Nicholas a strong motive for seeking him out and making sure he was not in a position to make more mischief for them.

The best chance I would have of speaking with Adam was on our drive, I knew. Once we reached Trevarrah he would be off either to the mine or to oversee some work on the estate, and I would have to wait until late afternoon before I saw him alone again.

I was taut with apprehension as he handed me up into the trap, and I was quite unable to respond to his kiss of greeting when we were out of sight of the houses. Whereas yesterday the touch of his lips had excited such longing in me, today there was no such response.

Adam, of course, noticed it.

'Tamsin?' His eyes on my face were concerned. 'Is something wrong? Are you regretting yesterday?'

I could scarcely answer that. Part of me was indeed regretting that I had allowed such intimacy – and not only because I had behaved as no decent young woman should. If it were only that, perhaps I could have put aside any shame I might have felt for the impropriety, and any fears that I had made myself vulnerable for all kinds of reasons that I did not care to contemplate. Besides, had not Adam asked me to marry him?

But how could I even contemplate marriage to a man who might have had a hand in the death of my own brother?

'I did not sleep well,' I said evasively.

His eyes narrowed still further. 'Does that mean you lay awake considering my offer of marriage? If so, from the look on your face, I don't think I give much for my chances of your accepting it.'

He said it lightly, as though it scarcely mattered to him one way or the other. Perhaps he was the one doing some regretting, I thought. Perhaps he had suggested marriage as a sop to his conscience for ruining me, and now he was hoping that I would not take him up on it.

'To be honest, I gave very little thought to your offer of marriage,' I said tartly. 'I had other things on my mind.'

'Oh!'

That had certainly taken the wind out of his sails, I could tell.

I could avoid the issue no longer.

'After leaving you yesterday, I came by some information that disturbed me greatly,' I said. 'It concerns you and Nicholas – and my brother John. You remember John?'

Adam was no longer looking at me. His eyes were fixed firmly ahead and I could not read the expression on his face, though I was aware that he sat very still suddenly, very straight.

'Yes.'

'You and Nicholas were, I believe, friendly with him.'

'We knew him, yes.'

'And you will remember that he died in what was always assumed to have been an accident.'

'At Old Trevarrah mine, yes. It was a terrible tragedy.'

'It certainly was,' I said. 'He was just a boy, with all his life before him. He had always been warned to stay away from the old workings. But I understand the two of you and John were engaged in some boyish adventure to find some supposed treasure. Is that right?'

'The Penrose Treasure,' he said. 'Very likely. We spent half our boyhood searching for it.'

I was surprised enough to deviate from my planned line of questioning.

'There really is a Penrose Treasure?'

He laughed shortly.

'Oh yes. Passed down through the family for generations for safe keeping, its whereabouts known only to the squire. It was, as you can imagine, a great temptation for two boys to search for it, especially if you know what it is.' He glanced at me again, his eyes narrowed. 'Where is all this leading, Tamsin? What do you know of the Treasure?'

'Nothing,' I said. 'Nothing beyond that John was spending time with you and Nicholas searching for it. He even claimed, I am told, that he knew where it was hidden. And it cost him his life.'

'What are you saying?' Adam asked.

'I...' I looked at him, at the man I had grown to love, the man who had just yesterday lain with me in the rough bracken, the man who had asked me to become his wife. I looked at his hands, strong yet gentle, on the reins as he guided the pony, and the scar on his face gained fighting for his country. I looked at his eyes, unfathomable now, yet to me the most honest eyes I had ever seen, and I could not accuse him. I could not accuse him because I could not bring myself to believe he could have done something so terrible as to deliberately cause John's death; no, not even when he was a youth.

And I could not accuse Nicholas either. If I did, and all this came into the open, who knew what damage it would do? If Adam knew nothing of it and was as good a man as I believed, then it would cause yet more trouble between the brothers, as if there was not enough already. Adam would have it out with him, I had no doubt, and there would be yet another quarrel, and one that might yet end in him putting Nicholas out of Trevarrah. And even if he did not, Nicholas would know that I knew, and the situation would be impossible. I could not be under the same roof as him, not as Adam's wife, not as Isobel's companion – and Isobel needed me desperately.

No, no good could come of raking up the past now. It was all a long time ago. It would not bring John back. And I might well live to regret the consequences of speaking out. Perhaps it was cowardice on my part that made me think this way, but whatever, I could not, for the moment at least, bring myself to say what was on my mind.

'I believe John died because of the Treasure,' I said, floundering now for a way of extricating myself from this conversation without making the accusation I had intended. 'Perhaps he thought it was hidden in the old mineworkings and he was looking for it when he fell.'

'Are you sure that is all you mean?' Adam was looking at me very closely. 'Are you sure you are not saying there was more to it than that?'

The doubt flared in me again. Why should he say such a thing? How could he have known what was in my mind unless…? Or had I made myself so obvious?

'Was there more, then?' I asked.

He flicked the reins. 'How should I know?'

Again the accusation trembled on my lips; again I hesitated. As I did so, Adam reined in the horse and turned to me.

'I was not there when John met his death,' he said, 'so I do not know whether he was looking for the Treasure in Old Trevarrah mine or not. But one thing I do know. He had not found it. If he had, you would all be rich and living in luxury. Either from selling it, or from the reward my father would have been prepared to pay to get it back.'

I frowned. According to Joshua, John had said much the same thing.

'What is this treasure, then?' I asked. 'And if as squire it is now in your possession, why are you so worried about money?'

Adam shrugged helplessly. 'It is not in my possession, I am afraid.'

'But you said... You don't mean *Nicholas* has it, along with the house and...'

'No, Nicholas does not have it either. The secret of where it is hidden seems to have died with my father.' Adam smiled wryly. 'Perhaps we should begin to hunt again, as we did when we were boys!' The smile died on his lips suddenly; he reached for my hand. 'I'm sorry. In view of what happened to poor John, I should not have said that. But it is indeed vexatious to me that something of such great value should be we know not where. Too well hidden, Tamsin, in order to preserve it. So well hidden it may be lost for ever. We must continue to hope that we will discover its whereabouts, but, to be truthful, I hold out little hope. The area where it must be hidden... well, look around you!'

He gesticulated to indicate the mile upon square mile of open moor land.

'It could be buried anywhere between here and the sea. It could be, as you suggest, in one of the disused mineworkings. It could be in a cave, with the tides cutting it off from the world twice daily. It might have gone home to Camelford or Tintagel.'

'Camelford?' I repeated, puzzled. 'Tintagel?'

Adam smiled at me crookedly. 'Since your brother shared the secret, perhaps I should explain. And if you are to be my wife, I certainly should. It is, after all, part of our family's inheritance.'

'What is?' I asked.

'The Treasure.' He smiled again. 'Even if it *is* lost.'

'Well, I am certainly lost!' I said tartly. 'I haven't the faintest idea what you are talking about, Adam.'

'You must surely know who it is that legend has it was born at Tintagel?' Adam said. 'And who set up court at Camelford?'

I nodded, though I could not see where this was leading. 'King Arthur, of course. They do say Camelot was Camelford. But… it's only legend, surely?'

Adam shrugged and flicked the reins. The pony moved on, and he continued: 'I am telling you of the Treasure, Tamsin, and the story attached to it. The story which has been passed down through our family from generation to generation is that an ancestor of mine was one of the knights of King Arthur's Round Table. When Camelot was under threat of attack, many of the riches of the kingdom were removed for safe keeping, cared for in the homes and castles of the families of the knights. My ancestor was entrusted with a dinner service – platters and goblets, one for each knight, one for Arthur, and one for Guinevere. And this dinner service was a very special one. It was made of solid silver. So its value is two-fold. Not only is it worth a king's ransom, but also it is of enormous historical significance. That is the reason we always refer to it as the Treasure.'

'Oh!' I was stunned for a moment into silence. 'But if it's just legend,' I ventured at last, 'how do you know the Treasure even exists?'

'Oh, it exists all right!' Adam said. 'The only thing in doubt is whether it was ever used by Arthur. But my family has always trusted that it was and treated it reverentially. I saw it once, as a small child, when my father showed it to me and explained that one day it would be my responsibility to keep it safe. I remember gazing at it in wonder – great silver platters and goblets, all a-gleam. The monetary value, of course, was quite unimportant to me then. All I could think of was that Arthur and his knights had eaten from those plates and drunk from those goblets. I asked Papa if Nicholas could see them too, but he said they were for my eyes only. That I, as the elder, would one day be their guardian, and they would now be returned to their hiding place. Is it any wonder Nicholas and I made a game out of trying to find them? I told him about it, of course, and he was goggle-eyed at the thought of it. As was John, when Nicholas told him. Oh yes, we spent many hours searching for the hiding place. To no avail.'

'And you still do not know its whereabouts,' I said.

'No. As I told you, my father said that when the time was right he would reveal the secret of the hiding place to me, and thereafter I would be charged with its safe keeping. But, as you know, I was in America when he died. I can only presume that, when I left, he did not foresee that he would be in his grave before I returned, and he would be denied the opportunity to pass on to me the location of the Treasure.' He smiled briefly, that small, wry smile that could usually make my heart turn over, but which, this morning, had no effect upon me at all.

'I doubt he would have told me then in any case. He was not best pleased with me. I was somewhat wild in my youth, and he told me quite frankly that I would bring disgrace upon the family if I did not change my ways. Practically his last words to me were that he hoped serving as a soldier would instil some kind of discipline in me. And I think it did.'

'It's strange though that he did not pass on the information to Nicholas when he knew that he was not long for this world,' I said. 'As I remember it, he did not die suddenly, but was in failing health for some time. I would have thought he would have realized the secret might die with him.'

'Given Nicholas's vices, I doubt he would have been any more likely to trust him than he did me in my wild days,' Adam said. 'No, I think he must have hoped that he would live a while longer, as we all do. It's not an easy thing, accepting our own mortality, especially for a man as strong-willed as my father was. I fear that unless he confided in someone outside the family, who has not seen fit to speak of it, the Treasure is lost for ever.'

We were approaching Trevarrah now. As he reined in, Adam gave me a sidelong look.

'Who told you about the Treasure, Tamsin? Who said that it cost your brother his life?'

I bit my lip. 'I'd really rather not say.'

'Was it Isobel?'

There was something in his tone that brought me up short, spinning a whole new set of questions and half-formed ideas through my already overloaded brain.

Joshua had said that John had been sweet on Isobel – had he boasted to her, too, that he knew the whereabouts of the Treasure? Almost certainly she would have known that he and the Penrose boys were searching for it. Yet she had never once mentioned John to me since I had become her companion.

Because she thought remembering was painful to me? Or because, as Joshua had suggested, she knew that either

Nicholas, or Adam, or both of them, had been involved in his death?

Adam was still looking at me, waiting for an answer.

'No,' I said. 'It wasn't Isobel.'

Was it my imagination, or did the muscles in his jaw relax a little; some of the tension go out of his shoulders?

'I must go to her,' I said.

He nodded. 'And I have a meeting regarding the future of the mine. I'll see you this evening, Tamsin.'

He handed me down. It was only as I was walking into the house that I realized he had made no further mention of his proposal of marriage.

Isobel was in the small parlour. She looked very pale, I thought, and the bruise on her cheek was discolouring and even more noticeable. I made no mention of it, however. Her sensitivity on the subject of how she had come by it had been all too obvious yesterday. Instead, I asked after Nicholas.

'Oh, he's feeling rather sorry for himself,' she said, 'but he was very lucky. It's a flesh wound only. It could easily have been so very much worse.'

Well, that was true enough!

'It was certainly lucky that whoever shot him does not possess a very good aim,' I said. 'Either that, or they never intended to kill him at all. Just warn him, perhaps, that he could be an easy target if they so decided.'

'I'm not so sure of that.' Isobel smoothed her skirts over her stomach and I thought again that she had remained very slender in spite of the passage of the weeks, and wondered if the stress she was under was having a bad effect on the development of her baby. 'Nicholas said he heard a sound behind him just before the shot was fired, remember, and took avoiding action. I think it might very well have saved his life.'

She caught at my hand. 'Oh Tamsin, I cannot tell you how glad I am that you are here with me! There are things going on under this roof… I would be so afraid if I did not think I had a friend! But then, I told you that, didn't I, when I asked you to be my companion?'

'You told me you were afraid of pregnancy and child-birth,' I reminded her with a straight look. 'You made no mention of anything else.'

Again Isobel's hands flew to her stomach, again I felt a qualm of anxiety for the healthy progress of her condition. 'Oh yes, that too!' she said. 'But I don't suppose I should be so afraid of my vulnerable condition if it were not for… all these other things.'

I bit my lip. There *were* dark secrets in this house, I felt sure. There was animosity and jealousy, there were, I suspected, unrequited passions. And over it all hung the threat of ruin – a ruin brought about by Nicholas's wild ways – and the wild ways of Adam before him, no doubt.

As for Isobel, I had long suspected she had not been entirely honest with me about her reason for wanting my company, and the bruise on her cheek was evidence that she did indeed have something to fear. Yet she had never pressed me to stay at Trevarrah overnight, except on the occasion of the ball, and I would have thought that the evenings and nights would have been the time when she would have been at most risk from a bullying and violent husband.

But just at that moment, for all that I was concerned about her, Isobel's fears, real or imagined, were not my most pressing concern. There were too many other things on my mind, things that affected me personally.

Yesterday, I had given myself to Adam in a moment of passion. Yesterday, he had asked me to be his wife and I had been overjoyed. Today he had scarcely mentioned it, and I could not help wondering if he was having second thoughts.

And hanging over me like a dark cloud from which I could not escape was the suspicion that Adam had been involved in John's death. I had shied away from asking him directly; the strength of my feelings for him had made a coward of me. But somehow I had to learn the truth, however unpalatable it might be. For John's sake, so that his soul could rest in peace, and for my own, for I could not continue with the uncertainty. However much I longed to believe that Adam was entirely innocent, however much I longed to be his wife, I could not spend the rest of my life wondering if he had been responsible for the death of my brother.

'Isobel,' I said urgently, 'these *other things* you speak of… Do they have any connection with the Treasure?'

Her eyes flew up to mine, wide and dark; what little colour there had been in her cheeks drained away. Her mouth opened as if to speak, then closed again. She swayed slightly and I was afraid for a moment that she was going to faint.

'Why do you ask that?' she whispered.

I steeled myself. 'Has it?' I persisted. 'And do you know anything about why and how my brother died?'

A startled expression crossed her face. 'Your brother?'

'My brother, John,' I said. 'When they were boys together, he and Nicholas and Adam were searching for the Penrose Treasure. John told them he knew where it was hidden. And then he drowned at Old Trevarrah. Do you know anything about that?'

'No – no! I know nothing!' She shook her head violently from side to side. 'Nothing, I tell you!'

I did not believe her. She did know something, I was sure of it. For all her protestations, the guilt was written all over her face.

'Isobel...' I began, but before I could pursue my questioning I was interrupted by a loud hammering on the front door. I broke off, startled, and as I hesitated, the hammering came again, followed by a commotion – men's voices, raised in anger, and the indignant squeaking voice of Mary, the kitchen maid.

'What in the world...?' Isobel looked alarmed now.

'I'll go and find out.'

Both puzzled and frustrated, I marched into the great hall. Three men were there – the same three men as had accosted Adam that night as he drove me home. Mary fluttered anxiously.

'I tried to stop them, Tamsin, but they've forced their way in!'

'How dare you come into the house without being asked!' I was too annoyed at being interrupted, just as I had been on the point of getting the truth of John's death out of Isobel, to be frightened by these arrogant bullies. 'What do you want, anyway?'

'Nicholas Penrose!' The same man as before was the spokesman. 'He owes us a great deal of money, and we intend to make sure we get it!'

I was bristling now. 'Adam has already told you, this house belongs to him, not Nicholas. If you touch anything, you'll be sorry!'

'So, the mighty Penroses are hiding behind a woman's skirts now, are they?' the man said unpleasantly.

'Adam is not at home,' I said coldly, 'and Nicholas is in no condition to receive visitors. He was shot yesterday in the shoulder – as no doubt you know. And if you do not leave this house this instant, I shall send for the constable and have you arrested for attempted murder.'

The look of astonishment on the man's face was genuine, I had no doubt. I knew in that moment they had not been responsible for shooting Nicholas. But I was not about to relinquish my advantage. 'Please leave at once!'

The man stood his ground for a moment. 'And who are you, I'd like to know?'

'I,' I said haughtily, 'am Tamsin Hardy. I am betrothed to Adam Penrose. And if you do not do as I ask, and quickly, you will have him to answer to.'

–

They left. I think I had taken the wind out of their sails. They made a few more threats, as much to save face, I think, as anything else, but they left.

I closed the front door after them, a little shaken, but also jubilant. I had seen them off single-handed and it made me quite heady with a sense of power. I went back into the parlour dusting my hands.

'I don't think they'll be back in a hurry, though I do think Nicholas would be wise to settle his debts with them without delay.'

Isobel was staring at me wide-eyed.

'What did you say to them?'

'I told them I'd have them arrested for shooting Nicholas.'

'No.' She was still staring at me. 'I thought I heard you say...' she paused, as if unable for a moment to form the words. 'I thought you said that you were betrothed to Adam!'

'Oh!' I gave a small awkward laugh. 'That!'

'You were just trying to frighten them?' she asked. 'It can't be true, surely?'

I hesitated. What could I say?

'He has asked me to marry him,' I admitted.

For a long moment she looked at me agape, and I thought her expression was one of horror. Then she gave an incredulous little laugh.

'Adam has asked you to *marry* him?'

I nodded. 'Yesterday.'

And suddenly her face was wreathed in smiles.

'Oh Tamsin, that is wonderful news! I can scarcely believe it! You are to be my sister-in-law! Oh, there's nothing I'd like better!'

She opened her arms to me, and as we embraced I felt an enormous flood of relief. I had suspected Isobel would not want Adam to marry anyone, least of all me. It seemed I had been wrong.

But alongside the relief was an equally strong feeling of something that might almost have been panic. I had not yet given Adam my answer, yet in an unthinking moment I had, it seemed, committed myself.

With all my heart I hoped I would not live to regret it.

Fourteen

When Adam brought the trap for me in the late afternoon Isobel came out with me. Once again we had seen nothing of him all day and I was glad of that, for I felt awkward that I had told Isobel the news before giving Adam a formal answer. I had wondered whether I should admit as much to her, and ask her to say nothing until I had had the chance to speak with him, but pride forbade it.

Now, as she went towards him, I could only watch helplessly and try to hide my discomfiture.

'Well, Adam!' she greeted him. 'You are a dark horse and no mistake!'

Her blue eyes seemed to challenge him, and once again I was painfully aware of the intimacy that remained between them.

Adam looked at me questioningly.

'Isobel knows that you have asked me to marry you,' I said awkwardly.

'And I must say I am relieved to know that you have come to your senses at last,' Isobel said. 'Tamsin will make you a good wife. I only hope you will treat her well.'

After her seeming delight at my news it seemed an odd thing to say, when congratulations would have been more appropriate. Adam, however, appeared unfazed either by the fact that Isobel was appraised of his proposal, or by her strangely cool reaction to it.

'I assure you, Isobel, I have no intention of doing otherwise.' He looked at me again, one corner of his mouth lifting. 'And I am glad that you are so delighted at the prospect of being my wife, Tamsin, that you could not wait to share the news.'

My face flamed. 'It came about because… Oh, it's a long story. I'll tell you on the way home.'

I made to climb up into the trap.

'A gentleman would help his future wife,' Isobel said reprovingly.

Again that half-smile. 'And if she would give her future husband the chance, I would do so gladly. It is no indication of a lack of respect for her, I assure you.'

'I hope not.' Still there was that strange edge to Isobel's voice. 'So what are your plans, Adam? I cannot prise out of Tamsin when the wedding is to be, let alone where you intend to make your home.'

She had not so much as mentioned that to me, but my flush deepened. Her meaning was all too clear and Adam could not fail to grasp it.

'We have not yet had time to discuss such things ourselves,' he said. 'When we have, I promise you, Isobel, you will be the first to know.'

'I certainly hope so. You owe me that, Adam, at least.'

I was growing more uncomfortable by the minute; I was mightily relieved when Adam took up the reins and urged the horse to move off.

'So,' he said to me as we headed for the track, 'it seems you have decided to accept my proposal. This morning I was less than hopeful. Perhaps it was all the talk of hidden treasure that changed your mind.'

'Of course not!' I said sharply. 'And I'm very sorry that I let it slip in front of Isobel before speaking to you again.'

'Don't apologize, or I'll think you are having second thoughts,' he said wryly. 'I'm very pleased, Tamsin. You have made me a very happy man and I promise you won't regret it, whatever Isobel might say.'

There was almost a question in his tone, as if he was wondering what she had said to me. I ignored it.

'I should explain how it came about,' I said primly.

'There's no need...'

'You should know in any case,' I persisted. 'Those men came to the house – the ones who accosted us a few weeks ago.'

I went on to relate what had happened, and Adam's face darkened.

'The devil they did! Oh, Nicholas has created a fine old mess for himself – and for me, too. Well, there's nothing for it. I shall have to find the wherewithal to pay them what he owes, or see him in a debtors' gaol.'

'You'd do that?' I asked.

He shrugged. 'I cannot see that I have any choice. But I'll let him sweat a while longer. It's time he learned his lesson, if such a thing is possible, which I have to say I doubt. When the cards are on the table or the dice roll, Nicholas seems unable to help himself.'

'And you were as bad once yourself, from what I can make out,' I said.

'Young men do foolish things,' Adam said lightly. 'I am not proud of the way I behaved, and I know I caused my father much heartache and anxiety. But at least I have learned the error of my ways.'

Young men do foolish things. Doubt niggled at me once more. I had said no more to Isobel about my dreadful suspicion, for the moment had passed, and with it my resolve to try to learn the truth, but now, once again, it was there, niggling like a thorn in my flesh.

'Well, at least it seems we do not have to keep what is between us a secret any more.' Adam glanced across at me. 'Perhaps it is time I renewed my acquaintance with your mother. You have no father, I know, whom I should ask for your hand, but at least I can assure your mother that I intend to take very good care of you. In her own way she worries about you, I am sure.'

Warmth trickled through my veins, washing away the doubt.

'That is a kind thought, Adam,' I said. 'But perhaps it would be too much of a shock for her if we suddenly announced that we are to be wed. Let her get to know you first, and become used to the idea that we are friends.'

'Oh Tamsin!' That crooked smile quirked the corner of his mouth. 'Still delaying the moment then?'

'No – really!' I protested. 'Apart from that one time when you came to the house, it's years since she set eyes on you. And on that occasion, if you recall, she thought you were your father. I really think it would be best if she got to know you a little first.'

'Then we'll rectify that at once,' he said decisively. 'This very afternoon.'

'But not to mention marriage...'

'Not to mention marriage, if that's what you think best. Just to begin to plant the seeds.'

'You do understand, don't you, that she can be very confused still at times,' I cautioned. 'I'm never sure what she might say or do...'

'I understand that. Stop worrying, Tamsin!' He reached for my hand, pulled me towards him. Though my skin prickled at his touch and I yearned with my whole being to be in his arms, I was afraid that once again I would be unable to control my desire for more, still more, and we would end up lying in the bracken as we had yesterday.

'Adam – no…' I protested weakly.

He raised an eyebrow. 'You don't want to kiss me?'

'No… yes… of course I want to kiss you! Too much! That's why… Adam, we must not do what we did yesterday again. Not until we are wed. It's dreadfully wrong, and…'

'Wrong? How can it be wrong?' he demanded. 'When two people love one another…'

Love. The word I had longed to hear. My heart lifted, my senses spun a little closer to that vortex that I knew was waiting to suck me in; the vortex of desire so compelling that it eclipsed all common sense, all good intentions.

'But, as it happens,' Adam went on, 'I agree with you. I don't want you to be with child when you come to me up the aisle. I don't want people saying that I am only marrying you to save you from ruin. Yesterday we may have got away without any… consequences. But we won't be lucky for ever. Not when there is such fire in my loins and you are so ripe for the picking.'

I felt the flush beginning again in my cheeks at his frank choice of words.

'You make it sound like…'

'Like all of nature? And so it is! But I intend to curb my instincts until I have you in the marriage bed. So you have nothing to fear from giving me a kiss.'

I still looked doubtful. Heaven alone knew I had been unable to curb my own, and everyone knew a man was far less capable of control than a woman!

'In any case,' Adam said, 'I would scarcely be able to face your mother, knowing I had just lain with her

daughter, and the fact written all over us. Even if she is...
confused. I suspect she would know, just the same.'

'Just a kiss, then?'

'Just a kiss. You have my word for it.'

'Very well then.'

The moment his lips were on mine, I felt that treacherous response stirring the deepest part of me. My lips
moved beneath his, my arms wound about his neck, my
body pressed against him, drawn by that unseen force like
a metal filing to a magnet. How could I have fooled myself
for even a moment that a kiss could be enough? For me,
with this man, it never could be.

I clung to him and felt as if my heart was being sucked
out of my body; sharp, insistent twists darted deep within
me, the whole of my skin felt sensitized.

And then Adam drew back, smiling down at me.

'By God, Tamsin, you are a temptress and no mistake!
"A kiss," you say, "no more." And then you do everything
in your power to set me afire!'

'No! I...'

'You are quite right,' he said. 'One kiss will lead to
another and then on to something else. I think I should
get you home as quickly as I can before you try me too
far.'

'I'm sorry,' I said humbly.

And: 'So you should be!' he said. But there was no
rancour in his tone. 'I tell you, Tamsin, I am very much
looking forward to having you in my bed!'

He clicked the reins and, as the pony broke into a trot,
I was left marvelling at his self-control, and ashamed by
my lack of it.

It was Adam's usual practice to drop me off at the end of the track leading to our home, but today he trotted the pony along the row of cottages. I glanced at Ruth's windows, suddenly self-conscious, but of my sister there was no sign. I guessed she was working in her kitchen and I was glad of it. Unaccountably I was nervous enough at the prospect of encountering Mammy with Adam at my shoulder; it would have been doubly awkward if Ruth became curious and decided to come around and see why Adam had accompanied me home.

I wondered what she would think when she heard the news. She was somewhat in awe of the Penrose family. She had never grown comfortable with them as I had, and they were her husband's employers into the bargain.

I opened the door and Adam followed me into the kitchen. Mammy was sitting in the chair beside the fire, a piece of tatting in her hands. Old and forgetful she might be, but she had never lost the knack of making beautiful things, and it helped her to pass the time whilst I was out all day.

'Mammy,' I said, 'I've brought someone to see you. You remember Adam, don't you?'

'Adam?' Her faded eyes were puzzled.

'Adam Penrose,' I said. 'Ralph's son.'

'Oh!' She smiled suddenly, that lovely smile that could transform her face and make it young again. 'Oh yes! You came before, didn't you? And I thought then as I thought now that… Oh, I am a foolish old woman!'

'I believe I reminded you of my father,' Adam said easily. 'Everyone says the same – that I take after him. I'm quite used to it.'

Mammy was trying to rise. She had, I imagine, been sitting in one position for too long and her legs had gone to sleep.

'Don't get up, Mrs Hardy,' Adam urged her. 'I don't want to disturb you. I only came in to bid you good day.'

'Well, it's good to see you, Adam. But, my goodness, it certainly is hard to believe how like Ralph you've grown! He'd be proud of you, and that's a fact!'

'I hope he would be, Mrs Hardy,' Adam said. 'It's a sad thing for me that he met his maker while I was far away and I never had the chance to say goodbye, nor to show him I was no longer the ne'er-do-well he thought me.'

'Oh, he knew that was just youthful high spirits! Why, he said as much to me the last time I saw him.' Mammy had become quite animated. '"The army will be the making of him" – those were his very words. And it pleased him, ill as he was, to think that.'

'You saw him after his illness struck?' Adam asked sharply. 'But I understood he was confined to his bed all of those last weeks.'

'He sent for me,' Mammy said. 'Oh, he was very poorly, but...'

'He *sent* for you?' Adam repeated.

'You must have got that wrong, Mammy,' I said, embarrassed. 'You know how confused you get.'

'Of course I haven't got it wrong!' Mammy said crossly. 'He sent for me and I went to see him.'

'Now why would he do that, Mammy?' I asked her gently. 'It wasn't Ralph you used to work for. It was his wife, and that's a very long time ago.'

'There's plenty you don't know about Ralph and me, my girl!' Mammy said tartly. 'Plenty you'll never know. I went to see him, and...' Her eyes clouded suddenly. 'Oh, what's the matter with me? It's all going again! Why can't I remember?'

My embarrassment was deepening by the moment. I sought desperately for some way of changing the subject.

'Have the children been in to see you today?' I asked.

'Mm…? Oh yes, I think so…' But clearly she had gone off into some world of her own.

I looked at Adam, imploring him to understand. He smiled.

'That's beautiful lace you're making, Mrs Hardy. As fine as ever I've seen. Is it to trim a gown for Tamsin? She'll need a fine one soon…'

'The key,' Mammy said. Her face was taut with concentration.

'Mammy…'

'The key!' she said again. 'He gave me the key and said I was to give it to you.' She turned to me. 'Can you get it, Tamsin? I don't feel at all safe on that stool.'

'Mammy, Adam doesn't want that old key!' I spoke as patiently as if she were a child. 'It's nothing but rubbish, discarded long ago.'

'It's Ralph's key!' Mammy was becoming agitated. 'He gave it to me to keep safe for Adam. And I was to tell him…' She broke off and her face puckered. 'Oh, I don't know what I was to tell him! Oh Ralph, I'm so sorry! It's gone… all gone… I must remember! I must! He said to tell Adam…'

I turned to Adam.

'I think perhaps it's best you go.'

He nodded. I could see he was as anxious as I was about the effect his visit had had on Mammy, but when he spoke to her his voice was soothing and he smiled at her.

'It's time I was leaving, Mrs Hardy. But I'll come and see you again soon, and perhaps by then you will have remembered what it was you were to tell me.'

Mammy was wringing her hands, quite distraught. 'I don't know! Oh, foolish woman that I am! I don't know...'

I went with Adam to the door.

'I am so sorry,' I said. 'She's not mad, really she's not, but she does get the past and the present all mixed up in her mind. Seeing you confused her...'

'Strangely enough, she did not seem confused to me.' Adam's face was thoughtful. 'Forgetful, yes, and agitated because of it, but clear enough about what she remembered.'

'What she *thought* she remembered.' I was still mortified by Mammy's insinuation that there had been something between her and Ralph that went beyond the relationship of an employer and employee. 'She's alone too much and reality becomes skewed. I'm beginning to think I'm wrong to leave her all day.'

'When we are married, you won't have to,' Adam said. 'In fact, there's no need for you to leave her all day now. There's room in the trap – she could come with you to Trevarrah.'

'And what would Isobel have to say about that?' I asked.

His mouth hardened. 'What Isobel says is neither here nor there. It is my house, and I think it's high time I became master of it. Summer's coming – your mama could sit in the grounds in the sun and nap the days away, or chat to Pol as she prepares vegetables. The company would do her the world of good.'

'That's very kind,' I said. 'We'll talk about it.'

'Do more than talk.' Adam swung himself up into the trap. 'And as for kind – it's simply practical. How can you rest easy if you're worried all the time about your mother? Much better that she should be where you can keep an eye on her. Especially since Trevarrah will soon be her home in any case.'

I said nothing. I was not so sure how Mammy was going to take to being uprooted from the house she had lived in for so many long years, but I could not see what the alternative was either.

As the trap moved off, I turned to go back inside, but Ruth's door opened and she emerged, cautious, but round-eyed with curiosity.

'Has he gone? That was Adam Penrose, wasn't it? What was he doing in Mammy's house?'

'He stopped by to see Mammy.' I took a deep breath. 'Ruth, there's something you should know, but I want you to keep it to yourself for the time being. Will you promise me you'll do that?'

'Well yes – if you want me to.' Ruth's eyes were rounder than ever. 'But what…?'

'Adam has asked me to marry him,' I said.

'What?'

I smiled briefly. 'It's a shock to you, I expect. It's a shock to *me*! But we… well, we've grown close these last months, and…'

'You and Adam! Lawks, Tamsin, I can scarcely believe it! You mean that I am to be related by marriage to the Penroses?'

'Yes,' I said. 'Oh, I know we've always looked on them as local gentry, but Adam is still a man like any other.'

Not like any other, my heart reminded me. *The only man who has ever set my pulses racing and my skin a-tingle. The only*

man who has ever made me forget myself so that I behaved like
a common slut and could not care...

'Anyway,' I went on, 'I don't want Mammy told just yet. I want her to come to accepting it gradually. So, Adam came in to see her and begin to get her used to the idea of him being around. But she did get into a dreadful state. He seems to remind her of Ralph as he used to be, and she started burbling all kinds of nonsense – that Ralph had sent for her when he was taken ill, amongst other things, and that she had been to Trevarrah to see him.'

Ruth frowned. 'That's not nonsense, Tamsin. She did go to see him, not so long before he died.'

It was my turn to be astonished. 'What? She went to Trevarrah?'

Ruth nodded. 'Yes. Dr Warburton came with a message that he wanted to see her. He offered to send the trap for her, but Mammy said she'd rather walk as it would cause too much talk if she accepted his offer.'

'But why?' I asked. 'Why would he send for Mammy?'

'I don't know,' Ruth said. 'I asked her about it, of course, but she wouldn't say. Quite secretive, she was – and you know how Mammy can keep her lip buttoned when she has a mind to. All I know is that she was very distressed when she got home. I think it upset her, seeing Ralph so poorly.' She hesitated, biting her lip, then went on: 'And though there may have been nothing in it, I have to tell you that Alice Weaver reckoned there was talk once in Mallen that there was something going on between her and Ralph Penrose, if you take my meaning.'

'Oh my goodness!' I closed my eyes briefly. 'You mean...?'

'It's just talk, Tamsin,' Ruth said. 'And it all happened a long time ago – if it happened at all.' She smiled slyly.

'But if there *was* anything in it… well, perhaps I shouldn't be so surprised about you and Adam. It could be just history repeating itself. Though he's free to do as he likes, of course, and his father was not. Whatever, I shouldn't worry your head about it.'

Not worry my head! Why, it was spinning!

'There's something else,' I said, dragging myself back from the edge of a morass of confused thoughts and emotions, 'Adam has suggested I take Mammy with me to Trevarrah each day for the time being, so that she is not here on her own so much and—'

'Whatever do you mean?' Ruth asked sharply.

'Just that I do not think it is good for her to spend so much time alone in her condition,' I explained.

At times, when she thought some criticism of her was implied, Ruth could be quite fiery. This was apparently one of them.

'Are you saying I neglect her?' she demanded. 'Because if so…'

'Of course I'm saying no such thing!' I replied hastily. 'But you have your home and children, Ruth, and—'

'I'm in and out of her house all day!' Ruth protested. 'Of course I don't leave her alone for too long! Charlie was with her for a good long while this morning, and she had her midday meal with us. Why ever should she want to go to Trevarrah?'

'I didn't say she wanted to.' I hastened to try and pour oil on the troubled waters. 'I just thought…'

'There's no need for that at all!' Ruth cut in indignantly. 'I can't believe you would suggest such a thing, Tamsin. She's far better off in her own home with me to care for her.'

Through the open door of her cottage came the thin wail of little Billy.

'I shall have to go,' Ruth said. 'We'll talk again later.'

I nodded, relieved at the interruption. 'Yes, of course. Go and see to Billy.'

I went back into the cottage. To my alarm, in my absence Mammy had dragged the stool over to the dresser and climbed upon it to reach down the jug, which was already in her hand.

'Mammy!' I said sharply. 'What do you think you are doing?'

And then, it seemed, everything happened at once. The pot slipped from Mammy's grasp, she made a sharp unthinking move to try and save it and lost her balance. As the jug fell, smashing to smithereens on the flagged floor, I rushed forward to try to save Mammy.

Too late. Before I reached her she had fallen, her head cracking on to the flagstones amidst the slivers of pottery.

'Mammy! Oh, dear God!'

I was on my hands and knees beside her. For a moment she lay quite still, dazed by the fall and the knock to her head, and my heart came into my throat.

'Mammy! Don't try to move now! Just lie still for a minute! Oh, why did you have to climb up on that stool? It's not safe!'

'Oh!' Mammy's hand went to her head, rubbing it. Her face was screwed up with pain. 'The key! I had to get the key!'

'Never mind the silly key!'

But, incredibly, she was struggling to sit up, scrabbling amongst the bits of pottery and the strewn contents of the jug until her fingers reached it. She folded it in the palm of her hand, pressing it tight against her breast as if it were some precious jewel instead of a lump of useless tarnished metal.

'Oh Ralph!' It was just a whisper, more to herself than to me. It was as if she had forgotten her fall, forgotten that I was there beside her, forgotten everything and gone faraway into a world of her own.

Anxiety ached in me. What damage had she done to herself now – and all because of her obsession with this key? What was my dear Mammy coming to?

'Oh Ralph!' she whispered again. 'I won't let you down! I'll do it now. It's going to be all right now.'

'Mammy...'

She looked at me and it was as if the cloud had lifted from her face. Her eyes were clear now, the same clear eyes I remembered, the clear, kind eyes that had been my refuge and my hope through all the years of my childhood and my growing.

'Do stop fussing, Tamsin!' she said. 'I bumped my head, that's all. And I remember now! I remember what it was that he wanted me to do. But I need you to help me.'

'Of course I'll help you, Mammy,' I said. 'But first let's get you up off this floor!'

Mammy was small and light as a child, and, astonishingly, she seemed scarcely the worse for her fall. She winced a little, it is true, as the weight went on to her leg, but not so much as to give me cause to think she had done it serious damage, though she would, I felt sure, have a bump on her head the size of an egg by tomorrow. I fetched the dish of butter and rubbed a knob of it into the sore spot, as she had used to do for us when we were little and fell over and banged our heads, and she grumbled a little about the mess it would make in her hair.

'We can always wash it out under the pump in the yard,' I teased. 'You'll decide the grease isn't so bad when you are faced with a stream of cold water, I'll be bound!'

She shook her head. 'What a slattern Ralph would think I've become! He'd never give me a second glance now. All lines and wrinkles – and greasy hair to top it off! You make the most of your looks while you still have them, Tamsin. Goodness knows, they're soon gone.'

The allusion to Ralph made me uncomfortable again. 'Why do you keep talking about Ralph today?' I asked. 'I think you should be careful what you say, or secrets may come out that you'd really rather keep to yourself.'

A sweet smile lit her face.

'He was a good man, Tamsin. I've heard it said he was a hard one, too, but he was never anything but good to me. And that boy is so like him! It gave me a fair turn to see him standing there – like seeing a ghost. Yes, I can see why Ralph thought so highly of him, for all that he'd led him a merry dance. I can see it all, now that I've remembered. Oh, I've been tardy, though! How long is it now that he's been home from the war?'

'He came home in the autumn, I understand,' I said, 'and now it's spring.'

'Oh! So long!' Mammy said. 'And when was my accident?'

'In December,' I told her.

'Then why didn't I…? Oh, I was ill, wasn't I? That's why I didn't go to see Adam right away! I had a bad chest and I could hardly draw breath. Yes, that's the reason, of course!'

'Mammy, you are talking in riddles,' I said, though I could not help remarking that her recollection of what had happened was clearer than at any time since she was attacked. 'I still don't know what in the world you are talking about.'

And she looked me straight in the eye, shaking her head a little as if despairing of me for being dim-witted and dull as an overused carving knife that has not seen a steel in a twelvemonth, and said the very last thing I had ever expected to hear her say.

'Why, the Treasure, of course, Tamsin! The Arthurian Treasure! What else could it be?'

The relief of remembering made her light-headed. She had known all the while that there was something she had to do that was vitally important, and struggling to recall what it was had made her head ache. Now, at last, the mists had lifted. She looked at the key she held tightly between her hands and remembered how it had come into her possession.

It had been Dr Warburton who had brought her the message that Ralph wanted to see her. He had stopped by after a visit to Trevarrah and passed on Ralph's request. And he had been blunt regarding the seriousness of Ralph's condition.

'You'd better go soon if you want to see him alive,' he advised her. 'He's a very sick man, and though I am doing all I can for him, I fear he's not long for this world.'

The news had shaken her. Though it was long years now since they had decided that, for the sake of both their families, they must end the passionate affair that had consumed them, yet, when time had quenched the fires, affection had remained. She had seen him but rarely over the past years, but the old bond was still intact, a friendship which was as constant as the seasons, unchanging as the rugged Cornish landscape. To know that soon he would be gone for ever beyond her reach was an ache deep within her, a heaviness in her heart and in her limbs as she walked with the vigour of a woman half her age across the moors, where the gorse was in full glorious yellow bloom and skylarks soared on the warm summer breeze.

She had found him every bit as ill as Dr Warburton had described. He lay in the great four-poster bed where once they had shared hours of stolen loving, scarcely able to move his heavy frame unaided. His breathing was laboured, his cheeks unhealthily flushed, though there was a clammy pallor to the skin around his sunken eyes and he seemed to be dozing. The ache in her heart grew fiercer; it was dreadful to see him so, he who had once been so lean and strong.

When he opened his eyes and saw her beside his bed, he smiled faintly – a parody of the smile that had once made her pulses quicken and tempted her to dangerous ground where she knew she should not stray, and held out his hand to her.

'Rose. You came, then. It's good to see you.'

She took his hand and squeezed it. Unlike his swollen body, his fingers were all sinew and bone and there was a tremor in them.

'Well, of course I came!' she said. 'What else would I do?'

'I knew I could depend on you.' His voice was husky, tired. 'I wanted to see you one last time, my dear. And I have a favour to ask of you too. Something very important I want you to do for me. I am dying, Rose.'

'Oh, don't talk so silly!' she protested, though it was all too obvious he spoke the truth. 'You'll be up and about again in no time.'

'I doubt I'll ever leave this bed again, Rose. You know it as well as I, so don't treat me like a fool. Anyway, I'm ready to go. Most of life's pleasures have been denied me this last year and more, and I'm not afraid to meet my maker. But there's one matter unresolved, and I could think of no one to put my trust in but you.'

She cocked her head to one side, eyes narrowed.

'What are you talking about, Ralph?'

'The Treasure. The silver platters Arthur and his knights dined off at Camelot. And the goblets too. You know I told you long ago how the Penroses had been their guardians for generations, the secret of their hiding place passed down from father to son.'

'I remember.'

The scent of his skin as she lay in his arms replete from lovemaking. His voice, low and muffled against her hair, talking of what sounded like nothing but a romantic fairy tale...

'Adam must be the next guardian, but I have never yet revealed to him where I put them for safe keeping. He was too young and wild, and I suppose I thought there was plenty of time – that I would live for years, if not for ever. Now my time is almost gone, and Adam is far away on the other side of the world. When he comes home – pray God he will come safe home – I shall be in my grave and unable to tell him what he needs to know. Will you tell him for me, my dear?'

'I?' She was startled. 'But surely Nicholas...'

He shook his head sadly. 'Nicholas, I'm afraid, is every bit as bad as Adam ever was – worse, for he's old enough to know better. He'd gamble away hundreds of years of legend and history in an evening if he knew where to find it. No, I can't trust Nicholas. But Adam... he'll have changed for the better by now, I trust. Fighting for his country will have made a man of him. What I am asking, Rose, is that when he comes home you will come to see him and tell him what I am about to tell you. Will you do it? For me? For old times' sake?'

She spread her hands helplessly. 'Well – yes, I suppose so.'
With an enormous effort he shifted his bulk, leaning towards her
and lowering his voice as if he thought the walls had ears.

'The Treasure is hidden at the Old Trevarrah mine,' he
rasped. 'There is a false wall in the old engine house with a cavity
behind, large enough to take the chest containing the Treasure.
Tell Adam that. He'll find it – though he scarcely needs to. It's
safer left where it is. Just so long as the secret is not lost. And
one more thing...'

With another enormous effort he reached out to open the
drawer in the table beside his bed and fumbled in it, eventually
managing to retrieve a heavy key, discoloured with age.

'This is the key to the engine house, Rose.' He held it out to
her. 'Take it and keep it safe until you can deliver it into Adam's
hands.'

She hesitated. 'Supposing Adam... supposing he does not
return? What then, Ralph?'

He sighed wearily. 'You will do whatever you think is for
the best, Rose. Maybe in time Nicholas will mend his ways. If
not...' He gathered his strength. 'But Adam will return. I know
he will.'

She took the key, a little unwilling, yet unable to refuse.
'Thank you, my dear. Now I can die with an easy mind.' That
brief smile, a mere shadow of the one she had known and loved,
yet recognizable still. 'It's been good to see you one last time,
too. I've thought about you a good deal over the last years, you
know, and never more than in these last months when I've been
tied to my bed. We should never have parted, Rose.'

'We had no choice.'

'There's always a choice. We should have had the courage to
break free and follow our hearts.'

'And what of the families we would have been forced to leave
behind? I couldn't have lived with the guilt, Ralph, and neither

could you. Not if you are the man I think you are. We would never have spent an easy night. Better to keep our dreams safe inside. Better that at least our memories are unsullied.' She leaned over and kissed him, her lips cool on his flushed cheek, and for a moment his gnarled hand grasped hers so that the key pressed into her palm.

'Goodbye, dear Rose. I doubt we shall meet again in this world. God take care of you.'

'And you, my love.' Tears pricked behind her eyes; her voice faltered. 'And don't worry any more. I'll do as you ask.'

He sank back against the pillows, exhausted.

In the doorway, she looked back at him for just a moment, this shell of the man he had once been. At least he looked at peace now. Her heart full, she turned and left.

She never had seen him alive again. Not so long afterwards, news had reached her that Ralph had gone. She had attended his funeral, a shadowy figure watching from a distance as his coffin was lowered into the Penrose family grave, keeping her tears inside.

There had been nothing to do then but to wait for Adam's return. But fate had intervened, first with the debilitating illness which kept her housebound, and then the strange attack, of which she could still remember nothing.

But at least she had remembered her promise to Ralph, remembered what he had asked of her. Nothing else mattered.

'I need your help, Tamsin,' she said.

And knew her dear daughter would not fail her.

237

Fifteen

When Mammy finished speaking there were tears in my eyes. All this and I had known nothing of it! To me, Mammy had always simply been Mammy, the one who had tended and cared for me when I was a child, and for whom I now tended and cared as best I could. I loved her with all my heart, yet now I realized there was so much about her that I did not know at all.

I had always imagined there had never been anyone for her but my father; now I was seeing a woman who had once been young and vibrant and in love, just as I was in love with Adam. Yet all this she had kept hidden deep inside. Her secret. Her passion, her heartache.

The bond between her and Ralph must have been strong indeed. She was the one he had trusted and turned to at the end, for all that they had had little contact these last years. And now she was trusting me with Ralph's secret because she was too frail to be able to do what he had asked of her.

'You must give the key to Adam,' Mammy said, 'and tell him where the Treasure is hidden. That was what Ralph wanted. Adam will know what to do.'

I nodded, remembering what Adam had said to me. He had feared the secret of its location had died with his father. Yet all the time it was concealed within the walls

238

of a ruined building he must pass a dozen or more times every single week.

I remembered too how he had talked to me of his plans for reopening the Old Trevarrah workings. Would he have come upon the hiding place if the engine house was renovated? Very likely not. Though the roof had fallen in and weeds grew thick around the door and windows, the walls were still as stout as ever they had been, built to last for generations. He might have worked within feet of the Treasure and never known.

'I'll tell him tomorrow,' I said.

'And give him the key.'

'I think,' I said, 'that you should give it to him yourself. I'll ask him to come and see you again.' I smiled. 'To think you tried to give it to him this very day and I thought you were talking nonsense!'

'Well, I expect I was,' Mammy said. 'I couldn't remember what it was for, could I? All I knew was that it was important. I expect he thinks me a fine fool, Tamsin!'

I put my arm about her.

'I'm sure he thinks no such thing, Mammy. Now, don't you think we should have some tea?'

That night I went to bed happy. It sang in my veins, that happiness. Partly because Mammy was so much more her old self, but mostly because I was going to be Adam's wife.

Until now I had not really taken it in. Everything had happened so fast, and events crowded in so thickly, I had not had the chance to savour it. Why, I had not even been certain he was serious about his proposal, or whether or not I should accept it if he was. But now...

I closed my eyes and let myself float on a tide of excitement and happy anticipation.

I loved him; not for a moment could I doubt that. And though he was a man of few words, I could almost believe that he loved me in return. Why else would he ask me to marry him? I had nothing to offer but myself. He could have had his pick of girls from the best families in the county, yet he had chosen me.

And I could scarcely believe that once Mammy had also loved his father. It was as if what could not be between them was now being fulfilled through me and Adam. And it felt so right, a crown for my own happiness.

I fell asleep at last, cocooned in drowsy contentment. But sometime during the night my pleasant dreams became confused, and when I woke, before dawn, it was to an edge of something like foreboding.

Nothing had changed, but there was a shadow over my happiness and I did not know the reason why. It frightened me, that foreboding, as it always did, but, with an effort of will, I pushed it away.

I was just being silly. It was my puritan spirit, nothing more, trying to tell me I had no God-given right to such happiness. Well, I wasn't going to entertain such notions for a moment. This was the most special time in the whole of my life. And I was determined not to let anything spoil it.

I went singing out along the track when it was time for Adam to come and collect me. I wondered if he might be early; I could not wait to see him, and hoped he might feel the same way. But he was not yet waiting and there was no sign of him on the moor land as far as I could see.

What would he say when I told him what Mammy had told me? He would be very surprised, I felt sure, to learn that all this time the key to the Treasure had been in the safe keeping of my own dear Mammy. And he would be relieved, too, for he must have been concerned that the inheritance that had been passed down through generations had seemed to be lost for ever.

What would he do with it? If he were to sell it, the value of the silver alone would put an end to all his money worries, but I did not think that was what his father had intended. The intrinsic value of the inheritance was price-less; it should be saved for future generations of Penroses, though it did seem a shame to think it was hidden away from view. A magnet for thieves it might be, and in more turbulent times perhaps it had been wise to conceal it where looters would not find it, but I would have liked to think that when we were married perhaps we could display it in our home, or at least make it accessible so that we – and our children – could enjoy it.

At last the trap appeared on the horizon; I started out eagerly to meet it. But as it came closer I saw not Adam in the driving seat, but Rudge.

Disappointment welled in me, and with it an edge of alarm, an echo of the foreboding I had felt when I awoke. Why had Adam not come himself, this morning of all mornings?

'Where is Adam?' I asked anxiously as I climbed up into the trap. 'Is he...?'

Rudge's faded eyes surveyed me for a long moment with something I might almost have taken for curiosity. The servants had no idea, of course, as yet, what was between us – or did they? Had it been there for all to see? Did they whisper behind closed doors? But if they did, it was likely they supposed that Adam was simply taking advantage of a country girl, companion to his brother's wife, and she too besotted with him to refuse to allow him to use her. Certainly it would never enter their heads that he would go so far as to even think of marrying her!

And Rudge, in any case, was no gossip. He was a solid man of the earth, slow-thinking and even slower of speech.

'He asked o' me to come for 'ee this morning, Tamsin,' he said at length.

'Well, yes, I can see that,' I said impatiently. 'What I'm wondering is why.'

'I'm not a one to ask questions,' Rudge replied after an annoyingly long interval. 'I just does as I'm bid.'

I thought I would get no more out of him, but after a few moments he added: 'He's off to Plymouth on some business or other as far as I do know.'

'Plymouth!' I exclaimed. 'Whatever business can be taking him to Plymouth?'

Rudge merely shrugged his narrow shoulders, clucking to the pony, and we had no further conversation.

As we approached Trevarrah, a tall figure on horseback emerged from the stable block, and even from a distance I knew it was Adam. There was no mistaking Lancelot, and Adam's seat upon him was distinctive too – straight back, long stirrups. My heart missed a beat, as it always did at that first glimpse of him, and I was very glad we were in time for me to speak to him before he left for such a long journey.

As he neared, I could see that he was indeed dressed for some business meeting, in a smart redingote and light-coloured breeches, though he wore no hat.

'Tamsin!' He reined in, and Rudge did likewise. 'I'm sorry I could not come for you myself today, but it was imperative I made an early start. I have had word from an acquaintance in Plymouth that he may be willing to back me in the venture we discussed, and I must waste no time in speaking to him face to face before he can change his mind! It does mean, though, that I shall likely be away from Trevarrah for a few days.'

'A few days!' I echoed, dismayed.

Adam nodded. 'I can't see that I can get there, attend to my business, and be back any sooner.'

'But...' What I had to tell Adam was making me burn with impatience. 'Could we have just a few moments alone?' I asked.

He frowned. 'Can't it wait until I get back?'

'I suppose so. But it really is very important.'

'Well, just as long as you make it quick. I really should be on my way.' He moved impatiently, and, as he did so, something caught my attention.

A button was missing from his redingote.

Disbelieving, I flicked my glance down the well-fitting garment.

Silver. All the other buttons were silver.

And one was missing.

My heart seemed to stop beating. Oh surely...! Surely not...!

But there was no denying it. The remaining buttons were identical to the one I had found on the floor of Mammy's cottage on the day she had been attacked, the button I had kept because it might be a clue to the identity of the person who had savagely beaten her and left her for dead.

There could be only one explanation. That person was none other than Adam.

'Make it quick, then, Tamsin,' Adam was saying.

My head was spinning round and round.

It was Adam who had attacked Mammy. But why – why?

The Treasure. It must have been because she knew the whereabouts of the Treasure and had possession of the key to its hiding place, and somehow he knew it. But why attack her? It made no sense. According to what she had told me, it was Adam to whom Ralph had asked her to reveal the secret. She would have told him of it willingly.

Or had she been confused even before that day? She had, after all, been ill. Had she taken him for Nicholas? They were quite similar in appearance, and if she had believed Adam to still be in America, perhaps she had refused to divulge the information entrusted to her. Had he then lost his temper and tried to beat the information from her? I could scarcely believe it – yet I had seen with my own eyes what a terrible temper he possessed when roused, and how it could transform him from the man I loved to a monster.

Even worse, Isobel had accused him of being the one to shoot Nicholas in anger, and Joshua had risked capture to warn me of him, saying that he believed one or both of the Penrose boys had been responsible for the death of my brother.

I had discounted it all because I wanted to. I had fallen under Adam's spell, and love and desire had made me blind. But now I could ignore the facts no longer.

Adam must have been in Mammy's cottage that terrible day. The missing button proved it. And I felt sure it had been torn off as she fought for her life.

'Tamsin?' Adam was looking at me curiously and his tone was impatient. 'If you want to speak to me alone, you'll have to get down from the trap.'

Somehow I found my voice. 'It doesn't matter.'

'I thought you said it was important.'

'No, really. It will keep until you get back.'

Adam shrugged. He looked irritated, impatient to be gone. 'Very well. I'll see you in a few days' time.'

He turned Lancelot, kicked him to a canter.

I watched him go in a haze of misery and confusion. Was this the man who had made love to me and asked me to marry him? He had not even kissed me goodbye.

Not that I wanted him to. I shrank from the thought of the intimacy that had been between us, just as I knew I would have shrunk from his touch.

How could I have allowed passion to blind me so? And how could I still feel such turmoil, as if my heart was being wrenched from my body?

But one thing was certain. I could not give him the information for which he had beaten Mammy to within an inch of her life.

And I certainly could not marry him.

—

What was I to do? As Rudge drew up outside the great front door my thoughts were still whirling in crazy, wretched circles.

It must have been fate that had made him put on that redingote today, and fate that we had arrived at Trevarrah before he had left for Plymouth. It must have been fate that had drawn my eyes to the missing button. Another moment and I would have told him the secret of where the Treasure was concealed.

Well, I could not tell him now. His father would never have intended the Treasure to pass into his hands if he had known how unworthy of it he was; that he was capable of attacking and half-killing the woman Ralph had loved and trusted with the secret, in a cowardly and greedy attempt to discover its whereabouts. Perhaps Mammy had known that and that was why she had refused to tell him, but now it was lost in the mists of her memory, along with the identity of her attacker.

Whatever, I could not believe it would be right to tell him. But I could not keep it to myself either. It was the Penrose family treasure and it belonged with the Penrose family. I must pass the information on to one of them.

And that person must be the one I trusted. My friend, Isobel.

–

I found her in the small parlour working at her loom. She looked up as I came in and I think my distress must have been written all over my face, for her welcoming smile faded.

'Tamsin? Is something wrong?'

'Oh, Isobel!' I hardly knew where to begin. As I stood there, hesitating, she got up and came to me, taking me by the arm.

'Come and sit down, my dear. What is it?' Her small face puckered with anxiety. 'It's not your mother, is it? She's not worse?'

I shook my head wordlessly and looked around.

'Nicholas…? Is he…?'

'Nicholas has gone to the mine. He shouldn't have – his shoulder is still paining him badly – but he insists he is fit, and, when Nicholas makes up his mind to something, I am powerless to persuade him otherwise. Adam has gone to Plymouth on business. So we won't be interrupted.'

She led me to the sofa, and gratefully I sank on to it, sitting bolt upright and pleating my skirt between my fingers.

'Is it Adam?' Isobel pressed me. 'Has he done something to upset you?'

Something to upset me! It was such an understatement I did not know whether to laugh or cry. I did neither. I drew a long, trembling breath.

'You know how my mother lost her memory as a result of the terrible beating she took on the day I came home to Mallen? Well, yesterday afternoon she fell from a stool and banged her head again. And her memory has come back to some extent.'

'Her memory has come back!' Isobel exclaimed. 'You mean she has remembered who it was that attacked her?'

I shook my head. A lock of hair came loose and I twisted it behind my ear.

'No, and I hope she never does.'

'But why? What can you mean?'

I glanced at her. Her expression was intent, her eyes as sharp as her voice had been. I looked away again, unwilling to hold her eyes.

'It's such an unlikely story, and yet… well, it seems that Mammy and Ralph Penrose were good friends.' I hesitated, wondering if I should admit that once they had been much more than that, and deciding against it. It had no relevance, really, and would only cause unnecessary embarrassment. 'Just before he died, Ralph sent for Mammy, and she came to see him.'

Isobel nodded. 'Yes, I knew that.'

'You knew?' I repeated, surprised.

'Nicholas and I were away at the time, visiting in Truro. But the servants do talk,' Isobel explained. 'I don't know how Ralph thought he could keep it secret from us really. And the family have long known that he and your mother had been… close, so we guessed he had asked her here whilst we were out of the way, for the sake of propriety, so that he could say his last goodbyes.'

'More than that,' I said. 'There was something he wanted her to do for him.'

'But what?' Isobel breathed.

'You will know, no doubt, all about the family Treasure,' I said. 'The silverware supposedly used by King Arthur and his knights, and guarded by successive generations of Penroses. I expect that, like Adam, you think the secret of its hiding place died with Ralph. Well, it did not. Ralph confided it to my mother. She was to tell Adam of it on his return from America. That's what she remembered yesterday.'

'Oh my goodness!' Isobel's voice brimmed with sudden excitement. I glanced at her again and saw that her eyes were shining and high spots of colour had risen in her cheeks. 'Oh Tamsin, that is wonderful! We truly thought the Treasure was lost for ever! And now you say your mother knows where it is hidden!'

'Yes.'

'But why are you so upset?' Isobel asked, puzzled. 'It's nothing to be upset about, surely?'

'I'm afraid there's more.' My fingers resumed the pleating of my skirts. 'I came to Trevarrah this morning eager to tell Adam what my mother had told me, but…'

'But he had already left for Plymouth.'

'No. We met him on the road.'

'Oh! Then you have told him already. Oh Tamsin…' There was something like dismay in her voice now, but I scarcely noticed.

'No, I have not told him. Something happened to prevent me.' I broke off, biting my lip. 'The day my mother was attacked, I found a silver button on the floor of her cottage. It must have been torn off in the struggle, I think. I kept it, thinking it might identify her attacker.' I hesitated again, then went on in a rush: 'Adam was wearing a coat with silver buttons when we met him this morning. And – oh Isobel – one of them was missing!'

Her hands flew to her mouth, her eyes widened above them. 'You mean…?'

'It can only have been Adam who attacked Mammy,' I said wretchedly. 'Why else would a button from his coat turn up in her house on the very day she was beaten and left for dead? That's the reason I am so upset, Isobel. To think that Adam… I can scarcely believe it of him. Why on earth he should have done such a terrible thing, I don't know. But it must have been him, mustn't it?'

I turned to her imploringly, suddenly desperately hoping that she would argue for Adam, tell me that I was wrong, and there must be some other explanation. That he had been at Trevarrah all day on the day Mammy had been attacked. Anything, anything at all that would exonerate him and lift this terrible weight from my heart, release me from this waking nightmare. But she did not.

Instead, along with the shock, I saw something I recognized as pity on her delicate-featured face.

'Oh Tamsin,' she said softly, 'I think I know the reason.'

'What...?'

'Wait here,' she said, 'and I will show you.'

She rose, left the room, and I heard her going upstairs. I got up myself, pacing the room whilst I waited, and the black cloud of wretchedness followed me, weighing me down.

A few minutes later she was back. In her hand was a folded sheet of paper. She held it out to me.

'Read this, Tamsin. It's a letter Ralph wrote to Adam just before he died. He entrusted it to old Trudy to pass on, though why he should have been so secretive, I can't imagine. His illness must have given him strange ideas, I suppose. But Trudy was taken ill herself before Adam came home, and had to retire to live out her days with her sister. I came across the letter when I was packing up her things.'

'What does it say?' I asked.

'Just read it,' Isobel repeated.

I unfolded the paper and ran my eyes down the heavy, sloping script. In places, the words were difficult to decipher, as if Ralph's hand had been shaky and his sight failing him. But there was no mistaking the content.

Ralph was telling Adam he had shared the secret of the family inheritance with someone he trusted implicitly, someone who would relay the information to him when he returned from the fighting in America. No name was mentioned, but of course, as I now knew, that person was my own dear Mammy. I raised my eyes, full of pain, to Isobel's.

'You think that, like you, Adam guessed that it was Mammy who was the person Ralph referred to,' I said dully.

She nodded. 'I am sure that he did. In fact I know so, for we discussed it. Nicholas and I had not seen the contents of the letter, of course, until Adam came home, because it was sealed into an envelope and addressed to him. And at first he did not make us privy to what it said. He was waiting, I suppose, for whoever it was who had the information to contact him, as his father had said they would. I expect he did not want Nicholas to know about it, though, as his brother, he had every right. Well, you know how things are between them. Anyway. When no one came forward, he became impatient. He asked us if we had any idea who the person could be, and we suggested your mother, knowing as we did that she had visited Ralph shortly before he died.'

'And you think that Adam went to see her instead of waiting for her to come to him,' I said miserably.

'I think that must be what happened,' Isobel agreed. 'We had heard she was ill, and urged him to wait, but then word reached us that she was at death's door and unlikely to live out the winter. He was afraid, I think, that if she died, the secret Ralph had entrusted to her would be lost for ever. I can only think that he sought her out without our knowledge and...'

I shook my head, still hoping against hope to find some way of exonerating Adam from the terrible crime of attacking my poor Mammy. The button was only evidence, after all, that he had been in the house, and now Isobel had explained that. Clearly Mammy had not revealed to him the whereabouts of the Treasure, or it would not still be missing. But perhaps, for some reason, she had decided the time was not right. Perhaps Adam had left, none the wiser, and the attacker had been someone else entirely...

But even as I struggled for some explanation other than that Adam had been responsible, Isobel went on: 'You know what his temper is like. If your mother refused to pass on the message for some reason, it's quite possible that he became enraged and tried to beat it out of her.'

I bit my lip. She was only putting into words what I did not want to think. I did know Adam's temper; I had witnessed it with my own eyes. The image of the way he had gone for Nicholas was all too clear in my mind's eye, and for a horrible moment I seemed to see him attacking Mammy with the same uncontrolled violence.

It was unbearable, quite unbearable. Bad enough to envision anyone beating my poor, defenceless Mammy. But that it should be the man who had evoked in me feelings I had never experienced for any other was painful beyond belief.

'But why should she refuse to tell him when Ralph had charged her with doing so?' Still, in spite of everything, I was in denial. Still I was trying to find a way of rebutting the charges I myself had laid against him.

'Perhaps she saw him for what he is,' Isobel said gently. She took my arm and led me back to the sofa, where she sat holding my hand tightly in her own. 'Oh Tamsin, I have tried to warn you about Adam. But you were too besotted by him to listen. And I... well, I tried to spare you the worst of it. There are a great many things I only hinted at. For my own sake, I am ashamed to say, as well as for yours. But now I think it is time that I told you the whole truth.'

Sixteen

A prickle of cold dread whispered over my skin. In spite of everything, I was still clinging to the desperate hope that Adam might not, after all, be the one who had harmed Mammy. Now Isobel's serious face, her whole demeanour, warned me. She was about to tear that last tiny shard of hope from my grasp.

Isobel must have been aware of the turmoil within me. Her thumb gently stroked the back of my hand as if to comfort me, but her light-blue eyes, holding mine, were uncompromising. She would not spare me from the things she thought I should know.

'Adam is, I am afraid, a very ruthless man,' she said now. 'It has always been so. When his heart is set upon something, he will not allow anything – or anyone – to stand in the way of his getting it. It has always been the same. He will plot and plan, and use every weapon at his disposal – including that devastating magnetism he undoubtedly possesses – in order to get what he wants. And if his scheming and his wiles fail, then I am afraid his darker side takes over. He cannot bear to be thwarted. The rage starts deep within him and consumes him. He can no longer control his impatience for whatever it is he desires. He then uses brute force to go after what he wants. Often with terrible consequences.'

'The Treasure,' I whispered.

'Yes, the Treasure is one of his obsessions, and always has been,' Isobel said. 'From his youth he has been crazed in his desire to possess it. He and Nicholas spent many hours as boys searching for it. For Nicholas it was nothing more nor less than a childish game. But to Adam it was so much more. He was obsessed with finding it. Your brother John often accompanied him and Nicholas on their quest, and one day John taunted him, saying he knew where it was hidden. Adam tried to make him tell; John held out. He said he would lead Adam to it, but only if he could take a share. Adam agreed, but he had not the slightest intention of keeping his side of the bargain. John led him up to the Old Trevarrah mine and intimated to Adam that the Treasure was hidden in the old workings. Adam told him to lead the way. John started to descend to the first level. He was on the rickety old ladder when Adam made his move. He pushed him, Tamsin. He pushed your brother to his death to ensure he would tell no one else of the Treasure's hiding place, and would make no more demands for his share. He murdered your brother in cold blood. I know, because I was there.'

I could scarcely breathe. So it *had* been Adam who was responsible for John's death. And it had been no accident. But…

'But the Treasure is not in the old workings,' I said.

'No, we know that now,' Isobel said. 'Adam searched that day, even as John gasped for breath in the muddy waters far beneath, and he has searched since, most thoroughly, I assure you, and found nothing. It was during his searching that he discovered what he thinks is evidence of a goodly seam of copper, which he is set upon excavating if he can obtain the wherewithal to finance the venture. Yet another reason for him to seek the Treasure with renewed vigour. For if he finds it, he will sell it to the highest bidder, make no mistake of it. He will dispose of the family inheritance for his own gain without a second thought.'

I remembered the conversation I had had with Adam. 'But he said that *Nicholas*...'

'What else would he do but attribute his own greed to his brother?' Isobel asked. 'But in truth he knows that Nicholas would never agree to such a thing. For all his failings, he is an honourable man at heart. The inheritance has been the sacred charge of the Penrose family for generations. And now, if Adam can get his hands on it, it will be lost to its rightful home for ever. But he cares nothing for that. He killed, even as a boy, to make it his own. He killed your brother, and all for nothing. I know that for a fact, and it is why I have no doubt in my mind that he came close to killing your mother too in his crazed obsession to discover its whereabouts.'

I was icy cold now, although it was quite warm in the parlour; icy cold and trembling.

'But if he had killed her, then the secret would have been lost for ever,' I said.

'In his blind fury he would not have thought of that,' Isobel said. 'All he would see was someone standing in the way of what he believes is rightfully his. Afterwards, of course, he regretted his loss of control, I have no doubt. He always does, if it has failed to gain his objective for him. In this case, he would have realized how close he had come to killing the one person in the world who knew the whereabouts of the Treasure. And that it was his own fault that the secret was locked away within the memory that he had caused to fail by his own actions. But he lived in hopes, I am sure, that one day her memory would return.

And he wanted to ensure that when it did he was in a position to know about it.'

'Through me,' I whispered.

Isobel nodded. 'Yes. I am sorry, Tamsin, truly sorry. Adam has been using you, not a doubt of it. By pretending to be in love with you, by putting you under his spell, and now, the wicked man, by asking you to marry him, he has ensured that he will be in a position to hear of anything your mother is able to remember. As I said, he is totally ruthless, with a heart of stone. But you must not be taken in by him and his charms.' She squeezed my hand again. 'I hate to disillusion you so, Tamsin. I hate to tear your dreams apart. But if you go on with this, you will only be hurt more. Adam is not in love with you, and never has been. Believe me, I know. For although I wish with all my heart it were not so, Adam is still in love with me.'

For a moment I could not speak. My heart was heavy as lead; it felt like a weight pressing down in my chest. I had long suspected there was still something between Adam and Isobel, and tried to tell myself it was nothing but the echo of a past love. Now Isobel was telling me different, as further proof, if such were needed, that he had been using me all along and everything that had meant so much to me had been nothing but a hollow charade.

'Adam has another obsession besides the Treasure,' she went on now. 'And I am afraid that I am that other obsession. Adam thought that when he came home he would find me waiting for him, the dutiful girl he had left behind. But I had changed, Tamsin. Once I had been in his thrall, just as you are, though I was also afraid of him

– of his dark moods and passions, and his terrible temper. With him gone, I was free. I fell in love with Nicholas and wed him, and that should have been the end of it. But, as I have said, Adam is not the one to let go. He refused to accept that I was now his brother's wife. The rivalry that was always between him and Nicholas was increased a thousandfold – jealousy is a terrible thing. He has done his utmost to turn me – and everyone else – against Nicholas. I am sure he has maligned him to you.'

I could not answer; I sat with my head bowed.

'Hasn't he?' she pressed me.

I nodded wretchedly. 'He has said Nicholas has gambled recklessly,' I agreed. 'And that the estate is in financial difficulties because of it.'

She laughed bitterly. 'I thought as much. After all that Nicholas has done to try to hold things together in his absence, after he has risked everything with a loan from those men who came here in order to try to make the estate pay… It was *Adam* who brought the family to the brink of ruin with his excesses. That was the reason his father sent him off to join a regiment. If he had remained here he would have ended up in prison and the estate sold off to pay his debts. And he has not changed. *Adam* is the gambler, just as he is a cold-blooded murderer.'

I thought of the morning when Nicholas had been shot and how Isobel had screamed hysterically at Adam, accusing him of trying to kill his brother.

'Do you think it was Adam who shot Nicholas?' I asked.

She bit her lip. 'I have no proof, but yes, I am sure it was him. Do you remember how you found me that morning nursing a blackened eye? I told you that I had banged it on the closet door. I don't think you believed me, and you were right not to do so. But I think you assumed, wrongly, that it was Nicholas who had struck me. It was not. It was Adam.'

'Adam struck you? But why, if he loves you? And why then shoot Nicholas?'

'I told you, he won't let me go. He came to my room that morning, demanding I leave Nicholas and return to him. When I told him I would never do such a thing, that black temper of his consumed him and he did what he always does in one of his rages – he hit out at me. And even as I sat there sobbing but still defiant, he threatened that if I would not leave Nicholas of my own volition, then he would free me from him for ever. At the time I thought it was an idle threat. I could scarcely believe that even a man like him would shoot his own brother in cold blood. But as you know, when he saw his opportunity, he did just that.'

My head was spinning. I had wondered, it was true, if it might have been Adam who had fired the gun that wounded Nicholas, but I had thought that if it was, he had done it because Nicholas had struck Isobel. Now even that excuse had been snatched from me.

'But surely he must know that you would be even less likely to return to him if he had murdered your husband?' I protested weakly. 'Your husband… and the father of your child.'

Isobel's eyes fell from mine. She rose and took a few faltering steps towards the window. Her back was towards me but I could see that her hands had gone to her stomach, covering it protectively. Then she turned and there was anguish in her eyes.

'I'm afraid, Tamsin, that Adam has an additional reason to be obsessed with me now. An additional reason for wanting Nicholas out of the way.' Her chin came up; the anguish in her eyes became something like blazing hatred.

'The baby I am carrying, Tamsin, was not fathered by Nicholas. The baby I am carrying is Adam's – and heir to the estate and the Penrose Treasure. Now do you understand why he will stop at nothing to be rid of Nicholas and once more make me his own?'

—

After all that had been revealed to me this terrible morning, I had thought nothing could shock me ever again. But I was shocked now by her words, shocked to the core, the numbness in me startled to raw awareness, my every sense reeling, my pain even more acute, if such a thing were possible.

'Adam is the father of your child?' I whispered through lips that felt stiff. 'You and he…? But I thought you said…'

'I said that he would not accept that what had been between us was over,' she said tautly. 'That is the brutal truth. Adam made advances to me, and when I rejected them he took me by force. He raped me, Tamsin.'

'Oh dear God!' Thoughts raced through my brain like a heath fire in dry brush. 'But how can you remain here with him at Trevarrah under such circumstances? How can Nicholas allow it?'

'Nicholas does not know.' She came to me, dropping back beside me on the sofa and taking my hand. There was urgency in the movement and in her voice. 'And he must not know, Tamsin. God alone knows what he would do if he learned the truth. And I could not live with the shame either. It's best for everyone that he believes that he is my baby's father. I have kept my own counsel and I have only shared my terrible secret with you because I believe you should know the truth about what Adam is capable of. But you must not tell anyone. Do I have your word on that?'

'But…'

'Promise me, Tamsin! Promise me it will go no further!'

I nodded. 'Very well, I promise.'

'You can see now, though, why I was so afraid to be here alone. Why I so desperately wanted you to come here as my companion.'

'Yes.'

'I'm only sorry that it has brought such heartache for you. I had no idea that Adam would make a play for you. Him being so obsessed with me, I never thought of such a thing. But I should have done. I should have realized that your mother's involvement with Ralph rendered you vulnerable. Can you forgive me for placing you in this position?'

'Oh, Isobel, there's nothing to forgive. You are my friend and always have been. It's not your fault.'

For a moment we sat there in silence, holding hands very tightly. Then Isobel drew a deep breath and let it out on a long sigh.

'So there you have it, Tamsin. The whole terrible story. Adam's obsessions and Adam's greed. I have shocked and upset you, I know, but the time had come when the truth had to be told. For your sake, I should have broken my silence earlier. I owed it to you, but I could not bring myself to destroy all your dreams and illusions.'

'I understand, truly, Isobel.' My lips were forming platitudes that were not strictly true. I did not understand how she could live with such terrible secrets, but then, at this moment, I did not really understand anything. I did not understand how I could have been so wrong about Adam. He had inspired a sort of madness in me, I supposed, that had blunted all my perceptions. I did not understand how any man could be so truly evil, and that I could be so unaware of it that I had given myself to him, body and soul. I did not understand, nor did I want to.

But of one thing I was certain. His father would never have asked Mammy to pass on to him the whereabouts of the Treasure if he had known what a monster he had spawned. He would never have trusted him to be its custodian. And, if it had not been for a missing button on his redingote, I would never have known either. I would have given him the information without a moment's hesitation and the inheritance would have been his, just as he had intended. To that end, he had seduced me and broken my heart, and there was no other way it could have ended. For when he had what he so desired, he would have discarded me like a broken toy.

Tears pricked behind my eyes. I blinked them away. I would not allow myself to think about that now – I simply could not bear to. There would be plenty of time later – too much time, far too much time. The rest of my life, perhaps, for I could not imagine I would ever be able to come to terms with the enormity of Adam's betrayal, or my own naive folly. It would be more than never again being able to trust a man – worse by far was the fact that I would be unwilling to trust my own judgement. There would be tears for my lost love and my shattered dreams, and plenty of them. There would be regrets. And there would be emptiness where recently there had been so much happiness and hope and anticipation. But I would not dwell on it now. I would turn my thoughts to the purely practical, which was much less painful to deal with – and a great deal more urgent.

I was in possession of the secret of the location of the Treasure. For Mammy's safety and my own, and, to ensure that it passed into the hands of the rightful guardians, I must share that information. Not with Adam, as I had intended, but with the one member of the Penrose family I trusted implicitly.

And she knew it too. As if reading my thoughts, she twisted on the sofa so that she was facing me, and took my other hand, so that between us we formed an unbreakable circle.

'I'm sorry to ask you at a time like this, Tamsin, but if you know the whereabouts of the Treasure, I think it would be best if you tell me now. I suppose for the moment, with Adam gone to Plymouth, you are safe enough, for I don't trust him for a moment. There's no telling what tricks he will get up to if he suspects for a moment that your mother's memory has returned. You are quite sure he doesn't know, aren't you? You didn't say anything to arouse his suspicions?'

'No, nothing...' But suddenly my blood ran cold.

Yesterday afternoon when he had come in to visit Mammy, she had been on the point of remembering. Snatches had been coming to her – the fall from the stool had merely clarified them. And she had more or less said so in front of Adam. I had thought she had been talking gibberish, but I had not known then what I knew now. She had spoken of the key, and said Ralph had bidden her give it to Adam. She had talked, albeit ramblingly, of her last visit to Trevarrah. Adam had heard it all, and whilst it had been lost on me, it would not have been lost on Adam.

'What is it?' Isobel asked, seeing my sudden expression of horror.

'He does know her memory is returning!' I whispered, and went on to tell her what had happened. Isobel's eyes widened in horror.

'There's a key – and he knows your mother has it?' she asked.

'Yes – the key to the old engine house at Old Trevarrah Mine,' I said. 'That's where the Treasure is hidden, in a cavity in the walls. She didn't tell him that, of course, but she was mumbling about the mine. He might guess.'

Isobel's expression grew even more grim. 'The key to the old engine house! Yes, he might very well put two and two together. He knows that key is missing. He searched for it high and low when he wanted to go there to assess how much work would need to be done to make it serviceable again. In the end he came to the conclusion it was lost, and said the door would have to be broken down to gain entry, but of course he hasn't resorted to that yet, for he has no firm backing for the project – nor likely to have, with his reputation. He didn't take it, did he?'

I shook my head. 'No. It was hidden out of sight in a jug on the top shelf of the dresser. Mammy wanted me to get it for him, but as I say, I was embarrassed by what I thought was her nonsensical rambling, and told Adam he'd better leave.'

Isobel stood up. There was a determined expression on her face.

'Then there is no time to lose. We'll take the trap and go and fetch it at once. And make sure your mother is safe too.'

Though she had not put into words what was on her mind, realization came to me in a cold flood. I got up too, sick with dread.

'You don't think…? Is it possible that Adam hasn't gone to Plymouth at all? That he's just using that as some sort of cover, and in reality he intends to go back to the cottage for the key?' I said, still hoping she would tell me I was being foolish and Adam had indeed gone to Plymouth.

But: 'I don't know,' she said tautly. 'I wouldn't put it past him.'

Fear for Mammy threatened to engulf me. Once again I relived that moment when we had found her beaten and half-dead on the floor of her cottage. Adam had almost killed her once in his attempt to discover the whereabouts of the Treasure. If he had gone to see her whilst pretending to be on his way to Plymouth, and if she was unable or unwilling to give him the key and tell him what he wanted to know, then it was quite likely he would do so again.

'Oh Mammy!' I groaned, then caught Isobel's arm. 'Let's go quickly!'

'We will. I'll drive like the wind.'

'Shouldn't we let Rudge drive us?' I suggested. 'It might be good to have a man with us just in case.'

Isobel snorted. She was no longer the meek little girl I knew, but fiery and determined.

'I don't want the servants knowing of this, and in any case, Rudge would be no good against Adam! He's an old woman. We'll stop at the mine and see if Nicholas is there. But in case we can't find him…'

She crossed to the bureau, opened a drawer and took out a pistol. I had never seen it before; now I stared in surprise at the gleaming barrel and the jewel-encrusted handle. A corner of Isobel's mouth twisted wryly.

'I learned to shoot with the boys when I was a child,' she offered. 'But I never realized I might have to turn a gun on one of them.'

She slipped the gun into her reticule and the reticule on to her wrist.

'Come on then, Tamsin. What are we waiting for? I'm sure no harm has yet befallen your mama, but all the same...'

I ran to the hall to pick up my shawl whilst Isobel went to instruct Rudge to make the pony and trap ready again for our use.

My heart was thudding, the urgency pumping in my veins, and I was cold with fear.

Not of coming face to face with Adam, nor of anything he might do to me.

My fear was for my poor dear Mammy. The secret Ralph had entrusted to her had already cost her her health and memory, and almost her life too.

If I was right and Adam had put two and two together yesterday and decided to act, covering his tracks with the excuse of going to Plymouth, then it might yet cost her dearer still.

Seventeen

I remember very little of the drive home to Mallen except that it seemed endless, and though Isobel, who surprised me with her competence, put the pony to a fast trot, the ground beneath his feet and the spinning wheels of the trap passed with frustrating slowness. The only thought in my mind was Mammy's safety. Adam's betrayal of me seemed unimportant by comparison, and the Penrose Treasure less important still. I hoped against hope that, if Adam had called upon her today, she had given him the key and told him what he wanted to know. I could not care less what happened to the Treasure, just as long as Mammy was safe.

She would tell him... wouldn't she? Why, yesterday she had been on the point of doing so, if only she could have remembered what it was she had to tell. But supposing that her memory had returned regarding other matters too now that the door had been opened? Supposing she remembered it was Adam who had attacked her? Then I could not see that she would be willing to part with the information. She would know that Ralph could not have wished Adam to have it if he had known the kind of man he had become, and she would doubtless put what she saw as her duty to Ralph before her own safety. Frail she might be, but my Mammy was not the one to be bullied into submission.

'Can't you go any faster?' I urged Isobel.

And: 'I'm going as fast as I dare,' she said. 'It won't help anyone if we lose a wheel or hit a stone and overturn.'

She was right, I knew, and I tried my hardest to curb my impatience – and my imagination, which was running riot.

We stopped at Wheal Henry and Isobel ran into the cluster of buildings in search of Nicholas. This was no good for her in her condition, I thought anxiously as I saw her pick up her skirts and skitter over the rough ground. I was already concerned that her pregnancy was not developing as it should. All this activity and anxiety could well cause her to miscarry her child.

And then I had the awful thought that maybe that would be for the best. To be pregnant as a result of being raped by a monster, to have to pretend it was her husband's child… oh, it must be a living hell for her. I did not think that I could have borne it with such fortitude if I were in her place. But all the same, I was ashamed to think for even a moment that it would be better if the poor, innocent baby should be denied the chance of life.

A few moments later Isobel was back.

'Nicholas is not here,' she said. 'He's somewhere out on the estate. I've left word that if he returns in the next hour he is to come directly to Mallen, but I'm not confident that he will. He could be gone all day. I think, Tamsin, we are going to have to deal with whatever comes our way by ourselves.'

'And we will,' I said.

And added silently: *Just as long as Mammy is safe! Oh please, dear God, let her be safe, and I'll never leave her alone again!*

At last — at last! The row of cottages that was Mallen appeared on the skyline. Those last few hundred yards seemed endless, then we were trotting along the track.

Alice Weaver was at her door, sitting on a stool in the warm sunshine and shelling early peas. She glanced up in surprise to see us and called a greeting.

Surely, I thought, nothing terrible could have occurred? Surely Adam could not have come and attacked Mammy again and Alice not seen nor heard anything? But he had come before and no one any the wiser. My heart thumped again, painfully, in my chest.

I was out of the trap even before Isobel had brought the pony to a complete stop, and running to our cottage door. I yanked it open with a sharp, panicky movement. Then I stopped short, my breath coming out on a sob of relief.

Mammy was in her usual chair, little Billy on her lap.

Charlie was sitting at the table, playing with his wooden soldiers. And Ruth, alerted by the sound of the door opening, appeared in the kitchen doorway, a dish in one hand and a drying cloth in the other.

'Tamsin! What are you doing home at this time of day?'

'Oh…' I broke off, uncertain how to explain myself without alarming them. 'I came home for the key, that's all.'

'The key?' Ruth looked puzzled. 'What key?'

'A key that Ralph entrusted to Mammy until she could pass it on to Adam Penrose,' I said. 'A key that…'

'Tamsin!' Mammy interrupted me. 'What passed between us is not for anyone else's ears! I should not have told you if I had been in a position to do what Ralph asked myself. Please don't repeat it. Not even to Ruth.'

Ruth and I exchanged a glance.

I thought she was better. Is she wandering again? Ruth's eyes said, and my eyes flicked to the kitchen, suggesting Ruth should return there so that I could speak to her out of earshot of Mammy.

Ruth seemed to understand.

'Well, if that's all, I am going to finish washing those dishes. Is Billy all right with you for a little longer, Mammy?'

'Of course he is, the lamb! He loves his old granny, don't you, my angel?' Mammy shifted him on her lap and planted a kiss on the top of his head.

I retrieved the key from the top shelf of the dresser, where I had returned it, and slipped it into the pocket of my dress. Then I followed Ruth into the kitchen.

'What is going on, Tamsin?' she asked in a low voice.

'There's no time to explain now,' I said, just as softly. 'I'll tell you everything later. But I want you to do something for me, Ruth. Don't leave Mammy alone for an instant today. Could you take her home with you? And bolt the door.'

Ruth's curious expression turned to one of alarm. 'But… ?'

'If Adam Penrose should come calling, don't answer the door to him. Don't let him anywhere near Mammy. He's dangerous, Ruth. I believe it was him who attacked her, and he may do so again.'

'Adam Penrose?' Ruth's voice was frankly incredulous. 'Oh surely not!'

'Just do as I say,' I said. 'Leave those dishes and find some excuse to take Mammy to your house. She'll be safer there – and you'd have more warning if Adam should come here.'

'Tamsin?' Mammy called. 'What are you and Ruth whispering about?'

'Nothing, Mammy,' I called back, and spoke again to Ruth in a low voice. 'Please, Ruth, just take my word for it that Mammy is in danger of her life from Adam. But don't say anything to alarm her. I'll be home again as soon as I can.' In spite of her bewilderment Ruth nodded, and I knew I could trust her to do as I asked. There was enough of a bond between us for Ruth to know I must have good reason for it, even though she did not understand what it was.

'I'm going now, Mammy,' I said, going back into the living room. 'But I shall be home earlier than usual this afternoon, I expect.' I ruffled Charlie's hair. 'Be a good boy for your mammy and granny, Charlie.'

He ignored me, totally immersed in his game, and I hurried out.

Isobel had turned the trap. She looked at me questioningly as I climbed up.

'He hasn't been here,' I said.

'You have the key?'

My fingers closed over it in the pocket of my skirts. 'Yes.'

She relaxed. 'Good. May I see it?'

I got it out, holding it in the palm of my hand, and she nodded. 'It certainly looks as if it could be the key to the old engine house. I can scarcely believe the Treasure has been so close by all this time and the key at Trevarrah until recently and we knew nothing of it. Ralph certainly knew how to keep a secret.'

We drove in silence then, each, I suppose, occupied with our own thoughts. Mine, certainly, were so chaotic

I could scarcely string them together. Now that the immediate anxiety for Mammy's safety had been assuaged, the enormity of Adam's betrayal hit me anew, and the knowledge that he had used me so callously was a pain around my heart so sharp I did not know how to bear it.

I should never have allowed myself to be mesmerized by him, I thought wretchedly. I had wondered how it was that someone like him could want someone like me. But the real reason for his attentions would never have occurred to me in a thousand years. Why should it? I had not known that my own mother held the key, literally, to the whereabouts of the Treasure. And even if I had known, I would never have believed that anyone could be so wicked – especially not Adam.

What a chance he had taken, coming to the house! Supposing that seeing him had triggered her memory and she had remembered that it was him who had attacked her? My blood ran cold as I envisioned what might have followed. But Mammy was safe enough for the time being. Ruth would make sure of that. And once Adam learned that Nicholas knew where the Treasure was hidden, and that he had the key, then it would be between them, and my worries would be over.

Not so Isobel's. I glanced at her, her small face set and determined as she concentrated on driving the pony, and felt a pang of anxiety on her behalf. Heaven alone knew what other outrages there would be before this was over.

Although I was oblivious to everything but my racing thoughts, the journey back to Trevarrah was so familiar to me that, the moment we veered from the usual path, I was aware of it, and I realized we were heading instead in the direction of the Old Trevarrah mine.

'You are going to see if the key fits the lock of the old engine house?' I asked.

Isobel nodded. 'I'd like to be sure.'

The trap bumped over the uneven ground and before long we had reached the old mine. Isobel reined in and we climbed down.

I glanced towards the shaft, hidden now by undergrowth, where my brother had fallen to his death, and shivered. In my mind's eye I saw him as he had been, a thin, whippy lad with a shock of reddish-brown hair as unruly as my own and much the same colour. But he had been small for his age and he would have been no match for the taller, stronger Adam. I thought of how afraid John must have been in those last few minutes of his life, excitement at the prospect of finding the Treasure turning to dread and then to panic, an adventure on a sunny summer's day turning to a waking nightmare and ending in death. White-hot anger rose in me, making me forget my personal heartache and shame, drowning any feelings I might still have for Adam.

How could I ever have thought I loved him? He was a monster, nothing less, and I should not waste a single regretful thought on him. All I cared about now was making sure the Treasure, for which he had schemed and in whose pursuit he had committed such terrible acts, was beyond his reach.

Isobel and I approached the engine house. Nature had reclaimed much of the land and all manner of weeds and brambles flourished in the shelter of the stout walls. We had to push our way through to reach the door and pull away the thick tendrils of ivy which clung to it.

'We shall soon know, Tamsin,' Isobel said. There was a faint flush in her cheeks and a taut eagerness in her voice, and I realized just how much this meant to her.

I fished the key out of my pocket and handed it to her. It seemed only right that she should be the one to unlock the door.

Her hands were trembling slightly and at first she was unable to slot the key into the lock. Then metal grated on metal, but still the key would not fit in snugly.

'Oh Tamsin, I don't think…' Isobel sounded dreadfully disappointed.

But I had noticed something odd about the heavy wooden door. For a moment I couldn't think why it looked wrong somehow, then I realized what it was.

'It's upside down!' I said. 'Something must have happened to the hinges at one time, and instead of mending them and replacing it the way it was, they've turned it upside down and rehung it!'

'You're right!' Isobel turned the key upside down too and it slipped into the lock a little awkwardly.

'Turn it as if you were locking the door instead of unlocking it,' I said.

'I know!' The edge of excitement in her voice was sharper than ever.

The key creaked and turned, and she pulled on the door, which now opened outward rather than inward. It was stiff; I lent my strength and together we managed to drag it ajar before it became stuck again in the thick tangle of undergrowth.

A musty smell came out to greet us, a smell of decaying vegetation and disuse. We kicked and yanked at the undergrowth until the door was open wide enough to allow us entry, then Isobel slipped through and I followed. The

273

floor was damp and cold beneath our feet, and weeds sprouted in the corners and along one wall. Part of the roof had fallen in, so there was a pile of rubble, bird droppings and a few bedraggled-looking feathers. But enough light came in through the hole in the roof to allow us to see easily enough.

'So where is the Treasure?' Isobel asked eagerly.

I began to make a circuit of the walls, looking closely for any clue as to which one might conceal a cavity, and Isobel did the same, moving around in the opposite direction. Then: 'Here!' she cried excitedly.

I crossed to where she stood. There *was* something different about the wall here if you looked closely enough. The stones were a little smaller and less even, they protruded slightly and the binding agent between them was darker over the area of a small square at about chest height.

'This is it! It must be!' She began to run her hands over the stones, trying to find a loose one, and picking at the mortar between.

'You'll never do it with your bare hands,' I said, but I had reckoned without Isobel's determination. As she persisted, a little shower of dust cascaded to the floor. I looked around for something to help loosen it and my eyes lit upon a shard of roof slate.

'Try this,' I suggested.

Isobel took it and began chipping away at the mortar until she could work her fingers into the crack and get a grip on the stone to loosen it. And at last the stone came away in her hand, so abruptly that she cannoned back into me.

There was no doubt now. The wall did indeed conceal a cavity. Isobel reached inside and gasped.

'It's there, Tamsin! Oh, I was so afraid Ralph might have tried to mislead us! He was such a wily one. But it's there! The Treasure really is there!'

'I'm glad,' I said.

'Come and feel it for yourself!'

In truth, I did not want to. I was relieved it had been found, but I wanted nothing whatever to do with it, this so-called inheritance that had caused so much trouble and misery and cost precious life. But Isobel was insistent. I took her place and slid my hand and arm through the aperture as far as it would go, reaching down into the cavity.

My fingers touched cloth; I worked them about and felt smooth metal. I was glad then that Isobel had insisted, for now I knew beyond doubt that the Treasure was indeed here, and my part in finding it was over. I straightened, withdrawing my hand.

'Turn around, Tamsin,' Isobel said. 'Very slowly now.'

The tone of her voice was quite different. Soft, yet strangely compelling. It puzzled me. I did not turn slowly at all; I jerked my head round and froze in utter shock.

Isobel was a couple of feet behind me now. In her hand she held the small gun which she had put into her reticule for protection in case we should encounter Adam.

And it was pointing directly at me.

So startled was I that in that first moment I felt no fear. Not only was my body frozen, but my thoughts too, so that my mind was nothing but a total blank of bewilderment.

'Isobel?' I whispered questioningly.

'I really am very sorry about this, Tamsin,' she said, 'but, as I'm sure you realize, I have no choice.'

'What are you talking about?' I blurted.

'What I have to do, of course. You have led us to the Treasure, and for that we shall be eternally grateful to you. But I'm afraid you know a great deal too much. You'd talk, my dear, and I must ensure you don't do that.'

The first flash of fear penetrated the haze of catatonic shock. Isobel had brought her gun on our expedition not to protect us should we encounter Adam, but to dispose of me when I had led her to the Treasure!

I could scarcely believe it – gentle, sweet-natured Isobel, whom I had thought was my friend! But there was no mistaking it. The gun was pointing unwaveringly at my heart and Isobel was regarding me with an expression of calculation and perhaps a little regret.

She meant to shoot me dead – quite suddenly I was in no doubt of it. Why she should need to, I could not understand, but this was no time to be puzzling over her motives.

'I wouldn't say a word, Isobel,' I said urgently. 'Not ever – I promise!'

'Oh, but I'm afraid you would, my dear. When you realized the truth… no, we have decided. It's for the best. All the loose ends must be tied up so that we can have a fresh start. We have come too far now to risk everything falling about our ears.'

We… Isobel and Adam. She was under his spell just as I had been. She was doing this for him. The thought of them plotting my death together was yet another sharp pain in my heart.

'Isobel!' I said desperately. 'He's not worth it! Really he's not! He's evil. Just look at the way he's treated *you*. He raped you. He beat you. And he'll do it again. You mustn't let him manipulate you this way.'

She laughed, a haughty, proud little laugh.

276

'No one manipulates *me*!'

'But Isobel, you told me yourself, not more than an hour ago. You said...'

Her lip curled. 'I said a lot of things, Tamsin. But I'm afraid I distorted the truth. Adam didn't beat me, or rape me.' She laughed again, unpleasantly, so different from the Isobel I had thought I knew so well that it was a shock in itself.

'Why, I'm not even pregnant!' she said.

I stared at her, almost uncomprehending. Yet hadn't I thought it was strange how little difference the passage of the weeks had made to her small frame?

'You're not pregnant?' I repeated.

'No, thank goodness. I should hate to have a baby growing inside me. But it seemed to me that saying I was, was the best way to persuade you to be my companion. I needed you close by, Tamsin, so that I was kept informed as to your mother's condition. I never for one moment thought the situation would continue so long, but I knew I could always pretend I had suffered a miscarriage if the time came when you began to suspect the truth. But that won't be necessary now. Everything has worked out very nicely. Better than we dared hope.'

We again. They had both lied to me and used me. Adam and Isobel plotting together. Caring nothing for me, only for the Treasure. They had thought I would lead them to it and I had done just that. And now my purpose was served, they had no further use for me. But as Isobel had said, I knew too much for them to simply allow me to return to my old life.

I looked at the gun, held unwaveringly in Isobel's small hand.

'So you are going to shoot me in cold blood.' A nerve jumped in my throat but my voice came out surprisingly level. I had realized instinctively, I think, that my only chance now lay with remaining as calm as I could manage and trying to buy a little time.

'Shoot you?' She laughed again. 'Oh no, Tamsin. Nothing so obvious. The fewer questions that are asked – the less suspicion that is aroused – the better.'

'So.' I swallowed at that nerve, which now felt like a lump of food stuck in my throat. 'What are you going to do?'

Her gaze met mine, as unwavering as the gun in her hand.

'It's what *you* are going to do, Tamsin. We are going for a little walk. Not very far. Just to the old mineshaft. What could be more fitting than that you should choose to end your life in the same way that your brother's was ended? You are going to jump into the dark muddy waters that flood the lower levels of Old Trevarrah mine.'

Ice-cold horror washed over me, but somehow I held her gaze defiantly.

'And what if I refuse?' I asked. 'You can't make me, Isobel!'

'Oh, I think I can!' she replied silkily. 'A gun is a great persuader. And if in the event you deny me, then I shall shoot you and push you down the shaft anyway. It will be a long time before they recover your body, and by the time they do, I doubt a bullet hole will be very evident. Everyone will think you decided to join your brother John and share his death. Shall we go, Tamsin?'

She made a small but meaningful gesture with the pistol, but I stood my ground.

'How can you do this, Isobel?' I demanded.

She shrugged. 'Oh, quite easily really, when so much is at stake. And it is a neat plan, you must admit. I really think I have been rather clever, don't you? Whilst you have been even more naive than I thought possible.'

'I trusted you, Isobel,' I said harshly. 'I thought you were my friend.'

'Oh, I suppose I was once,' she said carelessly. 'When we were children. But only because I was lonely. I only had the two boys and their friends for company, after all, and they didn't want me following them around all the time. Though it wasn't long before *that* changed. And I realized what fun there was to be had from making them fall in love with me – do anything I asked of them.'

Oh, the vanity of her! It was as repellent almost as all the other dreadful things of which I was learning she was capable. But it gave me a glimmer of hope. Vain people loved nothing better than to talk about themselves and boast of their achievements, and I was a captive audience. Every moment I could keep her talking about herself now was a moment longer that I was still alive. A moment I could spend trying to work out a way of escaping what she and Adam had planned for me.

'I can see that it must have been fun playing Adam and Nicholas off against each other,' I said. 'They were both in love with you then, and still are, I suppose.'

She smirked. 'Oh yes. I don't let my conquests go so easily! And in the old days, of course, it wasn't only them. All their friends were in love with me, too. Your brother John was no exception. He worshipped the ground I walked on. All I had to do was to allow a little favour here, then lower my eyelashes demurely there, and he would follow me like a lovesick puppy dog. It was pathetic, really. But then, *he* was pathetic.'

The smirk became a sneer. 'He cried like a baby that day in the old mineshaft, when he realized his way out was barred and he was going to die. I wonder if you will do the same?' Anger flared in me to hear her speak of my brother so, anger that for the moment blotted out my fear and overcame my caution.

'You stood there and watched whilst Adam tormented him!' I cried. 'You did nothing to help him! How could you, Isobel?'

'Adam?' she repeated. 'Oh, it wasn't Adam who pushed him. It was me.'

'You?' Even given all that I had lately learned, her bald admission still had the power to shock me.

'Oh yes, it was me. Adam wasn't even there — or Nicholas. It was only John and me.' She smiled, actually smiled, at the memory. 'He was going to show me where he thought the Treasure was — though he was wrong, of course. I wanted to beat the boys at their own game — take a silver salver or a goblet home with me to show them and tease them with it. I was so piqued when John came back empty-handed from the levels where he had been searching. I told him he was no more use to me and I wasn't going to let him come back up. When he tried, I stamped on his hands and then one of the rungs gave way. He was clinging on by his fingertips. All I had to do was to give him a little push. He screamed when he fell. It seemed a very long time before I heard the splash. And then I went home.'

I was so shocked and angry I could scarcely speak.

'You are truly evil, Isobel, and I never knew it. To think I felt sorry for you! Why, you're worse even than Adam and Nicholas. From what I can make out, whatever they do, it's because their temper gets the better of them. But you... you calculate and lie and deceive. But don't think you'll get away with it, because you won't. In the end you'll overreach yourself and get your just desserts. And you won't get away with killing me, either. My family know I would never do away with myself. Mammy knows...'

'Oh yes, your mother knows a great deal too much too,' Isobel said. 'She'll be dealt with, never fear, just as anyone else who is a danger will be. In different ways, of course, so as not to arouse suspicion.'

'You are mad!' I cried, horrified. 'Mad as well as evil!'

'Don't say that!' There was a wild fire suddenly in Isobel's light-blue eyes, her calm destroyed. 'I am not mad! Don't ever say that!'

'Oh but you are!' I had found a chink in her armour and I was going to pursue it. A dangerous course of action, perhaps, but if she lost her temper and shot me here where I stood, she would never be able to drag me to the mineshaft to dispose of my body, and there was a chance that suspicion would fall on her and Adam. I had warned Ruth about Adam, and she knew I had driven off with Isobel. It would not save me, of course, but it might save Mammy.

'You are quite mad!' I persisted recklessly. 'Was your mother mad too? Is that why you were left alone in the world and had to be taken in by Ralph Penrose?'

'Don't talk about my mother!' Her small face worked. 'My mother was...'

She broke off as the sound of a horse approaching at a gallop reached our ears. A little smile curved her mouth again.

Adam, I thought, my heart lurching into my throat. It must be Adam. He had not gone to Plymouth at all, just lurking somewhere until Isobel had persuaded me to tell her all I knew.

'So – your lover is here to collect his treasure and help you dispose of me, is he?' All my pent-up emotions made my voice shrill.

She frowned. 'My lover? What are you talking about?'

'Well, Adam, of course!' I snapped.

'Adam?' She laughed. 'Adam is not my lover! I realized a long time ago Adam was not the one for me. He has too strong a will of his own. Especially since he came home from the war. Nicholas is far easier to handle and always has been. That's the reason I chose him.'

The hoof beats had slowed and stopped; a tall form appeared in the doorway behind Isobel.

Not Adam, but Nicholas.

He stood there, drumming his riding crop against his thigh, looking at me with a twisted, triumphant smile.

'So, you have led us to the Treasure then, Tamsin,' he said. 'At last. And my wife has you under control, I see.'

Isobel smirked. 'I convinced her it was Adam who had been using her,' she said. 'And luck was on our side too. When I suggested you borrow Adam's coat when you visited her mother that day, I was only thinking it might help conceal your identity if you were seen. But Tamsin saw Adam wearing it today and noticed it was missing a button that she had found in her hovel.'

'It came off when the foolish old woman struggled with me,' Nicholas said. 'How very fortunate for us!'

In that moment, I knew. It was yet possible that Adam had pursued me for the same reason as Isobel – to be the first to learn the whereabouts of the family treasure. But everything else that Isobel had told me had been a pack of lies. It had not been Adam who had attacked Mammy but Nicholas. It had not been Adam who had killed John. He had not beaten Isobel, nor raped her. I doubted very much that he had been the one to shoot Nicholas either.

My heart leaped with joy and the sheer relief of it. Adam was not a murderer, nor a thug, nor a rapist. In spite of my predicament, the realization set my spirit free.

But what good could freedom of spirit do me now? I still faced the barrel of a loaded pistol, alone, in an isolated spot where no one would hear, no matter how loudly I might cry for help, nor hear the crack of the pistol either. And I now faced not just Isobel but Nicholas too.

I could see now why Isobel had said it was necessary for me to die. I could see why she had insisted I would talk. Of course I would! And the person I would talk to was the very one who would come between the pair of them and the Treasure they had schemed for.

They would stop at nothing to ensure that did not happen.

Eighteen

'Tamsin is proving a little difficult,' Isobel said. 'I have told her of the fitting end we planned for her, but she does not seem willing to play her part.'

'It's as well that I am here then.' Nicholas tapped his riding crop against his thigh again, the only sign that he might be tense and anxious. Otherwise his demeanour was that of everyday social intercourse. 'When you called at Wheal Henry, we decided it was best you proceed alone with Tamsin until our objective was achieved, but it did occur to me that I would be needed to complete the exercise. Tamsin is not the one to give up easily.'

'In the end she will, though,' Isobel said. 'She has no choice.'

She lowered the pistol a little, flexing her fingers as if they had become cramped. Whilst it had been only her and me, she had needed the pistol to ensure I did not overpower her, I supposed – and I could have done it, too, for I was stronger than she was, I felt sure, and fighting for my life would make me stronger still. But now that Nicholas was here, she could relax a little. With a man as lithe and powerful as Nicholas barring my way, I had no hope whatever of escape.

'So – the Treasure is here in the old engine house,' he said now, his eyes going to the brickwork Isobel and I had opened up. 'Who would have thought it?'

He came further into the building and instantly I tensed. If he was going to investigate the hiding place, perhaps I could make it to the doorway and run for my life. But I knew I would not get far. I could not ride, nor drive the trap. They would catch me easily – if they did not put a bullet in me first.

'I think we'll leave the Treasure where it is for the time being,' Nicholas said. 'It's been safe enough here for the past twenty years or more, and it will be safe enough a while yet, so long as we lock the door. No one else knows it's here, I assume?'

'Tamsin's mother knows,' Isobel said. 'But we can deal with her as soon as we've dealt with Tamsin. We shall go to visit her – and find her dead.' Her mouth twisted into an unpleasant smile. 'Suffocation should be easy enough with a woman as frail as she is, and there will be not a mark on her body to arouse suspicion. I don't really think anyone will be in the least surprised that she has breathed her last.'

Again I felt a flash of outrage and fury. How dare she talk so casually and callously of murdering my mother!

'You won't find it so easy!' I said spiritedly. 'She's not alone as you think. In fact, she's likely not in her cottage at all!'

Isobel frowned. 'She was certainly there an hour ago,' she said, as much to Nicholas as to me. 'And I saw no one else.'

'Let's not worry too much about the old woman,' Nicholas said. 'She's been rambling for weeks, hasn't she? No one is likely to pay any attention to what she says. They'll take it as so much nonsense – especially since she will be deranged by grief at the sudden and unexpected loss of her daughter. Why, it might even finish her off and do our work for us. Who knows? No, the one we have to worry about is Adam. But even he has played nicely into our hands. What good fortune he chose today of all days to go off on one of his fruitless meetings to try to persuade some old crony of his to invest in his mine!'

'And what good fortune he has as yet been unsuccessful!' Isobel put in. 'If Old Trevarrah had been reopened, it's possible the Treasure might have been discovered by pure chance.'

'But it was not,' Nicholas rejoined. 'And he had no idea we were on the point of finding it in any case.'

My heart missed a beat.

'But the letter!' I said. 'The letter his father wrote to him telling him that someone would contact him regarding the whereabouts of the Treasure...'

'Oh, he never saw that!' Isobel laughed. 'Surely you don't think I would be so foolish as to have shown it to him? I found it, just as I said, in old Trudy's possessions, but Adam was still in America. When he came home, I never told him there was any letter!'

Again, in spite of everything, my heart lifted. He hadn't known! He hadn't been using me at all! But my momentary relief was short-lived, replaced by a renewed sense of horror as Nicholas said lightly: 'Adam will be easy enough to deal with. In fact, I have already made plans. He was getting far too close to Tamsin for my liking. He'll meet with an accident on the road between here and Plymouth. A highwayman or footpad will put an end to him – or that's what everyone will say happened. And with Adam out of the way, the Treasure will be mine, to do with as I choose.'

'And mine!' Isobel said sharply. 'You wouldn't have it without my help, Nicholas.'

'That's true enough, my love. I lost my head – and very nearly lost the Treasure because of it. Whilst you have been a very clever girl.' The look he gave her left me in no doubt; Nicholas was utterly entranced by Isobel, and, evil as I now knew her to be, I could still quite see why. Pretty as a picture, apparently demure and sweet, yet clever and dangerous, Isobel wielded the sort of power that would utterly entrap a man, especially a man like Nicholas.

'We are wasting precious time,' she said now. 'And I am growing tired of the game I have been playing with Tamsin.' She raised the pistol again, pointing it once more straight at my heart. 'Let's take a little walk, Tamsin. To the old mineshaft.'

I drew myself up, determined not to make this easy for them, though I held out little hope of a favourable outcome.

'I am going nowhere.' There was a little tremble in my voice; I hated myself for it.

'Don't be foolish, Tamsin.' Nicholas took a step towards me, grasping me firmly by the wrists, and Isobel moved behind me. Through the thin fabric of my bodice I felt the hard ring of the pistol's muzzle in my ribs. She jabbed it harder, and as she did so, Nicholas dragged me towards the door.

The sun was high now, and after the dim light in the engine house the brightness of it almost blinded me. I began to struggle then, desperately, as they manhandled me the short distance through the gorse towards the overgrown mineshaft.

Nicholas used his riding whip to beat a path to its rim, still holding me fast with his free hand, and I knew that now we were so close it would be easy enough for Isobel to put a bullet into me and push me over the edge and no one the wiser.

'Go on, Tamsin,' she urged me now. 'Into the mine, there's a good girl.'

The panic was making me shake and waves of, first hot, then cold ran over my skin. But my mind was strangely clear as I sought for a way to trick them. Perhaps if I were to climb down into the shaft beyond their reach they would not care to come after me. They would never simply go away and leave me alive, of course, no matter how long I clung to the old ladder, but if I could somehow make them think I had fallen, then perhaps there was a chance.

Taking a deep breath and controlling the sob of fear that rose in my throat, I dropped to my hands and knees and lowered myself into the shaft. A fetid stench rose to greet me, the stench of stagnant water, and as my feet slithered on the slimy rungs, I had a terrible vision of my poor brother clinging here all those years ago and Isobel stamping on his hands until he lost his grip and fell.

A rung had given way beneath him, she had said. My searching foot found emptiness and I guessed it must have been the very rung beneath the one on which I now stood.

'Jump, Tamsin!' Isobel urged me from above. 'Put an end to your misery. You may as well. There is no escape.'

Briefly I wondered why neither she nor Nicholas had simply pushed me whilst they had the chance, but though I could no longer see her face, the gloating in her voice gave me my answer. She was enjoying this, just as she had enjoyed torturing John. She wanted to prolong the pleasure of having me in her power, my life in her hands. Why had I never realized what a cruel woman she was?

How well she had hidden the dark side of her nature beneath her pretty manners and gentle smile! But then, she had had long years of practice.

Though my every instinct was crying out to me to climb back up the wooden ladder to sunlight and fresh air, I knew I must not. At least, down here in the dark, evil-smelling mineshaft, I was out of their reach. It was my only chance. Somewhere soon must be the narrow tunnel opening to the first level. If I could find that and climb into it, then at least my feet would be on something more solid than these treacherous rotten rungs. But the darkness made it impossible to see, and I clung on where I was for a moment, trying to fight my rising panic.

'Jump, Tamsin!' Isobel urged again, and echoing down the shaft I heard Nicholas's voice, as clear as if he were standing right beside me.

'Leave her. We'll find something to block the shaft so she cannot get back up again.'

A fresh wave of panic rose in me like a hot tidal wave. Oh dear God, they were going to leave me here to die like a rat in a trap! There was plenty of old debris lying around the abandoned mine, quite large enough to cut off not only my escape, but also the very air I was breathing. I would never be able to dislodge it; already my arms were aching from the effort of supporting myself. Soon they would be too tired to do even that, and certainly not strong enough to move a heavy barrier.

Again I fought the urge to climb back up the ladder and face whatever they might do to me, and grimly concentrated on keeping my precarious hold on the ladder. But the fear and desperation were making me sob softly.

Above me I could hear the sound of something being dragged across the ground, and willed myself to think again. If I could only find the level, was it possible there was another way out of the mine? Certainly there would be air shafts, or the men would never have been able to remain below ground long enough to work the copper. Well, I knew for a fact there were, for they peppered the moor. But I doubted they would be equipped with ladders, since they were for the purposes of ventilation only.

But if only I could find one, it would better my chances of staying alive for a while at least. Someone might pass by this way, and if I heard horses' hooves or voices above me, then I could call for help. The chance of someone passing the very spot before I died of hunger and thirst and pure fear was slim, I knew, yet I clung to it. My only alternative was to accept certain death.

Gathering every bit of my courage, I tried to reach the next rung below the one that was missing. I stretched down so that the muscles in my calf cramped, and I had to draw back. There was nothing for it. I would just have to lower myself by my arms, trusting that my feet would encounter the rung before I was left hanging by my fingertips. And trusting too that it would not give way beneath me.

I drew a deep breath, preparing myself, and something slid over the aperture above me, blocking out what little light there had been.

I was on the point of launching myself into the unknown when I thought I heard what sounded like a shout.

At first I thought it was in my own head, a sort of silent scream. And then it came again. A man's voice. A roar of rage.

I froze. There came a loud thud and almost simultaneously Isobel's voice, shrill now: 'What are you doing?'

Someone was there undoubtedly! Someone other than Isobel and Nicholas. I drew a deep breath of fetid air into my lungs and screamed. 'Help! Help me!'

More thuds, the unmistakeable sound of punches being thrown, accompanied by Isobel's sharp cries of protest and the sort of grunts and groans that men make when they are fighting. I expected to hear the crack of Isobel's pistol at any moment, and shouted at the top of my voice.

'Be careful! She has a gun!'

Then there was a loud crash directly above me that made me shrink against the ladder. Something – or someone – had fallen on to the timber that Isobel and Nicholas had dragged across the mineshaft. Almost simultaneously I heard a splintering sound as the wood, rotten with age, gave way, then something I realized was a body hurtled past me, catching my shoulder and almost causing me to lose my hold and fall with it. Moments later, amid the trail of loose stones it dislodged, it hit the dark water below with a splash so loud it echoed and re-echoed around the passages and caverns. And at the same moment Isobel screamed.

'Nicholas! Oh my God! Nicholas!'

For a long moment I hung there on the ladder, frozen by shock. Nicholas had fallen down the shaft! Then I was sobbing again, and every sob was a name. Adam. It must be Adam! By some miracle he was here! He and Nicholas had fought and Nicholas had met the fate he had planned for me. Even now I could hear him struggling feebly in the filthy, oily water. But I was too frightened and too exhausted to feel even a moment's pity for him. Closing my ears to the sounds of his struggles, I began to climb.

The shattered remains of the boarding was dragged aside, blessed light and air came rushing in. Strong hands reached down to mine, steadying me, helping me up. I pulled myself up, rolling breathless into the prickly gorse, and looked up at my rescuer.

Not Adam at all. Joshua Tripp!

And he would be unarmed!

'Isobel has a gun!' I gasped. Even as I said it, she came rushing at Joshua. 'Look out!' I cried.

But Isobel no longer appeared to be armed; she was quite hysterical, grabbing wildly at Joshua's arm, beating at him with her hands…

'Save him! Save Nicholas!'

Joshua brushed her off as if she were a fly. 'You'll be lucky.' Unhurriedly, he crossed to pick up the gun, which she had dropped in the gorse.

'He'll drown! He'll drown!' She was sobbing and screaming.

'Aye, very likely,' Joshua said, unmoved. 'And so he bloody well should. I ain't a-risking my neck fer the likes o' him.' His voice was as calm and slow as if nothing untoward was happening at all. 'An' it'll be too late by now, I reckon, any road.'

'No one deserves to die like that!' I whispered. I leaned over the open shaft, but there was no sound now from below, no splashing, no cries.

I tried to rise to my feet and suddenly the world was swimming about me. I made one last effort, but everything was going away from me, voices, sunlight, Isobel's heart-rending sobs, everything.

I knew no more.

The ground was moving beneath me with a jolting motion. I opened my eyes and realized I was lying in the trap. Joshua was driving it; Nicholas's horse, tied up to the rear, trotted behind. Of Isobel there was no sign.

'Joshua!' I said faintly.

He looked back over his shoulder. 'Oh – you'm come around, then.'

'I fainted! Did I faint?' I felt vaguely surprised; I had never fainted in my life before.

'You did that – and hardly to be surprised at.' He chuckled. 'Well, that were an old carry on, and no mistake!'

'You saved my life, Joshua!' I said. 'But what are you doing here? I thought you'd long gone – to Bristol, to find employment.'

'Couldn't bring meself to go,' he said. 'This round here's my home. I found a corner for meself in one of the old mine buildings – it's snug enough this time o' year – and I've been living off game. I went out this morning, checking my traps, and when I got back… well, I could scarce believe my eyes at what were happening! You down the old mineshaft and they two up top gloating… It's a good job I can move like a poacher still, is all I can say. I crept up close enough to take 'em by surprise and they never knew I was there till I caught a-hold of Mr Nicholas. An' now he's the one floating down there – or sinking. An' it's the best place for 'un, if you do ask me.'

I shuddered. I couldn't bear to think of it.

'And Isobel?' I asked. 'Where is she?'

'Still there as far as I do know. And if she wants to chuck herself down the shaft too, well, it won't be no loss, will it?'

'Joshua!' I felt a flash of anxiety for the man who had saved my life. 'You could end up being blamed for both their deaths!'

He shrugged. 'They'm deaths I'd be proud to own to! But I can't, can I? 'Tweren't my fault Mr Nicholas fell on the rotten plank when I hit him, and if she follows him to damnation, that's her lookout. But I think I ought to clear off to Bristol, all the same, once I've got you safe back to your ma's. What with Nicholas drownded and me riding his fine horse… oh, I think I'd better make meself scarce.'

'You shouldn't have to run like a fugitive,' I said. 'I shall tell Adam how brave you were, and ask him to find you honest work and a little home of your own.'

'Adam?' Joshua sounded indignant. 'What's he got to do wi' it? You aren't still mixed up with him, I hope?'

I smiled weakly, aching suddenly for Adam. How could I ever have doubted him?

'Adam is a good man,' I said. 'And to be honest I think Nicholas was more weak than evil. Isobel was the truly evil one, and Nicholas was under her spell. He'd do anything…' I broke off, suddenly remembering what Nicholas had said about arranging for Adam to meet his death at the hands of a highwayman or footpad.

'Oh Joshua!' I said, beginning to shake again. 'I do believe Adam is in danger too! I've got to warn him! But how? He left for Plymouth hours ago…'

Again Joshua shrugged. 'Well, I ain't a-goin' after him, that's fer sure. Mr Adam is big enough and ugly enough to look after himself.'

'Oh!' I wrapped my arms around myself, feeling that I was lost in a nightmare.

Joshua had saved me, and in so doing also inadvertently saved Mammy from the harm Isobel and Nicholas had planned for her. But Adam was still in mortal danger. And if anything happened to Adam… I loved him with all my heart and the thought of life without him was more than I could bear.

A horseman appeared on the horizon riding towards us across the moor, but I was too preoccupied with my thoughts to even wonder who it might be. It was only as he came closer that I strained my eyes in disbelief.

That tall figure, sitting so tall in the saddle of his great horse… it couldn't be, surely? Adam was halfway to Plymouth by now… I must be imagining things.

Closer, closer still. Breath caught in my throat.

I was not imagining things! There was no mistaking who it was!

My heart gave an enormous leap of joy and relief.

'Adam!' I whispered. And then shouted: 'Adam!'

He came alongside, frowning to see Joshua driving his trap and Nicholas's horse tied up behind.

'What's going on?' he demanded.

'It's all right!' I cried. 'I'll explain everything! But, oh Adam, the most terrible things… Joshua has just saved my life. Oh, I've never been so glad to see you! But what are you doing here? You're supposed to be going to Plymouth…?'

Adam's eyes were narrowed. 'I was. I had a bad feeling that something was terribly wrong. I turned back.'

I could scarcely believe it. I knew all about premonitions and bad feelings, but I would never have imagined for a moment that a man as down-to-earth as Adam might experience the same thing!

I stumbled out of the trap; he dismounted from his horse. And with Joshua watching, in amazement, no doubt, I went thankfully into his arms.

I had terrible news to break to him, and good news too. But for the moment nothing mattered except that my head was on his chest so that I could hear the beating of his heart and his arms were around me. Nothing else mattered at all.

A little more than a year has passed now since that day. Adam and I are wed and Mammy is living with us in Trevarrah. Though Ruth had thought she would not want to leave her old home, she scarcely protested at all and I am sure she is happy there. I think it makes her feel close to Ralph.

As for Joshua, I did indeed persuade Adam to find work for him and he moved into our cottage when it became vacant, next door to the one which had once been his home. He has overcome his dislike of Adam and now shows him a grudging respect, though I think he still finds it difficult to entirely trust anyone who bears the Penrose name.

Isobel did not throw herself down the mineshaft after Nicholas. In spite of her distress, her instinct for self-preservation was, I think, too strong. Adam found her there, sitting in the bracken, crying and rocking herself – and clutching a silver goblet that was part of the Treasure.

Sometimes I wonder how I could ever have doubted Adam for a moment. But Isobel was so persuasive and so manipulative, and in my naivety I never thought to doubt her – another woman whom I thought was my lifelong friend. I should hate her, I suppose, but mostly I pity her, born with a terrible inheritance of her own. The inheritance of madness.

She inherited the condition from her mother, Adam told me. She had stabbed Isobel's father to death whilst he slept and then killed herself. Ralph had taken pity on the child and taken her in, and now Adam likewise felt he owed her a duty. He arranged to have her taken away to a place where she cannot do any more harm, either to herself or to others, and he pays for her to be looked after in comfort. Considering the terrible things she has done, I feel it is generous of him, particularly since he has had to borrow to pay the bills for her care, as well as setting the estate back on its feet. But at least we are looking forward to a more secure future. With Nicholas no longer holding him back, Adam has been able to secure backing for reopening Old Trevarrah, and it seems that when it is once again in operation it will provide the wherewithal not only to put an end to all Adam's financial worries, but also to give employment to local people for a good long time to come.

And we have more cause for celebration, too, for a month ago I gave birth to Adam's son – whom we have named Ralph. He is the most beautiful baby I have ever set eyes upon and we both dote upon him.

Sometimes, though he is far too young to understand, Adam shows him a piece of the Penrose Treasure. But he seems fascinated by the way the candlelight winks on the silver plate, and his chubby little hands reach out to touch it.

I have no doubt that when he is grown, the Penrose Treasure will have a safe guardian for yet another generation.

I suppose I should hate the Treasure, too, for all the trouble it caused. But I cannot hate that either. If Ralph had not entrusted the secret of its hiding place to Mammy, then none of this would have happened. I would no doubt still be in Launceston, working as a lady's maid, and I would never have met and married my darling Adam.

Life has brought me an abundance of riches worth far more than any treasure, however valuable, however sought after it might be. And I intend to make the most of every single precious day and ensure that those I love do the same.

—

She sat in the soft candlelight, at peace with herself and with the world. And in the dancing shadows she seemed to see the man she had once loved, a shadow himself, yet real – so real.

He was not as she had last seen him, grown old and bloated, barely able to shift his heavy frame, struggling for each breath, but as he had been before – young and lithe and handsome and strong.

'Ralph,' she murmured. 'I did not fail you. I did as you asked. The Treasure is safe now in Adam's keeping. And you would be so proud of him! He's a fine man, a wonderful husband and father, and a worthy squire too. Oh, he is your son and no mistake.'

She held out her arms. They no longer looked skinny and withered, but smooth and firm.

The candlelight flickered; the shadows moved. She seemed to feel his breath on her cheek, his strong arms encircling her.

'I knew I could trust you, Rose.' Just a voice in her head, nothing more, but it lifted her heart. 'And I knew I could trust Adam.'

She smiled, and her face was young again.

It would not be long now before they were together.

Until they were, she was more than content.